CANDLELIGHT

Supreme

"WHICH ROOM'S MINE?"

"What else but the master suite?" Logan told her.

At the door Lerisa hesitated. "Does it have a key?"

"Afraid of burglars?"

"Afraid of you," she sassed. "What assurance do I have you won't come prowling later on?"

"None," Logan admitted. "Not knowing will keep you on your toes, or your back, I guess, since you'll be sleeping."

"Come through this door after I'm inside and you'll be on your back permanently," Lerisa threatened.

"Go to sleep, my love." Logan smiled, refusing to be baited. "All your clothes are neatly unpacked. And I think when you see the bath you'll agree it has everything any woman needs."

"A strong lock and complete privacy are all I need."

D1738525

CANDLELIGHT SUPREMES

QUANTITY SALES

Most Dell Books are available at special quantity discounts when purchased in bulk by corporations, organizations, and special-interest groups. Custom imprinting or excerpting can also be done to fit special needs. For details write: Dell Publishing Co., Inc., 1 Dag Hammarskjold Plaza, New York, NY 10017, Attn.: Special Sales Dept., or phone: (212) 605-3319.

INDIVIDUAL SALES

Are there any Dell Books you want but cannot find in your local stores? If so, you can order them directly from us. You can get any Dell book in print. Simply include the book's title, author, and ISBN number, if you have it, along with a check or money order (no cash can be accepted) for the full retail price plus 75¢ per copy to cover shipping and handling. Mail to: Dell Readers Service, Dept. FM, 6 Regent Street, Livingston, N.J. 07039.

BEDROOM MAGIC

Alice Morgan

A CANDLELIGHT SUPREME

Published by
Dell Publishing Co., Inc.
1 Dag Hammarskjold Plaza
New York, New York 10017

Copyright © 1987 by Alice Morgan

All rights reserved. No part of this book may be reproduced or transmitted in any form or by any means, electronic or mechanical, including photocopying, recording or by any information storage and retrieval system, without the written permission of the Publisher, except where permitted by law.

Dell ® TM 681510, Dell Publishing Co., Inc.

Candlelight Supreme is a trademark
of Dell Publishing Co., Inc.

Candlelight Ecstasy Romance®, 1,203,540, is a registered trademark of Dell Publishing Co., Inc., New York, New York.

ISBN: 0-440-10831-4

Printed in the United States of America

July 1987

10 9 8 7 6 5 4 3 2 1

WFH

For my daughter Nanci

To Our Readers:

We are pleased and excited by your overwhelmingly positive response to our Candlelight Supremes. Unlike all the other series, the Supremes are filled with more passion, adventure, and intrigue, and are obviously the stories you like best.

In months to come we will continue to publish books by many of your favorite authors as well as the very finest work from new authors of romantic fiction. As always, we are striving to present unique, absorbing love stories —the very best love has to offer.

Breathtaking and unforgettable, Supremes follow in the great romantic tradition you've come to expect *only* from Candlelight Romances.

Your suggestions and comments are always welcome. Please let us hear from you.

Sincerely,

The Editors
Candlelight Romances
1 Dag Hammarskjold Plaza
New York, New York 10017

CHAPTER ONE

Lerisa glanced up as the flight attendant's voice abruptly changed from a businesslike tone to a throaty feminine purr when she greeted a passenger.

Obviously a VIP, she mused, staring curiously at the back of a man whose broad shoulders and towering height completely obscured her view of the other passengers directly behind.

Blocking the narrow aisle of the airplane, the stranger paused to show the attendant his boarding pass before turning his face toward Lerisa.

My dreams have come true! Lerisa reflected with rising excitement as she met his glance head-on.

Infinitely and totally masculine was the second description that came to mind. The first was sexy, virile, and so appealing that her stomach muscles clenched as she continued her observation.

Partially lowering her lids when he refused to look away, she tried to appear disinterested while peeking through a lustrous black fringe. Her lashes may have shadowed her thoughts from the man before her, but they did nothing to quell her instantaneous desire to know the dynamic-looking male specimen better.

When he turned away she watched, absorbed, and decided without the least hesitation that this was a man she'd like to make love with . . . which in itself was a pretty traumatic happening since she couldn't remember a single time in the last twenty-five years when that feeling had happened with such speed.

Continuing to stare surreptitiously, she was determined to give the handsome brute a business card before they reached LAX. Who knows? Maybe he'd be interested in her work or . . . after a hastily planned feminine coup during the flight . . . even herself!

Admitting that the man's front and back views were equally dramatic, Lerisa wasn't surprised to hear the light-hearted interplay of the eager attendant continue as she offered to take his carry-on luggage. She didn't blame the woman one bit when her smile widened and her blue eyes shone with open encouragement in response to his friendly manner.

"Thank you, miss," the stranger said when the slender blonde reached for his sturdy nylon bag to place in the closet area near the entrance.

As the attendant fumbled he moved fast, drawing Lerisa's attention to the strength of his biceps as he caught his luggage. The clenching muscles in his tanned forearms, with their sprinkled covering of fine dark hair, made her ache to feel them around her own slender shape.

"Careful," he cautioned, giving the attendant a sympathetic look, though it was obvious from Lerisa's view that it was a deliberate ploy on her part to delay the man from taking his seat. "I'd better do this for you."

Even his voice was a dream, Lerisa enthused as he easily disposed of his suit bag. After spending the last two years studying in France, it was like being welcomed home to hear the familiar American accent.

Unnoticed, she gave the man a more thorough scrutiny, concluding he was a walking seduction scene. She could still feel tremors running up and down her spine from his deep mellow drawl as he continued to talk with the attendant.

Seeing no reason to control her avid curiosity, Lerisa speculated on his occupation. Was he an executive? Probably not, she surmised. He didn't carry a briefcase or wear a three-piece business suit.

A man of wealth?

Unquestionably. The first-class seating, his obvious poise, plus the fine gold watch, indicated as much. His deeply bronzed skin presumably came from extended weekends in Bermuda or Palm Springs. No doubt with a willing female companion at his side twenty-four hours a day, she thought peevishly, wondering why she should care.

Could he be a famous sports figure? He had the muscles of an athlete, but she didn't recognize his features.

Eyeing his clothes, she continued to contemplate his life-style. Though casual, his attire was of the finest quality. Slim-fitting jeans hugged his thighs and were a deep shade of brown, somewhat like the dark russet hair waving around his aristocratic head. A short-sleeved knit beige shirt covered a wide chest she wouldn't object to exploring with her bare hands.

Lerisa looked down the length of his body, eyed his suede chukka boots, and then wandered slowly up the long length of the first awesome male package she'd seen in ages.

Unbidden, she gave a wistful sigh. This man was something else. A superbly built, powerfully attractive package of male perfection, and she intended that he remember her . . . not the flight attendant . . . after they reached California.

When the object of her thoughts looked down and

11

caught the open admiration in her eyes, he smiled. A long and appreciative smile that lit the depths of his vivid cerulean-blue eyes until they glinted, humorously acknowledging her bold glance with equal enthusiasm.

Lerisa returned his grin, not believing in her good fortune when he stopped at the vacant seat beside her. Suddenly she looked forward to every minute of the long flight from Paris to Los Angeles.

"It appears to be my lucky day," the stranger greeted her, settling his large frame with masculine grace on the adjoining plush velour. Despite the luxurious first-class seating, his knee and hand grazed her body when he fastened his seat belt and spread his long legs forward.

Lerisa's lashes lowered as she feigned interest in the contents of her purse. The accidental contact with her arm and leg was a touch he didn't appear to notice but she doubted she'd soon forget. Talk about sparks flying. He was a walking power plant!

"If I'd previously arranged it myself, I couldn't be happier over having you for a seat partner," he told her sincerely.

"That's nice of you to say." Lerisa thanked him in a voice so soft and ultrafeminine, she was surprised he could hear her. "Though I suspect it's false flattery because we'll be sitting next to each other for so many hours."

"Every word is the truth," he insisted, running his glance over her features like a connoisseur. "You're absolutely breathtaking."

Oh my gosh, Lerisa sighed, swallowing back the sudden lump in her throat as his devastating smile drew her eyes to his white, white teeth and well-shaped, seductive mouth.

As their eyes met and held, her heart was completely

12

won over. One glimpse, two compliments, and a single smile had done it.

Jolted by her thoughts, she lowered her lashes, knowing he'd be shocked if he could read her mind at that moment. Her fingers literally itched to paint the nude image she envisioned. She could picture the finished oil now. Not a vulgar depiction but a life-size canvas artistically and beautifully executed filled with his compelling physique. She had looked at him with a practiced eye and knew the planes and muscles of his body would equal his facial features. A face hewn to masculine perfection from tanned flesh drawn tight over hard bone.

It hadn't taken many life classes at art school to assess how a man would pose naked despite his outerwear. Rarely had she been wrong, she remembered with a teasing smile, reminded of the many excursions to Cannes and Lyon for weekend swimming parties. Her French boyfriends had all worn scandalously brief suits that left little to the imagination.

The crazy, impetuous interest in her seat partner was not as a model only, Lerisa admitted freely. Her thoughts had definitely turned to the erotic the moment she spotted his towering head and shoulders above those of the other passengers.

Determined at least to act detached, Lerisa pulled her eyes away. She glanced out the window as the ground crew busied themselves for takeoff and wondered why she bothered with the pretense of nonchalance. Her mind absolutely refused to concentrate on mundane flight preparations anyway when the opportunity to start a relationship with her ideal man sat inches away.

She stole a quick peek sideways, only to find he had not stopped scrutinizing her.

His eyes were keen and all-knowing as they roved over

her features with a thoroughness unlike any appreciative glance she had ever endured.

Lerisa felt as if she'd been appraised, found very much to his liking, and programmed back into his computer-bank memory for future reference. Though flattering, it was still a nerve-racking experience.

"Do you have an airline magazine?" she blurted out, the first thing that came to mind when he refused to look away.

"Yes, and so do you." The stranger pointed to it with a long, well-groomed finger. He took the one from his seat front and handed it to her. "Have two, they're free."

Lerisa accepted the magazine without comment. At least he hadn't mentioned how visible the one in front of her was. Only a blind person could have missed seeing the vividly colored glossy cover.

She crossed her legs, for the first time noticing how high the hem of her skirt had ridden. Apparently it had scooted up as she twisted in her seat to get a closer glimpse when he first appeared beside the flight attendant. She pulled her skirt down as far as its medium length would allow, noticing his keen eyes frankly admiring her nylon-clad knees and exposed legs.

"I was hoping you wouldn't do that. It's a shame to cover such feminine beauty." His eyes were alive with mischief when she quickly uncrossed her legs and placed both feet primly on the floor. "You have great-looking legs from this angle."

"You appreciate the female form, Mr. . . . er . . . ?" Lerisa questioned, fishing for his name.

"Call me Mark," he answered easily. "And yes, I do admire an attractive woman." He fastened his seat belt and settled back. "And you, Ms. . . . ?"

"Lerisa," she replied quickly, refusing to disclose her last name also. His continued comments were a good sign if she was to make any progress toward a close relationship longer than the eleven-and-a-half-hour flight.

"*Lay—risa,*" he drawled. "Gorgeous name for a gorgeous woman. As I was saying, Lerisa, you must realize, if you've ever looked in a mirror, that you are absolutely stunning."

Lerisa glowed, refusing to comment on Mark's smooth praise. His technique was flawless. The way he slowly rolled her name off his tongue the first time he pronounced it sounded like a drawn-out caress. His apparent intent to become better acquainted matched her interest.

When the plane taxied onto the runway Lerisa took a deep breath and sighed. She was acting ridiculously over the man. Just because it was the first time any male had affected her pulse beat to this extent was no reason she should not act more poised. After all, she wasn't a teenager anymore.

Mistaking Lerisa's sigh for nervousness, Mark asked, "Are you afraid of flying?" Totally at ease, he sympathetically placed his hand over hers in an attempt to quell her fear during takeoff.

Refusing to comment on his mistaken observation, Lerisa left her hand beneath his and burst out with the only plausible excuse she could think of. "I'm not the least nervous about flying but my ultimate destination causes a few flutters in my stomach when I think about it."

"Not bad news waiting on your arrival, I hope," Mark comforted.

"Hardly," Lerisa corrected in a soft voice. "I'm flying to my first job in the United States after years of intensive schooling."

"That doesn't sound like anything to be nervous about."

"It isn't really," Lerisa admitted honestly, glancing at Mark. "I guess I'm just a little apprehensive since my new boss has spent so much money. He paid for this first-class fare and offered an enormous fee for my services, plus picking up all subsequent expenses while I'm in his employ."

Mark gave Lerisa a wide smile that curled her toes with pleasure.

"I don't doubt you'll be worth every penny your employer spends whatever your . . . er . . . *services* . . . are." He squeezed her hand and released it.

"I certainly hope Mr. West feels the same."

"I can guarantee he will."

"Thanks for your confidence," Lerisa spoke politely. "But unfortunately his opinion is the only one that counts." She settled into the seat and wiggled her shoulders, hoping to relax the suddenly tight muscles.

Unaware when she moved that her full breasts stretched the soft cashmere of her sweater and outlined their thrusting shape, Lerisa looked over curiously as Mark inhaled sharply.

Barely able to take his eyes off Lerisa's voluptuous beauty, Mark probed, "What are the services you're rendering?"

It was torture to make small talk when he wanted nothing more than to take her in his arms and explore the sweet curve of her mouth in a passionate kiss. Kisses, hell! He stifled a groan. His damned arousal sent erotic signals to his brain that made him ache to sate himself deep inside her in the ultimate act of love. Satisfaction with a mere kiss was for immature school kids, not for a healthy adult male.

"Your occupation's strictly respectable, I presume?" Mark reiterated in hopes of breaking the train of his libidinous thoughts.

"I'm not into anything illegal," Lerisa laughed. "I assume that's what you suspected."

"Your silence did make me wonder," Mark teased. "I would prefer you be more specific."

"I'm an artist."

"I'd never have guessed that on seeing you for the first time," Mark admitted.

"Why?" Lerisa insisted curiously.

"Your clothes, for one," Mark explained, eyeing her long-sleeved gray sweater, straight skirt, and neat court shoes with medium heels. Lessening the severity of her outfit, the designer scarf picked up the exact green of her outstanding eyes. "Your clothing is perfect for a long flight but not as flamboyant or colorful as I imagined an artist would have in her wardrobe."

"I'm not bohemian enough, you mean." Lerisa chuckled, used to people's opinions of how artists should look.

"You read my thoughts," Mark teased back.

"Actually I normally wear wild, crazy colors, far-out clothes, and silk headbands to keep my hair out of my eyes while working. This trip I decided it best to tone down my true nature."

"Why on earth would you do that?"

"My boss is reputed to be a womanizer. I figure if I meet him looking drab and businesslike it will put him off and I can start painting without any unwanted distractions."

"It will take more than an unadorned sweater and simple skirt to make any man overlook your beauty," Mark promised warmly, meeting her gaze with amused eyes. "The man would have to be blind to ignore you. Surely hiding your true personality wouldn't slow down the average womanizer."

"My new boss is not average. He's dedicated his life to female conquests and is a notorious rake."

"Are there any of those left in this modern age of liberated women and changed morals?" Mark chuckled.

"At least one and he's the worst," Lerisa insisted. "He's wealthy, arrogant, and a handsome beast to boot."

"How do you know if you haven't met the man?" Mark came back quickly, his eyes flashing with ready humor at Lerisa's vehement look.

"My best friend told me everything she knows about the man, which was plenty."

"I'm listening," Mark told her attentively.

She looked at him and decided to explain from the beginning so he would understand just why she was filled with trepidation over meeting her boss.

"Jaclyn, my friend, painted a stunning nude picture of Josh. That's the man she loves and later married, though she didn't know he felt the same about her at the time."

"This sounds like a sexy love story," he interrupted, his tone warm with humor.

"Josh and Jaclyn's love affair is. My part is just the opposite, as you'll find out in a minute."

"What happened next?"

"Well, I wasn't supposed to see this revealing oil entitled *Stolen Idyll* but I did and commented that if I ever found a man who poses that well in the buff I'd cover my wall with nudes of him. Then she tells me about Logan West, who she thinks will be Josh's equal in every way. Talk about intrigued. I could hardly wait to meet this epitome of male excellence. But in the end the more I heard about the man, the less I wanted to meet him."

"Why the change of heart?" Mark probed.

"Frankly, after she described him to me in more detail, he sounded like the kind of oversexed maniac that will make out with any female with a pulse beat. I like a faithful man. One who devotes all his spare time and energy to me."

"Any male who did otherwise would be a fool," Mark assured her, all the time subjecting her to another devastating appraisal. "Getting back to Jaclyn," he asked in a straightforward manner, deliberately forcing himself back to their former conversation, "doesn't she like this Mr. West?"

"She adores him," Lerisa scoffed, as if her friend was no judge of character. She added as a sudden afterthought, "Of course her experience with men is very limited."

"Unlike yours?" Mark persisted.

"Unlike mine," Lerisa answered, making no further explanation.

"Is your inexperienced friend one of this . . . er . . . oversexed maniac's ex-conquests?" Mark queried with false seriousness, trying hard not to laugh at Lerisa's outraged manner.

"Oh heavens no," Lerisa admitted quickly. "She's been in love with her husband since she was fourteen years old. Too much in love to even look at another man."

"Then how would she know for certain this . . . er . . . *rake* . . . is as bad as she says?"

"Her husband's known this man for years and is one of his best friends, plus their social circle is the same. She told me my new boss is devastatingly single-minded when he's on the make."

"Most men are, Lerisa," Mark told her with a touch of humor. "As you should know if you're as experienced as you say."

"Agreed," Lerisa answered with a chuckle, remembering all the men she had been involved with through the years. "Are you?"

"Most definitely."

19

"Then you should understand my reasons for wanting to tone down my normal personality."

"What is your true nature?"

"Not drab or docile. Looks can be deceiving," Lerisa assured Mark. "Despite having black hair, I'm as fiery-tempered as any redhead."

"Volatile and outspoken as well, I presume?" Mark pointed out with keen insight. "Am I right?"

"Yes. It will be quite a change to make a dignified and somber entrance. And extremely hard to curb my tongue if we don't like each other."

"We hit it off immediately. This man's probably not one bit different from me. Do you agree this is a possibility?" Mark challenged.

"Not likely," Lerisa argued. "You look like a . . ." She broke off, trying not to gush as she explained her feelings of instant rapport with the man beside her.

"Like a what?" Mark persisted, unwilling to let her comment go unheard.

"Like a man of integrity and honor."

"But you just told me looks can often be deceiving."

"I hope not," Lerisa told Mark quietly. She knew the disappointment of finding he was lying would be devastating. "I'd hate to think that you have a devious mind intent on creating mischief or the lascivious mind of a rake."

"I've been known to be involved in subterfuge when it suited my purpose."

"That's far removed from the one-track mind of a sex pervert."

"A platonic relationship with you wouldn't interest me, Lerisa, so don't be misled."

Mark pinned her eyes with a look of such intensity, Lerisa felt her stomach churn with excitement. She lowered her lashes, needing time to gather her thoughts after that blatant revelation.

"Does my desire for you make me a womanizer?" he persisted.

"Actually"—Lerisa met his glance and smiled—"it makes you rather intriguing. I like men who aren't afraid to speak out. It's the sneaky, devious type of man I hate most. One with nothing but sex on his mind, like my employer."

With a noncommittal shrug Mark suggested, "Why don't you forget your boss? I'd rather enjoy our time together without any outside distractions."

"Me too," Lerisa enthused. Totally enthralled with the man beside her, she returned his open admiration with a dazzling smile that she hoped knocked him for a loop.

"Tell me about yourself, Lerisa. I'm particularly curious about all this experience you claim to have."

"Don't you like innocents, Mark?"

"I love them," he teased back, unperturbed. "I prefer sophisticates as companions, though."

"Any particular reason why?" Lerisa probed.

"Because the training period, if done right, would take longer than many of my past relationships have lasted."

"You're blunt, but I understand exactly how you feel. I've certainly never been interested in dating awkward, unskilled boys."

"Then we, my beauty, make a perfect pair." Mark picked up her hand, cradling it in his palm. He traced the length of each well-manicured capable finger before turning them over and rubbing a sensual circle around and around the sensitized skin of her palm.

Lerisa's stomach clenched with the excitement of Mark's touch. It was unlike any she had ever known. A simple caress, but designed to curl any woman's toes.

Not wanting Mark to comment on her reaction, Lerisa swallowed back a sigh of ecstasy and started to talk, calmly explaining about her lifelong love of art.

Before she knew it the "Fasten Seat Belt" sign blinked off. She had been so entranced with the man at her side, she had paid little attention to the plane taking off, reaching full altitude, and zooming forward at 560 miles an hour toward their destination.

Mark was an attentive listener, with the unique charisma to make her feel like the only woman in the world important to his happiness.

Interrupted by the flight attendant, Lerisa accepted a glass of white wine and a plate of tempting hors d'oeuvres.

"Thank you." Lerisa smiled, watching with interest as the woman fawned over Mark to make certain he had everything the airline had to offer. Herself included, she suspected maliciously.

To be fair, Lerisa didn't blame her one bit for giving the man beside her extra attention. After all, she was planning how she could proceed with a subtle interrogation of her own. Being indirect was hard on her nerves when she ached to demand that he give her a full biographical account immediately.

Lerisa took a sip of her drink, set it down, and bluntly asked, "Do you like living in Los Angeles?" Darn it, she scolded herself mutely. How obvious could one get?

"No, I don't," Mark replied, with glints of humor shimmering in his eyes. "You should taste the prawns wrapped in sweet pea pods, Lerisa. They're delicious."

Lerisa picked one up, dipped it in seafood cocktail sauce, and raised it to her mouth. She paused before taking a bite and flicked Mark a sideways glance. "I guess downtown Los Angeles isn't the ideal place for a man to settle. All that smog wouldn't be good for his children."

She inwardly kicked herself, wondering why she didn't just come right out and ask if he was married. She'd done it before without a qualm.

Taking a bite of the prawn, she choked when Mark sensed her indecisiveness and suggested, "Why don't we quit beating around the bush, honey? If you're interested, ask."

"Excellent idea." Impatient for Mark to explain his marital status, Lerisa waited. It was an effort to chew her appetizer without further comment. Damn the man, he knew darn well she was annoyed by his delayed reply.

"Simmer down, sweet, or you'll choke on your hors d'oeuvres again," Mark warned with a devastating humorous smile. "I'm not married or engaged and I don't think you are either, correct?"

"Right," Lerisa admitted, glancing at Mark with a pleased look. "I wasn't very subtle, was I?"

"No," Mark replied honestly. "But why should you be? I'm thirty-four and you must be eight or ten years my junior, which is well past the age of consent. Why be coy about our obvious attraction to each other?"

"As I guessed before, you are an honest man, Mark." Lerisa gave him a trusting smile. "I like that trait in a man."

"I'm honest when it suits my purpose," Mark contradicted, making no further explanation when Lerisa raised a finely arched brow in inquiry.

Lerisa continued talking with Mark through the leisurely dinner and what must have been hours afterward. His attention never veered, heeding each word as if she were the most fascinating woman in the world.

"Your turn, Mark," Lerisa apologized. "I had no intention of monopolizing the conversation for so long."

"You didn't," Mark assured her. "Every word revealed

another facet of your delightful personality to me. You're a very special lady, Lerisa."

"And you, Mark, are an exceptional listener." She unfastened her seat belt and reached for her purse. "If you'll excuse me for a moment, I'll freshen my makeup, then you can give me a summary of your life."

"Plenty of time for that later," Mark guaranteed, moving his legs aside so she could get to the aisle.

In the close confines of the rest room, Lerisa applied fresh lip gloss and a spray of perfume below each ear. She was anxious to return to her seat and learn more about Mark. He certainly knew the high points of her life, yet she hadn't given him time to divulge a thing about himself.

When Lerisa returned Mark had adjusted the seat and was resting with his head back, eyes closed, and hands lightly clasped in his lap. Despite the extra room in first class, his feet were thrust far under the seat ahead.

She stepped over his long legs without disturbing him and sat down. Openly staring, she admired the way his thick lashes, unusually dark on a person with red glints in their hair, shadowed his molded cheekbones. His high-bridged nose fit his aristocratic features perfectly. Asleep or awake, he had the most kissable mouth of any man she'd ever met.

"Sniff! Sniff!" Mark teased, inhaling in an exaggerated manner without opening his eyes. "You smell delicious, woman. It's going to be hard to catch up on my sleep with that heady fragrance floating in and out of my nostrils."

Pleased he liked her choice of perfume, Lerisa questioned softly, "Are you tired?"

"Beat," he told her, raising one hand to stifle a yawn. "I feel like I've been traveling forever." He opened his eyes and smiled. "Do you mind if we wait for my part of our life's story?"

"Not at all." Lerisa was instantly sympathetic to his need for rest. Traveling on a plane was never a picnic, and long flights could be a nightmare to your body time clock.

"Good girl," Mark whispered, shutting both eyes with a contented sigh. "You'd make a hell of a wife for a marrying man. Intelligent, gorgeous, and compassionate. Your boss is a very fortunate man."

"Go to sleep, Mark," Lerisa urged softly. "I'll be right beside you when you wake up."

"Hmm," he whispered huskily, "those are the sweetest words I've heard in months. Too bad we're not in my house, then they'd really mean something worthwhile." He turned his head toward her and gave a regretful sigh.

"Hush," Lerisa scolded. She lowered her seat to the same angle as Mark's. "You're becoming delirious."

Certain she was involved in the beginning of the love affair of the century, Lerisa didn't mind if Mark slept. It gave her more time to study him undetected. There was plenty of time later to find out everything she wanted to know about the most wonderful man she had ever met.

She stared at him with stars in her eyes, meditating with longing about the happy hours ahead.

Mark suddenly raised his lashes, catching Lerisa's unguarded expression. "Don't look at me like that, woman," he protested huskily, giving her a lazy grin.

"Like what?" Lerisa whispered, feeling her stomach clench when his voice lowered intimately and his hand reached out to touch her face.

"Like you want me to make love to you right here in the dimly lit interior of the plane." Mark stroked his finger down her smooth cheek, outlined the shape of her mouth, then reluctantly he returned his hand to his lap. "Do you?"

"It's a little too public, don't you think?" Lerisa answered wistfully. The thought of being entwined in Mark's strong-looking arms seemed like a wonderful idea.

"For what I want to do to you, it's a *lot* too public," Mark said with a groan. He reached out and threaded his fingers in Lerisa's silky black hair. Cupping the back of her nape with both broad palms, he gently drew her into his arms. "But it's not too public for this."

From the moment his mouth covered hers with a hunger and surprising possessiveness, she was lost. His hands imparted their own magic, caressing her tenderly as his lips parted hers with such shocking expertise that she leaned farther into him with an unbidden whimper of extreme pleasure.

As Mark continued his sensual exploration, lazily probing back and forth across her sensitive mouth, Lerisa forgot every caress she'd ever received.

Offering her tremulous lips with a sigh of complete capitulation, she clung to his neck. It was her first touch of heaven, and she ached to be in his arms so that he could stroke her from breast to thigh. She felt greedy for his undivided attention and wished with all her heart they were in the privacy of her Paris apartment.

Long, long moments later Mark pulled back, exhaling as if stunned. His clean breath fanned Lerisa's face as she shuddered, desperately trying to regain a semblance of composure also. Obviously shaken, his voice was harsh and disturbed. "You're one dynamite lady, sweetheart."

He breathed deeply for several seconds, holding her widened eyes with his sensual, intimate gaze.

She returned his stare, not believing the charged emotion still emanating between them.

"I remember being told at a very early age that it's dangerous to play with anything explosive," he whispered, unaware that his dilated pupils made his eyes appear black, betraying how disturbed he really was.

"Too bad," Lerisa objected softly, lowering her lashes in hopes that Mark would forget the warning and continue his caress.

Unable to avoid the temptation of soft pink lips, parted and willing, Mark gripped her shoulders and drew her close once again. He explored the sweet moist contours with delicate precision, each movement more erotic than the one before.

"I—I think the warning was sound," Lerisa stammered, making no attempt to pull away.

"Maybe. Maybe not," Mark conceded, letting his breath mingle erotically with hers. "For a kiss that was a stunner, I don't feel inclined to heed any parental advice if it keeps me from touching you."

"You'd better let go," Lerisa cautioned in a teasing voice as she looked over his shoulder. "I think the two elderly ladies across the aisle are starting to take notes on your technique."

Glancing to his right, Mark gave each white-haired senior citizen a wide smile, then turned back to Lerisa and warned, "I'm damned if I see anything noteworthy in what I've done to you . . . *so far.*"

With reluctance Mark released Lerisa, watching as she withdrew without further comment. Leaning back in his seat, he faced straight ahead, trying to control his heightened emotions. His damned jeans were so tight in the crotch now, they'd probably cut off the circulation to both his legs . . . or somewhere even worse!

Noticing Mark's obvious arousal, Lerisa gave him a compassionate, unembarrassed smile.

"Two kisses from you and I'm behaving like your . . .

er . . . rake of a boss," Mark grumbled, squirming to get more comfortable while waiting for his body to relax.

"Hardly," Lerisa contradicted with meaning. "Despite your physical reaction, they were still only kisses . . . not a seduction."

"The hell you say, woman," Mark contradicted, leaning over Lerisa's seat to grip her firmly by the shoulders. "My thoughts had us in bed from the moment I first spotted your gorgeous face raised so enticingly up to mine. By now I'm way beyond wanting to stop with a kiss or two and you damned well know it."

"There are no cold showers in a 747," Lerisa teased, pulling free of his grip with a soft chuckle as she tried to cool his heated comments.

"Well, I need one," Mark complained. He raised his seat up. "I think I'll order us a couple of drinks in lieu of anything better to suppress my craving to continue our love-making."

"Wonderful idea," Lerisa concurred, straightening her seat also. "Something icy with the flavor of lime sounds refreshing."

"Refreshing, yes. Mood altering, I'm afraid not." Mark's eyebrows drew together in a deep frown. "This is neither the time nor the place for adult games. My mind knows it, but my body refuses to be convinced."

"Poor man," Lerisa sympathized, barely able to suppress a satisfied smile. She also felt shaken from his fiercely controlled passion. It was marvelous for her ego to know he was as unnerved by their first caresses as she was.

She leaned her head against the seat, closed her eyes, and smiled, wondering if her current thoughts would surprise Mark. The taste of his mouth still lingered on her lips like an elusive potion overwhelming her with the need to savor him again and again. Along with the rest of his body from top to toe . . . front to back . . . each hard tanned inch of taut masculine flesh.

Waiting for her drink, she broke the silence by confessing, "That was a pretty heady interchange, Mark, considering we're virtually strangers."

"Hardly strangers after that conflagration!" he contradicted harshly. "My body's still aroused, and until today I've always been proud of my self-control."

"Point taken," Lerisa conceded in a soft voice. Accepting the frozen daiquiri from the attendant with a pleased thank-you, she took a long sip, then licked her lips with a satisfied sigh. It was delicious and the perfect remedy for soothing a throat suddenly gone dry.

Further disturbed by Lerisa's seductive actions, Mark gulped his whiskey in one quick swallow in hopes the fire in his stomach would take the heat from his body.

Unaware of Mark's physical reaction to the sight of her dainty tongue, Lerisa wondered if she should have curbed her feelings when they had kissed. Impossible. She couldn't have if she'd tried. Anyway, he was as aware of his effect on her emotions as she was of his response to her.

In bed she knew they would be magic together. Even more disquieting was her eagerness to experience that bedroom magic at the first possible opportunity.

"You kiss like a dream, sweetheart," Mark told her with such warm intimacy that she found it impossible to hold his gaze.

"It was special to me too," Lerisa acknowledged, hoping he'd think it was the potent drink that had loosened her tongue. In the face of such solicitous behavior, she knew darned well it didn't take a daiquiri to make her express her feelings.

"Special, hell!" Mark scoffed, meeting her frank look

29

with one of tenderness. "Kissing you was pure magic." He picked up her hand and caressed it lovingly. "Not wanting to sound like your boss on the make, I hesitate to confide how I feel about you already."

"Tell me," Lerisa insisted, dying to know his inner thoughts.

Mark caught and held her glance, admitting in a husky voice, "Right now I feel like taking you to my home and making love to you until we're both mindless with the beauty of it. I want to hold you in my arms all through the night . . . and I ache to kiss, taste, and caress each silken inch of your skin as you lie quivering with desire beneath me. That, I know, would be like nothing I've ever experienced before."

"That's pretty heady commentary to any woman," Lerisa acknowledged while trying to ignore Mark's continuous fondling of her hand.

"It's the truth," Mark vowed intently. "You looked like pure bedroom magic the moment I first saw you."

"Bedroom magic?" Lerisa repeated in a soft whisper. Those were the very words she had used about Mark. Could he have picked up her thoughts?

"Yes. Bedroom magic is the best way to express my reaction to your feminine appeal."

He raised her hand to his mouth and tenderly kissed each fingertip before stopping her breath with his husky admission.

"The promise of your response and revelation in your gorgeous eyes is more than any mortal man should have to endure when he's uncomfortably strapped in a seat at thirty-five thousand feet with an overattentive attendant apt to return any second."

"I think after that declaration it's time we both rested,"

Lerisa confided, feeling totally taken aback as she withdrew her hand and placed it in her lap.

She lowered her lashes, pretending to doze off and on until time for breakfast. Just being next to Mark was plenty to handle for the moment. Another caress and she'd propose to the man. For now she'd play it cool and sophisticated and let him make all the future plans when they landed in Los Angeles.

She could hardly wait to tell Jaclyn that the job she and Josh procured had brought more to her than a lucrative commission.

Aware of Mark's presence every second of the long flight, Lerisa bided her time as they finally landed and departed the plane for the long walk to customs. With his hand on her elbow she even began to feel more at ease about seeing her employer. After all, she thought smugly, the exalted Mr. Logan West would appear a mere shadow of a man in comparison.

Awed by Mark's presence going through customs, Lerisa was pleased to follow his lead as he headed toward the main exit door of their terminal and stopped.

Suddenly Lerisa felt awkward standing alongside her heavy suitcases and waiting like an imbecile while Mark stood silently by with his nylon carry-on bag casually slung over one broad shoulder.

What next? Surely now Mark would ask for her temporary address and phone number. Oh lord, what if he just walked away? She would die it would hurt so bad.

Interrupted as a uniformed chauffeur came up to her and identified himself, Lerisa looked at Mark, mentally begging him to make some kind of a commitment.

"Since you have a limo waiting for you, I'll say au revoir for now, Lerisa, my love." Mark pulled her into his arms and kissed her hard on the lips.

Lerisa squirmed closer, clinging to his shoulders with unashamed pleasure until he ended the kiss. Everything would be fine now. It had to be after that heady caress.

Surprisingly, Mark shrugged free of her hold when she tried to link her arms behind his neck to keep him near. He kissed her gently on the forehead and whispered for her ears alone, "Until we meet again, my love. It's been magic."

Without a backward glance he strode out the automatic doors and was soon lost from sight when a mammoth RTD bus came to a stop between them.

Lerisa smothered the shocked cry that threatened to spill from her throat at Mark's abrupt departure. She stifled the urge to abandon her luggage and run after him until he explained his surprising actions.

Au revoir, he had told her? Until we meet again? At least it wasn't a point-blank good-bye, she thought wistfully, giving a silent plea for him to return as suddenly as he left.

As long seconds passed Lerisa failed to justify Mark's unexpected parting. Her concern changed to anger and her independent personality asserted itself in absolute fury. With chin held high and back stiff, she proudly met the curious eyes of the man beside her.

"Let's go," Lerisa prompted the poker-faced chauffeur. "I've a job waiting and I'm ready to start work."

Blinking back tears, she followed him outside, across the crowded sidewalk, and stepped into a luxurious silver-gray stretch limousine. Alone on the vast velvet seat, she let the tears fall unheeded the moment her door was closed.

"The hell with you, Mr. Mark What's-his-name?" Lerisa scoffed bitterly. "Everyone my age should know magic isn't real. Especially *bedroom magic* with a damned sweet-talking stranger!"

CHAPTER TWO

Lerisa scrutinized Logan West's plush outer office with appreciation, though her nerves were still on edge from Mark's traitorous departure.

"Very impressive. In fact, I'm overwhelmed by the entire building," she told the pretty secretary seated decorously behind a mammoth desk.

"All Mr. West's real estate offices are both functional and beautifully decorated, Ms. Forbes."

"Call me Lerisa, please."

"I'd like that. I'm Mary Ann."

It was evident that Mr. West hired for brains and attractiveness. Lerisa liked Mary Ann's friendly manner the moment she welcomed her inside the tenth-floor office.

Of course the pregnant belly and wedding ring were a big surprise. From what Jaclyn told her she had expected to find a dozen voluptuous centerfolds parading around in harem outfits instead of one smiling, sweet-faced young woman.

Lerisa observed the bulging figure as Mary Ann stood to place some papers in a filing cabinet. Could she be carrying one of Mr. West's mistakes? she wondered maliciously. The baby, that is. Not the ring. She knew darned well from what Jaclyn had told her that the man was shy of long-term commitments. Especially legal ones with gold wedding bands attached.

She glanced at her watch and frowned. Less than a quarter of an hour left. Damn but she dreaded the meeting. If he made her wait even one minute past their eleven o'clock appointment, he could hire another artist! She was too angry to play games, even if she did want the lucrative commission.

"What's the delay?" Lerisa asked, trying hard not to take out her momentary anger against all men on the woman before her.

"Your appointment isn't for ten minutes, Ms. Forbes . . . er . . . Lerisa, and Mr. West's a stickler for punctuality."

"Bully for him," Lerisa shrugged, not bothering to hide her irritation. Unfortunately she was preprogrammed to actively dislike her employer, which didn't make for a good start to their working relationship.

To begin with he had insisted, despite her vehement argument against the idea, she come straight from the airport to his office. A damned-fool idea, since the plane didn't land until seven-thirty at night. He should at least have allowed her a night's stay in Los Angeles to sleep off any jet lag. Instead he demanded she neither call Jaclyn to say hello nor take the time to change her clothes until after their initial meeting.

She'd outsmarted the arrogant Mr. West on one command at least, Lerisa reminded herself smugly. The chauffeur had no choice but to stop at a gas station when she asked to use a rest room.

Thinking of Mark's statement on the plane about expecting an artist to dress far-out, she had changed her mind about making a dowdy impression. She'd knock Mr. West for a loop when he saw what she wore tonight. She

34

had changed from a drab peahen to a bright peacock in a matter of minutes.

Lerisa glanced at her offbeat attire and smiled mischievously. Vivid eyeliner covered the fatigue in her eyes and a darker shade of glossy lipstick had boosted her morale instantly.

Her hair had been a cinch. Thick and shiny, it fluffed out into a riotous tangle of black curls held dramatically in place with a kelly-green silk headband whose tails hung along her neck.

A royal blue, low-necked leotard deliberately exposed a creamy expanse of bosom. Her multicolored skirt was the pièce de résistance. Several hand-printed scarves of her own design were sewn together and belted at the waist to fall in soft folds just above her knees. The sharp-pointed hem directed one's eye straight to the thin straps winding crisscross down her calves to her sandal-clad bare feet.

"I love your outfit," Mary Ann complimented her. "Being six months pregnant and already bulging like a blimp, I envy anyone with a tiny waist."

"I'm colorful anyway," Lerisa acknowledged with a chuckle.

"You can carry that kind of ensemble off, being so tall and shapely. I'd look awful even if I wasn't going to have a baby."

"You look beautiful, as all pregnant women should," Lerisa told her sincerely. She stood up, deliberately looking at her wristwatch for the umpteenth time. Two more minutes to wait and she was either inside his office or outside his building.

"Happiness is supposed to show," Mary Ann volunteered shyly. "Mr. West, being such a super boss, insists I take regular breaks and go home the moment I begin to feel tired. I'm a junior typist, not his executive secretary."

"If he's so considerate, why the heck are you working at this ungodly hour of the night?"

"This is special." Mary Ann gave Lerisa a patient smile, the enthusiasm for her boss coming through clearly in her awe-filled voice. "Mr. West knows my husband takes a night college course on Thursdays and offered me a fantastic bonus if I'd come in just to welcome you."

"He did?" Lerisa queried. His consideration for a minor employee's comfort surprised her. From Jaclyn's narrative she didn't expect him to even acknowledge his female staff existed unless he wanted to make out with one of them.

"It's eleven o'clock sharp. You'd better go in." As Mary Ann opened the door for Lerisa she added, "I'm leaving now. It's been a pleasure meeting you. If I can help you in any way during your stay, feel free to contact me."

"Thanks, Mary Ann. I'll remember that."

Lerisa smoothed her skirt and raised her chin, ready to do battle with the man she had been reluctant to confront for nearly five months.

"One wrong word or leering look and Mr. West will find me on my way back to France so fast he won't remember what I look like," she murmured beneath her breath as she swept past Mary Ann's startled features and into her employer's inner sanctum as if she owned the place.

Perturbed at seeing nothing but the rear view of a high-backed executive chair entrenched behind a gleaming desk big enough to play paddle tennis on, Lerisa slammed the door and stormed forward.

"Mr. West." She interrupted the silence of the vast room. "I'm Lerisa Forbes and I'm damned tired of playing games. Kindly turn that monster of a chair around and introduce yourself or I'm returning to Paris tonight without so much as seeing a single glimpse of your supposedly handsome face!"

Logan spun his chair around, giving Lerisa such a devastating welcoming smile, she gaped in wide eyed disbelief.

"You bastard!" She spat out the two words bitterly.

He stared at the glossy-haired beauty before him. She was all he'd been impatiently waiting to see. His perfect image of an artist. A black-haired witch with eyes that flashed emerald fire beneath heavy black lashes.

As Lerisa mutely observed the open desire in Logan's eyes, she knew he expected her to continue her sharp tirade with added vehemence. As their eyes locked, her rage grew when he made absolutely no attempt to hide his unbridled expression of sensual interest.

Logan shifted in the deeply padded chair, cursing the discomfort of slacks suddenly taut. One cursory glimpse of her as he faced his chair forward and his body had hardened like a damned kid's. He couldn't remember a woman ever affecting him to the extent Lerisa did.

"Welcome to San Diego, *Ms. Forbes.*" Logan greeted her smoothly. It was a good thing her view of his intense sexual hunger was hidden by his desktop. If she observed his obvious arousal, she'd flail him alive with her sharp tongue, then attempt to flee as if threatened by Satan himself.

"Thank you, *Mr. West,*" Lerisa hissed through gritted teeth, wishing her clenched fingers were around his neck rather than hanging straight alongside her hips.

She stared him straight in the eye for a moment, not bothering to hide her mounting fury, then with slow deliberation thoroughly scrutinized his apparel.

Dressed in a deep brown three-piece suit, he looked the epitome of a business tycoon. Assured, wealthy, and in complete control in his surroundings.

The pristine white of his shirt and impeccable tie emphasized his deep tan. A skin color rare but unbelievably striking for a copper-haired rake!

"Mr. Logan . . . *Mark* . . . West, I presume."

"You presumed right, my beautiful bohemian artist."

Logan or Mark, Lerisa didn't care which name he used, since she hated them both equally, had the nerve to let his eyes travel up and down her figure with a look of such sensual appreciation, anyone would think he owned her.

"You look even more lovely standing in my office than you did sitting next to me in the plane, Lerisa," Logan complimented her. "I missed you, sweetheart."

"Well, I didn't miss either you or your fantasy figure, Mark What's-his-name, you damned devil!"

"Not even a little bit?" Logan teased.

"Not at all!" Lerisa stormed back.

She eyed Logan warily, debating what to do. He gave the impression of being totally relaxed, but she knew the moment she made a move toward his outer door to leave he'd pounce like the beast he was.

"I'd have been suspicious of you from the first but Jaclyn told me you had bright red hair. Your wavy locks are more brown than red."

"They've darkened since I heard about you and will no doubt turn solid gray now that we've met. You're one turbulent handful, woman."

"I'm as sweet as honey," Lerisa insisted saucily.

"To taste, yes," Logan went on. "But temperwise, no."

"I warned you," she reminded him.

"I know, and if I didn't think I could handle the merchandise, I wouldn't have spent so much money airfreighting it over."

Logan swiveled his chair back and forth, very much at ease, with his elbows on the chair arms and fingers peaked as he watched her speculatively.

"I hope you can deduct me as a loss on your income-tax return," Lerisa remarked rebelliously. "I haven't met a man yet who can handle me if I don't want him to, and you, Mr. West, are at the top of my list of undesirables."

"Think whatever you like, sweetheart," Logan warned with a knowing smile. "But when I want you I'll damned well make certain you want me first."

Taken aback by the sincerity of his advice, Lerisa paused, searching her mind for a way to exit with her pride intact and Logan sitting speechless in his chair.

"I like your outfit," he admitted, deliberately changing the subject. He slowly ran his eyes up and down her figure, not missing a single detail.

"You don't look too bad in your change of clothing either," Lerisa said between clenched teeth. "You must have an excellent tailor. It's a shame your expensive suit hides the body of the sneaky, devious type of man I hate most, as I told you on the plane."

"And do you remember my reply?"

"Yes. You said you were honest when it suited your purpose." Lerisa glared, hoping her furious look would make Logan tremble in his undoubtedly handmade shoes. "And did it?"

"Most definitely. I enjoyed each minute of our flight." He leaned back in his chair, casually clasped his hands together, and twiddled his thumbs as if he had all the time in the world. "Every single moment was delightful."

Lerisa moved to the front of his desk and leaned over, bracing herself on her outspread hands. She wasn't finished with the man yet and wanted to make certain he heard every word when she bid him a final farewell.

"Even hearing about my thoughts of working for a beastly womanizer?" she taunted in a voice filled with skepticism.

"Especially that," Logan assured her. His eyes were filled with devilry as he laughed at her attempt to put him in his place.

"Is that the underhanded way you conduct all your affairs?" Lerisa queried. "Business and otherwise?"

"No. Only the beginning of my love affair with you." Logan's darkened gaze moved from her face to her throat, then lower to the beauty of her shadowed cleavage.

"Ha!" Lerisa fumed. "Consider our affair a short one. Barely twelve hours, in fact. Lasting from Paris to Los Angeles."

She refused to acknowledge what his wandering eyes were doing to her equilibrium. It was as if he were caressing her, and it wasn't the least unpleasant.

"Sit down, honey. We've lots to talk about and your bodice is doing wild things to my heartbeat."

"My bodice?" Lerisa stormed back curiously.

"Actually, your breasts. You're so angry, you're unaware that your nipples have hardened and become enticingly visible beneath the thin material of your leotard."

"I'm leaving," Lerisa told him, straightening up, though she knew it did nothing to hide her full feminine contours. "Jaclyn was right. You're a . . . a . . . sexual pervert!"

"Hardly a pervert." Logan laughed off her sarcastic insult without concern. "I do admit I'm a man on the make and definitely single-minded in my pursuit of my next conquest"—he paused to emphasize the importance of his statement—*"which is you."*

"Don't hold your breath for that moment," Lerisa sassed. "Unlike you, I'm particular who I go to bed with."

"Good. That's the only kind of woman I'd ever want," he mocked, never short of a quick comeback.

"That's not what I hear," she spat in return. "You have

40

the reputation of bedding anything . . . whether it's free or a twenty-dollar streetwalker!"

"Rumor only," he answered, unperturbed by her continued insults.

"Do you deny my accusations?" She stood braced with hands on her hips.

"Yes and no."

"Liar!" Lerisa snapped, flashing him a haughty look. "My source of information is indisputable."

"Oh I agree I've had many women," Logan told her with complete aplomb. "But not a damned one's been free. They've all cost me in one way or another, but never as little as a twenty-dollar bill."

"Don't nitpick, Logan." Lerisa's features were stormy as she held his glance. She hoped he couldn't see the jealousy that forced her to continue her chastisement, despite knowing it was none of her business what the man had done in the past.

"You probably have a hot line direct to a madam and b-buy lovers by the gross!"

"Very few of my partners are call girls," Logan answered. "But I've found all women have a price. Whether it's a thinly veiled hint for an expensive piece of jewelry or a full-length mink . . . *afterward* . . . or an honestly stated set fee . . . *before*. The results are the same. Only the timing of the payoff differs."

"You're despicable!" Lerisa shot back.

"Why?"

"Because you're oversexed!"

"Hardly." Logan pinned her eyes, forcing her to acknowledge his point of view. "I'm a normal, virile, unattached male. I'm also completely frank to each partner regarding my desires, careful in my choice of sophisticates, and answerable to no one for my past."

"The hell with this!" Lerisa raged furiously, turning to run from the room. The damned brute had an explanation for every despicable deed he'd ever committed.

Logan leapt from his chair and stopped her before she'd taken two steps. With his greater strength he held her struggling form still, confident she wouldn't resist when he told her how he felt.

"Quit fighting me and listen. You're mine and you have been from the moment Jaclyn described you. She thinks we're a perfect match."

"What does she know?" Lerisa scoffed, wiggling helplessly to get away. "I told you she had no experience with men other than her husband."

"Jaclyn's smart enough to know you're the woman for me." He held her easily until she quit fighting his superior strength.

"The hell I am, you lying, deceitful monster." Lerisa kept both hands tightly clenched at her sides and met his eyes boldly.

"You're gorgeous, intelligent, and spirited." Logan stared back, completely impervious. "Perfect in every way."

"A perfect woman wouldn't have you on a bet."

"Wait and see, my love," Logan told her matter-of-factly.

Lerisa shifted, trying to pull away. It was like trying to move a mountain. Logan controlled her as easily as he would a young child, despite her standing four inches below six feet. She faced him bravely, knowing he couldn't curb her tongue. Not that it had done her any good so far, she admitted peevishly.

"You'd better quit squirming." Logan gave a low warning. "In case you haven't noticed yet, I'm fully aroused."

Of course she had noticed. How could she help but be

aware of something that size? The damned thing was throbbing right through the thin material of her skirt.

"I'm aware of your boyish lack of control . . . *again,*" Lerisa chided, lowering her lashes to hide the sensual intrigue in her expressive eyes.

"Good," Logan shot back. "Then you'll also realize . . . *being a woman of great experience* . . . that making love now will not only curb your bad temper but satisfy the past months' frustration you've caused me as well."

"Me caused you?"

"Yes. You refused to speak to me on the phone and took your damned sweet time answering my many letters. If I hadn't been so involved here, I'd have flown over and dragged you back to the States weeks ago."

Before Lerisa could comment on Logan's most absurd statement yet, he kissed her. Not briefly. Not softly. But with such lingering expertise that she let her firmly closed mouth soften and her lips part to accept his caress. When his kiss was finished it left her feeling ravished from head to toe and her sensitized skin imprinted forever with his loving touch.

Darn the man. Why did he have to be the only male that sent her senses soaring with a single touch?

"That's more like it," Logan informed her long minutes later. "There's no damned need to waste time arguing or trying to hold back your response to me. It won't work and you know it. You're much too passionate when I kiss you like this to freeze me out now."

With Logan's mouth once more in possession of hers, Lerisa asserted her opinion of his comments with a sharp kick on the shin. The moment her foot connected he thrust his leg intimately between hers and lowered his arms to cup her bottom with both hands. The pressure of his arousal was so shockingly exciting, her knees started to buckle and she was forced to grip his shoulders for balance.

"Be good, damn it!" Logan gasped when she squirmed against him in a vain attempt to get away. "I'm warning you, Lerisa," he reiterated as her struggles continued. "You're about two seconds away from getting laid in my office."

Lerisa stood stock-still, breathing hard. Logan's eyes were brilliant, dark with the depth of his emotions, and she knew he was what Jaclyn had forewarned her to be wary of . . . a very, very sensuous man.

She fluttered her eyelashes, giving him a false, flirtatious smile. "Is this better?" she asked sarcastically, all the while conscious of how well they fit in each other's arms and thinking that making love on his plush office carpet might not be too horrendous after all.

Remarkable, too, was the effort it took to continue being angry when she'd much rather follow up on the message his hardened body was sending to her own quivering body.

"Much better." Logan returned her smile with a satisfied grin. He looked into her eyes. They had darkened to a shimmering emerald, vacillating between outrage over his deceit and a sweet poignant desire to respond without restraint.

"You're gorgeous when you're mad," he whispered, unable to tear his glance away from her face.

"Then I'm my most beautiful right now," Lerisa spat back. "Of all the damned stupid, underhanded things for a grown man to do. Your ridiculous scheme takes the cake!"

"Would it make you feel better to know I did it because I couldn't wait any longer to see you?"

"Not one bit." She hesitated, aware he knew she was lying, then added scornfully, "And if it did I wouldn't believe you anyway."

Logan pulled her head into his chest with one hand, then stroked her back while he explained. "It's true. You've had me so tied in knots I haven't been able to work to maximum effectiveness for weeks. Jaclyn's extolled your virtues on and on until I couldn't wait any longer to meet you."

"You're crazy, Logan," Lerisa told him, refusing to be placated. "I owe you a big one for this idiotic charade and intend to get back at you as soon and as often as possible."

"Forget any retaliation. It won't work." His lips brushed the top of her head tenderly while his fingers explored her spine. "Admit you were curious about meeting me too."

"My initial inquisitiveness was soon overcome by better judgment. I told you on the plane how much I dreaded meeting you," Lerisa insisted in a voice muffled by his suit jacket. "That's why I put off coming over so long."

She eased forward a fraction, settling more comfortably against his warm frame. They fit perfectly, she thought. The top of her head nestled just below his firm chin. His hand continued to do terrific things to her taut spine and she hoped he'd never quit.

"I really did," Lerisa added, all the while burrowing her head deeper against his hard chest.

"I know it, honey," Logan soothed, unconcerned by her honest insults. "You kept putting me off with one stupid excuse after another for not coming here to do my picture."

"I didn't want to paint for you."

"Why not?"

"Survival instinct, for one. You're an awful man."

"Why did you accept my offer then?" Logan persisted.

"I needed the money," Lerisa burst out in a half-truth. She was always short of cash, but primarily her curiosity increased to the point where she could hardly wait to see if any male was as appealing as Logan was reputed to be . . . though darned if she'd confess as much to him tonight. No need admitting he far exceeded her most vivid fantasies as well as making most of her past boyfriends look like wimps.

"Jaclyn told me you have an ample monthly income," Logan continued to probe, hoping to catch her off guard so she'd tell him the truth.

"More than ample, but I like living beyond my means."

"Most women do." Logan grinned. "Apparently you need a keeper."

Lerisa raised her face from the warmth of Logan's broad chest. She leaned back in his hold and told him in a blunt voice:

"What I need is a good night's sleep and a rich sugar daddy. Either one would keep me from being subjected to a late-night interview for a job I don't want anyway."

Logan laughed at her unexpected reply. "I knew you'd be trouble, honey, but I didn't think you'd solicit my bed and my bank account within minutes of arriving."

"I haven't." Lerisa withdrew from Logan's arms and met his gaze. "First, I intend to sleep alone . . . and second, you're too young for a sugar daddy. I want an old patron of the arts. One who's physically able to shell out his money nonstop but too feeble to perform otherwise."

"You're suffering from jet lag." He took her arm and walked her to his office door. "Come on, sweetheart. We'll talk business tomorrow."

"Where are you taking me?" Lerisa demanded to know, not trusting Logan one bit.

"To my newest home. I think you'll like it."

"Why? Aren't you going to be there?"

Logan ignored her comeback and told her, "You'll like it because it has a large well-lit studio, a brand-new super-soft king-sized poster bed, and a private bedside telephone so you can call Jaclyn first thing in the morning."

"And you?" Lerisa demanded, knowing darn well he knew what she meant.

"And me"—he picked up her thoughts immediately—"I have numerous homes, plus a penthouse suite at the top of my office building. I can use each of them as I wish."

"Good," Lerisa sassed. "See you try them all during my entire stay!"

Annoyed by Logan's amused laughter, Lerisa decided to forget his arrogance and relax. What was the use of fighting? She was too darned tired to argue with the man anyway.

Barely aware of her surroundings, Lerisa let Logan escort her out of his office and into a gleaming Cadillac whose supple leather seats felt like heaven to her weary body.

She laid her head back, shut her eyes, and hoped she could manage to stay awake until she was in bed and Logan was securely locked outside the front door.

Miles later Logan gave the tail of her headband a tug. "We're home, sweetheart," he whispered close to her cheekbone.

Awakened immediately by that and a sexy nibble on her earlobe, Lerisa opened her eyes. "I'm home," she yawned. "You're not. Give me the key and it will save you a trip to the door."

"Forget it," Logan disagreed, stepping out to open the passenger door. He took her hand and drew her up from the low seat.

In seconds Lerisa was scooped up into his arms and carried up the wide walkway to an elegant English Tudor mansion. The bricked porch spread from each side of

47

elaborately carved double front doors wide enough to move a grand piano through sideways.

"What's the matter with you?" Lerisa demanded, despite the pleasure of being held tight in his strong arms. "I can walk as well as you do."

"Much better than me actually," Logan agreed with a twinkle in his eyes as he slipped a key in the ornate brass lock of one door and opened it. "My hips don't wiggle and my butt doesn't bounce."

"Shut up," Lerisa reprimanded like a tired child when he abruptly set her on her feet.

"Right this way, my sweet-talking witch." Logan bowed, spreading his hands wide as he extravagantly gestured that she enter and follow him across the stunning marble-floored entry with its vaulted ceiling to the carved oak stairway gracefully curving to the upstairs suites.

Lerisa obeyed, barely glancing right or left at the beauty of the large rooms. At the moment a bath and bed sounded more wonderful than a tour. She could snoop tomorrow.

"Which room's mine?"

"What else but the master suite?" Logan told her when he reached the end of the deeply carpeted hall.

At the door Lerisa hesitated. "Does it have a key?"

"Afraid of burglars?"

"Afraid of you," she sassed, meeting his glance with chin raised. "What assurance do I have you won't come prowling later on?"

"None," Logan admitted, giving her a hug and brief kiss on her delectable mouth. "Not knowing will keep you on your toes, or your back, I guess, since you'll be sleeping."

"Come through this door after I'm inside and you'll be on your back permanently," Lerisa threatened. "I may have a black belt in karate for all you know."

"Do you?"

"No."

"Too bad," Logan warned confidently. "Since I do. It might be fun to see who's better on the mats."

"I'm sure you are." Lerisa understood his double entendre, as he intended she would. "Jaclyn says you've certainly had plenty of experience."

"Go to sleep, my love." Logan smiled, refusing to be baited. "Inside the dressing room and your private walk-in closet are your clothes, all neatly unpacked. I think when you see the bath you'll agree it has everything any woman needs."

"A strong lock and complete privacy are all I need."

Lerisa stepped inside, pushed the carved door shut, clicked the lock with deliberate intent, then headed straight past the high poster bed. She ignored the ornate inlaid oak wet bar beside the spacious fireplace, barely glanced at the two roomy lounge chairs angled toward the hearth, and continued directly to the bathroom.

"Alone at last," she sighed with pleasure, awed by the stunning beauty of gleaming shell-shaped sinks in their mile-long marble countertop, a separate shower, and cushy ankle-deep carpeted steps leading up to a contoured tub with swan-shaped spigots of glistening metal looking suspiciously like gold.

Blissfully removing her sandals and dropping her clothes on a carpet the same emerald color as her eyes, she watched the massive tub fill while thinking of the entire sequence of events since meeting . . . Mr. Logan Mark West.

What a dream he was! Unfortunately it would take a few weeks to mold him into ideal husband material. Just about the same amount of time it would take to paint his picture, she thought, forming her plans with all the assurance of a general preparing for battle.

Not wasting any time luxuriating in the foamy bath water for more than fifteen minutes, Lerisa shut off the Jacuzzi jets and stepped out. Wrapping a soft-as-down bath sheet around her naked form, she headed for the turned-back bed.

Logan would die if he knew she slept in the buff, she grinned. His easily aroused body would need more than a cold shower to cool it down if he even suspected as much.

What a lover he'll make, she thought, easing between satin sheets on the softest bed she'd ever slept on. It was like floating and would be a perfect place to begin their love affair.

CHAPTER THREE

With her face burrowed deep in a fluffy goose-down pillow, Lerisa slowly woke to the unfamiliar sound of ocean waves gently breaking on the beach to the west of Logan's oceanfront property. She raised her head just long enough to inhale deeply and sigh, delighting in the salty, pungent fresh morning air.

It's ironic, she reflected with eyes still closed while indolently wiggling her hips back and forth on the heavenly soft mattress, the best night's sleep of her life would have to be in a notorious womanizer's bed.

Not bothering to stifle a yawn, she rolled over onto her back, rubbed both eyes sleepily, and recalled in vivid detail each moment of her previous day. It would be a long time before she forgot Logan Mark West's deceit on her flight to the States.

She had poured her heart out to the man, telling him how much she dreaded meeting her despicable employer. He had listened with such innocent understanding, she had been completely fooled. Totally entranced, too, she admitted with reluctance, yet eagerly anticipating their next confrontation.

Unfortunately his daring deceit and bold approach appealed to her sense of humor, though she'd never admit it to him without coercion. In fact, she'd never met a man so self-assured in his own masculinity. After introducing himself he had surged ahead with such confidence, it probably never occurred to him that he could ever be thwarted by a mere female.

"Damn you, Mr. West, you devastatingly sexy, lying monster." Lerisa broke the silence of the room with a sleepy murmur. "Today I intend to invent a scheme or two that will catch you by surprise. The chase may be on, but it won't run as straight or as smoothly as you expect."

Sitting up, she glanced at the bedside clock. Eight in the morning, California time. And that, she tried to convince herself, yawning again, was plenty of rest for anyone.

Her eyes were caught by the carvings on the antique bed. Intrigued, she studied the intertwined cherubic figures as they wound around the four heavy posts. They identically matched the chubby forms delicately carved into the head- and footboards. It was a surprisingly romantic bed for a thirty-four-year-old confirmed bachelor to own.

She surveyed the rest of his master suite from top to bottom and wall to wall, expecting to find at least one notched bedpost, numerous and varied adult sex toys, along with a library of lovemaking manuals on the nightstand shelves, plus mirrored ceilings reflecting her image from every angle.

Instead she found the bedroom beautifully elegant. It was a dream of a room and as tastefully furnished as any woman could want.

Her eyes moved past an opened sliding glass door and back again to stop curiously. She was certain that last night the entire wall had been covered by the drapes now drawn to both sides of the wide expanse of window. Presumably his housekeeper had entered from an adjoining outside room while she was asleep.

52

A full-length balcony beckoned with irresistible appeal. It was time to start snooping through Logan's house anyway, and that seemed a good place to begin. She wanted a clear idea of her surroundings before he dropped in, no doubt unannounced, and insisted she return to his office to complete last night's postponed business.

Unconcerned by her nudity, Lerisa threw the satin top sheet aside, slid off the bed, stood up, and stretched like a sleek, sensuous cat.

She glanced back at the shimmering gray sheets with their ruffled lace edging that covered the massive expanse of mattress and imagined Logan's naked form sprawled in the middle. A wistful smile curved her lips. It would be a challenge to test out Jaclyn's claim that Logan was reputed never to have left a woman unsatisfied.

A pleasure, too, if yesterday's kisses were any indication of his sensual expertise. She tingled just thinking about the shock of his lips, hungry and eager, on her mouth. They were the most physically exciting moments she'd ever experienced in her life.

Grabbing the carelessly dropped emerald-colored bath sheet she had used the night before, Lerisa wound it around her body. Forcing Logan and his skilled lovemaking from her mind, she tucked the ends in under one arm and began to explore the impressive room.

The pièce de résistance, not counting the bed, was an enormous ornate gold frame holding center stage over the fireplace. It's empty inner section appeared to be vacantly waiting for her painting of a nude.

The reason Logan commissioned her work was now obvious, Lerisa thought maliciously. He was getting older and apparently needed the added stimulus of a naked female form across from his giant bed to bring him to the full peak of desire.

Her arched brows drew together in a deep frown as she admitted with resentment that it was no wonder, too, considering the vast number of women he was reputed to have had. Any man leading such a dissolute life-style was bound to have a waning libido.

Although, she was compelled to admit when a rush of heat coursed through her veins remembering yesterday's actions, the devious devil had shown no sign of slowing down on either the flight or in his office. His damned libido rose faster than her hair-trigger temper!

Forcing her mind away from Logan's virility, Lerisa decided the furniture suited her aesthetic tastes completely.

She cocked her head, staring at the blank space inside the frame, and impetuously made a decision. A mischievous smile tugged the corners of her mouth into an enticing curve as she visualized the end result of her scheme.

Instead of starting the female form she'd been hired to paint, her first work would be a life-size nude of Logan. With his portrait mounted in the opulent frame centered directly across from her bed, the room would then be perfect. His boldly depicted image could return her stare with twinkling blue eyes as she began and ended each day with erotic fantasies that would shock the socks off her mother if she were still alive.

The only problem that she could foresee would be conning Logan into posing for her in the buff.

Shaking the wild tumble of uncombed curls back across her shoulders, Lerisa stepped barefoot outside onto the balcony floor. Hopefully the cool air would clear her mind of her sexy, imperious boss.

"Darn you, Logan," she complained in a clear voice. "You've completely taken over my thoughts, and no man has ever made that impact on me before. Furthermore," she continued speaking to herself, "I'm not certain I like it one little bit!"

Lerisa walked forward and leaned over the railing. Filled with rapture at the view below her, she stood silently inhaling the heady fragrance of salt in the damp morning air. Nothing in the world could compare with an ocean's aroma.

Awed by the uncluttered view of the Pacific as well as a sparkling free-form swimming pool in the midst of verdant landscaping, she looked at the vast grounds.

Towering eucalyptus spread their grayish-green leaves above heavy-needled cypress, giving complete privacy from adjoining property owners. A velvety lawn, as vividly green as her bath towel, spread endlessly.

Flowers grew in lush profusion along the borders. African daisies, some white with purple hearts, others a pure violet, intermingled with large crimson, saffron, and tangerine nasturtium. All were edged with brilliant mounds of lobelia of darkest purple, robin's-egg blue, and chaste white. It was a veritable work of art. Her eyes filled with delight thinking of wandering barefoot across the short-clipped grass among so much beauty.

"What a view! What a home!" Lerisa exclaimed wistfully, standing on tiptoe and stretching her arms high overhead. "I could happily wake up in this mansion every day of my life without any regrets at all."

"So could I if you were sharing my bed," Logan interrupted her joyous exclamation.

Lerisa spun around, returning his amused look with shocked eyes as he casually stepped from the bedroom onto the private balcony with a smile of greeting on his handsome face that would warm the coldest heart.

"How long have you been spying on me, Logan?"

"Just long enough to overhear that I made such an im-

55

pact on you yesterday that I've been in your thoughts ever since."

"That's only because I'm suffering from jet lag," Lerisa prevaricated without a qualm.

"Little liar," Logan laughed, seeing through her put-down easily.

She stared at him openly, making note of the casual blue denims and short-sleeved navy-blue shirt that suited his masculine physique so perfectly. A sharp breeze surged off the ocean and up the bluff to lift thick strands of hair above her brow. The color caught and held her eye, its sheen beneath the bright sunlight a glossy russet-tinted brown. A stunning color to look at, a hard color to duplicate, she thought, dying to get started on the painting of him for her bedroom wall.

"We'll make this our principal residence from now on since you like it so well, Ms. Forbes," Logan broke in on her thoughts in a convincing voice.

"Think again, Mr. West," Lerisa disagreed. She gave him a level look through hastily narrowed lashes, hoping it disguised the spontaneous joy she experienced from his unexpected appearance. "My time here is limited to the number of days it takes me to complete your painting."

"What about the fact that I'm the only man who has ever managed to completely control your thoughts?"

"What about it?" Lerisa's voice was deliberately casual, though her heart was still racing like a wild thing.

"That's what I asked you," Logan reminded in an even voice.

"Since you're so good at eavesdropping, you will also remember I said I didn't like it one little bit!"

"That's only a temporary problem," Logan assured her with a devilish twinkle in his eyes. "A good man should be able to overcome your outspoken resistance easily."

"A good man, maybe," Lerisa threw back at him. "But not you. You, Mr. West, are the exact antithesis of good, as your past reputation and yesterday's escapade proved."

"Rant on, honey," Logan prompted with considerable aplomb. "Whatever you call me makes no difference. The only important fact to remember is that I'm going to be your next and . . . more importantly . . . your *last lover.*"

"That'll be the day!" Lerisa denied vehemently. She didn't like the gleaming look of ruthless intent in his eyes one bit.

"And night too," Logan added with infinite seriousness. "I'm not one who is easily satisfied."

"So I've heard," she scoffed, jealously forcing the image of him making love to other women from her mind.

"You read me wrong, honey. I'm not talking about the short-lived relationships I've had in the past. I'm alerting you to the length of time I intend to keep you in my bed when we do make love. Our first bout will go on for hours, Lerisa." His eyes pinned hers, his husky voice warning of his intent: *"Maybe even days . . . or weeks."*

"You'll have to get me there first," Lerisa dared, raising her chin a defiant notch higher.

"That's the easy part," Logan informed her with complete self-confidence. "You're a very passionate lady."

His eyes swept her stormy features, lingered on the burgeoning curve of her high breasts, then returned to hold her mutinous glance with a look of total confidence.

"Since you approve of this home, I've decided to consummate the seduction here."

"Think again," Lerisa warned, giving him such a fiery glare that a lesser man would have trembled in his shoes and fled without further comment. "Now get out of here. I'm not dressed."

"Believe me, I'd noticed," Logan drawled huskily, holding her glance with eyes filled with admiration. Rather than leave, he stood his ground and watched with open amusement while she boldly looked him over in return.

"Out, Logan." Lerisa pointed to the door. "You're no longer welcome."

"I can't believe that," he continued with a self-satisfied expression on his face. "Especially after overhearing how much you care about me."

He knew his comment would increase her temper, which was a sight he doubted any man could witness without becoming aroused. He sure couldn't, as evidenced by the straining cloth across his crotch. Annoyed or sweet, she was the most stimulating woman he'd ever known and he could feel his body tremble just looking at her.

"Your impact on my senses will be even more short-lived than my days working for you are," Lerisa answered impudently, not liking his assured expression one little bit, though his obvious arousal did a lot for her morale.

"I think not, love," Logan soothed in a husky voice that caressed her taut nerves like velvet. "While you slept cozy as a newborn kitten, I made plans for your seduction and I'm getting more frustrated by the moment."

"You can stuff the part of your seduction that includes me," Lerisa, undaunted, warned. "I have my entire future planned and it doesn't include you, your gorgeous home, or your dubious lovemaking."

"Don't knock it until you've tried it," Logan suggested, using an old cliché.

"Try it?" Lerisa snapped. "I have no interest in even experiencing a small taste test of anything that the entire adult female population of California has undoubtedly sampled at least once!"

"Hmm," Logan mused, raising one eyebrow in deep

concentration. "Your choice of words must be a Freudian slip. The image of swapping taste tests with you leaves me damned near speechless."

"Forget it!" she burst out furiously. "You know darned well I meant that I have no desire to be another notch on your overcarved bedpost."

"You? Just another notch? Impossible," Logan contradicted with concern. "Never you, sweetheart. I warned you yesterday that I'm particular about my women."

"That sounds strange coming from a man who buys bed partners like most men buy lottery tickets."

"A quote from your best friend, Jaclyn, no doubt," Logan said. "I'd better speak to Josh. It sounds like her tongue needs curbing by her husband as badly as yours does by me."

"Don't waste your time on a phone call," Lerisa warned. "I'm here to paint one picture, then I'll be gone as quick as the jet will fly me back to Paris. In the meantime you can direct your sexual energies elsewhere, since you'd be the last man I'd consider for a lover."

"Don't bet money on it, honey," Logan pointed out emphatically. He stepped forward, stopping one stride in front of her. "You're just as good as had by me right now, Lerisa. You're mine and no one else's from this point on."

"Apparently you weren't listening. I'm no man's . . . and especially not yours!"

"Cut the crap, witch, and get the hell over here," Logan cautioned in a deep voice that brooked no argument. "Apparently it's time I sweetened your sharp little tongue with a kiss."

Lerisa braced herself, refusing to budge an inch. Her chin raised, alert eyes shimmering with sparks of excitement as she waited to see what Logan would do.

She stared openly, thought he had the most sensual

mouth of any man she'd ever known, and admired the deeply tanned skin that emphasized his white teeth. This is ridiculous, she fumed inwardly, drawing her arched brows together in a frown. She was looking at his damned sexy features like a love-starved old maid.

Logan returned her belligerent look, holding her glance with eyes that darkened to a deep indigo blue filled with loving awareness.

"Come to me, *Lay . . . risa,*" he drawled out her name huskily. "First we kiss, then we argue. You didn't even say good morning before you lit into me."

Opening her mouth to object vehemently, Lerisa changed her mind, moved forward until they were barely touching, and stopped. She raised her hands, placing them gently around Logan's strong neck, and softly sighed.

Unable to control her body's involuntary reaction, she let his exciting warmth invade her senses until she wanted nothing more than to be in his arms forever. She lifted her face, aching to feel the pressure of his mouth claiming hers as it had the day before.

Her eyes shimmered with excitement and eager anticipation. She couldn't have protested if she had wanted to when he placed his hands on her shoulders and drew her unresisting body tight to his.

Logan laughed softly at Lerisa's rapid about-face. "From anger to angel in a moment's time. You're quite a woman, and it's time you were thoroughly made love to."

He claimed her mouth in a kiss that lingered, lifted, returned, and leisurely continued as though he never wanted to draw away.

The moment their lips touched, a sweeping tide of emotion surged through Lerisa's body, causing her to tremble uncontrollably.

She felt Logan's hands move. With exquisite seductiveness one slid across her bare shoulder to fondle her tender nape while the other caressed the entire length of her spine slowly and steadily.

The pleasure of his restless fingers on the sensitive skin of her neck was nearly as addictive as the warmth of his broad palm cupping her bottom. His fingers stroked the rounded curves intimately, then tightened to pull her upward until she was held firm against the full length of his hardened manhood.

"Lovely witch," Logan murmured, not releasing her mouth as he began an exploration of the moist sweetness within.

"Womanizing devil," Lerisa scolded, aware of the heat of his arousal throbbing against her lower abdomen with persistent intent.

"Enticing witch," he groaned when she returned the stimulating touch of his tongue with the tip of her own.

"Sneaky devil," she whispered, returning each erotic caress with one equally sensual.

"Passionate witch," he growled when she pressed her full breasts into the thin material of his knit shirt and squirmed to get even closer.

"Demanding devil," she purred, unable to stand another second in his arms without dragging him off to her tumbled bed.

Finding it nearly impossible to curb his urge to thrust his maleness into the heated warmth between her legs, Logan temporarily sated himself by moving his tongue inside the moistness of her mouth in duplicate motions of the act of love. Never in his life had he wanted a woman like the one responding with such uninhibited joy in his arms.

Unmeasurable moments later, Lerisa reluctantly drew away, clinging to his broad shoulders for balance. The man's sensual expertise was a miracle. His kisses made her feel as if he had violated her most intimate self. What on earth would his complete lovemaking be like? Could she live through it? Better yet, could she live without it, once experienced?

Logan shuddered, inhaling deep breaths of air in an attempt to regain his earlier composure. A stunned whistle escaped his lips when he realized how near he had come to climaxing during their embrace. Never in his entire life had a woman affected him to the point that he nearly lost control during a single kiss.

"G-good morning, Logan." Lerisa clung to his waist, still needing his support until her legs regained strength enough to hold her weight.

"God almighty, sweetheart, I like the way you say hello," Logan groaned in disbelief.

"You . . . you . . . er . . . don't do too bad of a greeting yourself," Lerisa stammered breathlessly.

Logan eyed her smooth bare shoulders and the exposed cleavage, which drew him like a magnet. His eyes were black as pitch as he tugged the material enough to partially expose the creamy flesh of each rounded breast.

"I like your nightie." He trailed one widespread hand across the satiny fullness burgeoning over the left edge of her towel, held her widened gaze for a breathless moment as one finger lazily probed in the scented valley, then casually proceeded to caress the right side.

Shattered by his silent intimacy, Lerisa jerked back, self-consciously hitching the slipping velour towel securely across her bosom. It was amazing that the thing still decently covered her body after Logan's long, devastating kiss and taunting caress. If it had fallen down she wouldn't have objected anyway, she admitted truthfully. Right now the thinnest barrier between their skin touching seemed unbearable.

"As I said, I like your nightie, honey," he reiterated, enjoying the play of emotions in her gorgeous eyes.

"It's just your bath sheet," she whispered, leaving the balcony on legs that still felt decidedly wobbly.

Logan's glance lingered on the graceful curve of Lerisa's spine and shapely calves above slender ankles exposed below the towel.

She turned back, speaking over her shoulder, "Didn't you recognize it?"

"I'm familiar with my towels, but that wasn't the night attire I meant," Logan explained matter-of-factly as he followed her into the bedroom. "When I said I liked your choice of sleepwear I was speaking about your lack of any clothing at all. You have skin a monk couldn't resist touching."

"What are you talking about, Logan?" Lerisa begged. "Isn't this the first time you saw me today?"

"Second." His eyes were alight with devilry. "Earlier this morning, while you were still asleep, I crept—"

"You what?" Lerisa demanded, waiting with bated breath for his next damaging comment.

"I entered this room." Logan sighed, closing his eyes as if recalling the moment in explicit detail. "Believe me, it taxed my control to the limit observing your . . . er . . ."

"My what?" Lerisa demanded. Much to her pique, he took his own sweet time before resuming in a calm voice:

"Your *half*-covered nakedness beneath the thin, clinging sheet."

"Half-covered?" she urged, catching the additional emphasis he placed on that wording.

"Yes."

"Which half?" Lerisa insisted with a feeling of sudden vulnerability. It was completely possible she might have tossed the sheet off and lain totally exposed while asleep. If Logan saw her nude, she wanted to be awake and consenting. "Tell me, Logan."

Aware of her thoughts, Logan soothed her fears with a tender smile. "Your entire top half, which was actually your bottom side, since you were burrowed belly-down in the mattress like you never intended to leave."

"You're crazy," Lerisa insisted, hating the thought of him staring at her unobserved.

"Crazy for not stripping the damned sheet off and making love to you that instant."

"Darned fool," Lerisa scolded. "I thought for a moment you were a peeper as well as a pervert."

"I'll be guilty of both charges if you continue sleeping au naturel. I damned near took a bite out of your delectable-looking butt right then instead of the near future as previously planned. That silly sheet clung to you like a second skin."

"Because I sleep in the buff doesn't explain how you managed to enter my room," Lerisa voiced, changing the subject abruptly, since the thought of him nipping her backside sounded intriguing and she wanted to curb their relationship at least for a day or two.

She turned to face him, standing with both hands on her hips. "When I left you last night I deliberately locked you out of this room."

"I heard you," Logan told her, sitting down in a lounge chair as if he had every right to be there. He crossed his legs, nonchalantly letting one ankle rest on his other knee. Without removing his eyes from his polished leather loafer, he waited for her to speak. He could feel her temper grow as she prepared to demand an explanation.

"Well then," Lerisa stormed, "detail if you can how you came waltzing in here unannounced . . . *not once but twice* . . . through a securely locked solid wood door?"

"Would you believe I'm a magician?"

"I would not!"

"Well then," Logan contemplated. He raised his eyes from his shoe and deliberately let them trail from her bare feet up the slender length of limb exposed to his eyes and past the fingers tightly clenched on her shapely hips. He skirted back and forth across each voluptuous breast, with its hardened nipple straining the toweling, then reluctantly moved upward to her stormy features, framed by midnight-black hair tousled from a long night's sleep.

"Well then, what?" Lerisa insisted, finding it took every bit of poise she had to stand before him as if he wasn't giving her the most thorough scrutiny of her life. "Answer me, darn you."

"What was the question?" Logan requested with feigned innocence. "Somehow when my eyes got to your breasts I completely forgot what you asked."

"You know damned well what I said, Mr. West," Lerisa shot back. His composure was as annoying as his uninvited presence.

"As I recall," Logan mused, closing his eyes as if deep in thought, "you wanted to know how I entered your bedroom."

When he didn't come forth with an explanation as soon as she thought he should, Lerisa burst out wryly, "Did you put on your karate outfit and chop the door down with your bare hand, then replace it while I slept?"

"No."

"Did you play a gallant knight, climb up the balcony, and enter that way?"

"No."

"Then how did you get in here without me hearing you?"

"Actually I picked the lock," Logan told her in a disgustedly calm voice. His eyes briefly slid down to her thrusting breasts and instantly darkened with the telltale signs of passionate interest. "I'm very good at *getting into things.*"

"So I've heard," Lerisa acknowledged in a disgusted voice. She hastily closed her eyes, hoping to shadow her resentment as she jealously imagined the many women he had satisfied with his virile body.

When she glanced up Logan's undisguised desire left her shaken. To avoid commenting further she turned sideways, refusing to meet his look. She hated being so responsive each time his mood changed to one of passion. It made her feel vulnerable, which was something no man had ever succeeded in doing before.

A wide smile tugged Logan's sensual mouth as he rose and moved slowly forward with a determined expression on his face.

"Keep away, Logan." Lerisa straightened her shoulders, unaware that her silhouette enhanced her feminine contours with enticing clarity.

"As a matter of fact," he mocked, "I'm especially good at getting into things I desire."

"I—I'll take your word for it," Lerisa flung back at him, aware that she was treading on dangerous ground. It was obvious she had made no objection to any caress he'd given her to date, so why should he expect her to refuse him now?

Strangely enough, his erotic teasing fascinated rather than offended. Her overactive mind was crowded with images of testing his staying power at the earliest possible opportunity.

Unable to withstand another emotional onslaught on

her vacillating emotions, she turned her back to him and rushed across the plush carpet to the privacy of her dressing room.

She walked inside, calling over her shoulder in a clear voice, "No wonder you're so rich. You have all the skills a successful criminal needs."

"Or a womanizer intent on seduction," Logan corrected with a husky laugh. He smiled indulgently at her hasty retreat.

"Every despicable deed Jaclyn told me about must be correct. She especially warned me that you were relentless when in hot pursuit."

"Jaclyn's right," Logan admitted without concern. "Now get dressed or my . . . *hot pursuit* . . . and . . . *seduction* . . . will begin and end in the dressing room you fled to when it looked like I was going to make love to you."

"I didn't flee," Lerisa protested. "I sauntered in here to get dressed just so I can go look for your kitchen. I'm starving."

"Sauntered?" Logan disputed with a knowing laugh. "You retreated like a frightened virgin."

"Me?" Lerisa taunted in a voice filled with disbelief. Nonchalantly shrugging one bare shoulder, she commented without further explanation, "Men have been an integral part of my life since my fifteenth birthday."

"I don't have time to hear about that now," Logan insisted in a voice suddenly grown bitter. "Get dressed and hurry up about it."

"Why should I?"

"Because we have lots of unfinished business to take care of. Personal and otherwise."

"Great with me," Lerisa agreed, rooting through the many drawers until she found her underwear. "Though I intend to eat a huge breakfast before I discuss anything with you." She looked up, adding impudently, "Personal or otherwise."

"Tempestuous brat!" Logan laughed, peering into the dressing room as Lerisa gathered up wispy bits of vivid red lace. "I'll see you get anything you want, but you'll eat in my downstairs office while I explain what I want you to paint. Maybe with your mouth full I can talk undisturbed."

With that parting shot he left the room as Lerisa spun around to watch his departure.

"Hmm," she mused with a teasing smile. Logan may think her walk was better than his, but his backside was decidedly sensual, taut and compact. In fact, she just might sink her teeth into his tempting tush someday in the near future too.

Grabbing navy-blue jeans and a new blouse in a vivid cherry color that exactly matched her bra and panties, she admitted Logan's broad shoulders and long limbs helped emphasize his cute behind. What a sexy devil to work for, she mused with unconcealed admiration.

Feeling like a million dollars after a good night's sleep, a passionate good-morning kiss, and challenging verbal interchange, Lerisa walked into the bathroom. A quick shower, clean clothes, and she would feel ready to conquer the world. Logan included.

"It's too damned bad you don't want your ceilings painted, too, Mr. Logan Mark West," she giggled. "I feel my talents are equal to Michelangelo today and just might consider spending the rest of my life painting a miniature Sistine Chapel in each of your homes."

Lerisa added as an afterthought, speaking into the silent room, "Of course my painting time will have to be arranged between swapping passionate kisses for my fee. A fair exchange of labor if what I've experienced so far is any indication."

With those exciting thoughts milling through her mind, Lerisa rushed through her morning's preparations. She was eager to get dressed and see Logan's home office, which would no doubt be as lavish as everything else he owned that she'd seen thus far.

First, though, was a phone call to Jaclyn. Logan could wait while she told her former classmate everything that had happened.

Lerisa picked up the receiver and pushed Jaclyn's number into the bedside touch-tone phone. It would be wonderful to talk without the expense of an overseas call. Ever since her best friend had finished art school and married Josh, they'd barely had time to keep in touch. They had promised to see each other often during her stay in California and she wanted to set a date to meet as soon as possible.

"Darn it," Lerisa grumbled when she received a busy signal. "Oh well," she spoke out loud, "I'll reconnoiter the upstairs area, dial her again, talk a while, then go beard the beast in his den."

She left the bedroom, heading directly for the first door along the wide hallway. She entered, immediately suspicious as she noticed the unmade bed and distinctly male furnishings. Had Logan spent the night in the adjoining room?

Something else to find out, Lerisa decided, boldly entering a dressing room crammed with fine men's clothes in the size and colors that fit him to perfection.

That did it! She fled downstairs with all thoughts of further prying forgotten as she hurried to find out just what Logan thought he was doing sleeping here when she had insisted he stay at his other homes each night during her entire stay.

CHAPTER FOUR

Lerisa burst into Logan's office unannounced and slammed the door shut to get his full attention before voicing her outrage.

"Damn you, Logan, you devious monster. You fooled me again." Unconcerned that he was speaking on the phone, she continued to blast him contemptuously. "I told you you can't sleep here until I've finished my commission."

She stood just inside the paneled room with legs braced, hands clenched on each hip, and chin raised waiting for his reply. When he didn't speak she gave him her most disdainful look. Completely ignoring his upraised hand commanding her to be silent, she continued unabated:

"What's the first thing I find when I leave *my* room?" Her eyes shone with sparks of temper as she answered her own question. *"Your* bedroom, complete with its unmade king-sized playpen, that's what!"

Seated behind a highly polished desk that had been in his family for years, Logan placed his hand over the mouthpiece and slowly lowered the receiver.

"What made you think it was my room you were prying around in?" he asked in a laconic voice. His eyes narrowed with displeasure, pinning hers as she started to open her mouth to persevere with her tirade.

Deciding to replan her attack, Lerisa clenched her teeth

and swallowed nervously. She knew her momentary hesitation was all Logan needed to presume there would be no further argument.

She held his gaze resolutely, thinking how wrong she'd been about the color of his eyes. They were definitely a shimmering indigo blue instead of cerulean, as she'd first thought on the plane. Maybe his animosity affected them like his passion did. It was certainly obvious he was furious with her now.

Until that moment she'd never counted on his having a temper equal to hers. His disapproval intimidated her and she instinctively knew it would be wise to back off. Unfortunately resentment overcame her better judgment and she remained determined to tell him everything on her mind.

"Answer me, witch," he insisted, looking ready to wring her neck for daring to question his actions. "Why did you assume you were in my room?"

"Because the bed's been used, the closet is filled with your size clothes, and—"

"And what?" he cut her off in a firm voice, allowing his own furor to increase as she continued to censure him for his behavior when he felt she had no cause. "Tell me, Lerisa, before I really get mad."

"And the whole damned thing looks like a seduction scene except there aren't any mirrors on the ceiling in your room either." She lowered her lashes to shield her eyes from his anger, adding childishly, "Besides, I told you not to stay here last night."

"No one," Logan informed Lerisa in a controlled voice, "and that includes you, sweetheart, tells me when I can or cannot sleep in any home I own. Now be quiet a minute and listen."

He gave her a disgusted look, turned aside, then ignored

71

her, as if she weren't there, to resume his conversation unperturbed.

"As I was saying, Josh, before I was so rudely interrupted."

Logan leaned back in the chair, pointed to a serving cart, and indicated that Lerisa should lift the gleaming silver lid.

Thoroughly chastened, Lerisa readily admitted that Logan had every right to sleep where he wanted without being yelled at by someone in his employ. As quick to overcome her temper as she was to flare up, she ignored his frowning features and gave him a devastating smile of apology.

What did it matter now anyway, with the distraction of a neatly set table close by? Her last bit of anger was promptly replaced by the gnawing pangs of hunger.

Everything she could see looked and smelled delicious. A coffeepot, with its fresh-brewed aroma tantalizing her nostrils, waited beside two cups. Various sweet rolls and breads filled to overflowing a napkin-lined basket. Curls of butter and pots of jam rested beside an icy pitcher of orange juice.

Tossing her head at Logan, who continued talking, she walked to the cart and peeked beneath the lid. A sigh of sheer pleasure escaped her lips as she saw a steaming plate of ham and eggs with fresh hash-brown potatoes, crispy fried and golden, waiting to be consumed.

Inherently polite, Lerisa poured Logan a cup of coffee first. She carried it, along with the sugar and creamer on their silver tray, and set it on his desk.

As she placed the hot drink in front of him he reached over and grabbed her hand. Taking it to his mouth, he kissed her fingers gently, then gave her a smile that assured her all was forgiven on his part as well.

Feeling decidedly happier, she pulled a chair up to the cart, placed a napkin across her lap, picked up her fork, and prepared to taste the first good American-style country breakfast she'd eaten in years.

Raising the fork, filled with a tender slice of ham, to her mouth, Lerisa paused in stunned disbelief as Logan announced with his usual daring, "Sure I'll repeat it, Josh. I said I was getting married."

Logan gave Lerisa a tender loving smile that made her wonder what he could possibly do to top that solemn heart-stopping statement.

"I'm serious," he repeated, as if Josh didn't believe him the first time. "Since Jaclyn is the one responsible for my sudden downfall, I thought you should be the first to congratulate me."

All the blood drained from Lerisa's face on hearing his profound words. Her hands trembled as she set the fork down and looked him square in the eye.

Logan's words left her absolutely speechless for the first time that she could remember. Surely she wasn't expected to calmly eat her breakfast while the only damned man she could ever love calmly made plans to wed some other woman? But what would Jaclyn have to do with finding him anyone besides her?

Noticing Lerisa's shocked expression, Logan stood, walked around the desk, and motioned for her to come to him.

Without thinking she rose and went straight into his arms, hugging him about the waist while she gathered enough composure to let him know what a cold, heartless bastard he was.

One firm hand, as steady as her heart was unsteady, held her still. With her face directly over his heart, she breathed deeply of the clean male scent invading her nostrils and knew another imprint was registered on her senses not to be forgotten.

"I hate you, Logan," she whispered into his brawny chest as he laughed at something Josh said. "Even if I do love you too," she murmured beneath her breath, uncaring if he could hear her or not.

Love, Logan? Already? Impossible. Or was it? Thoughts ran through her mind with the speed of a computer. Obviously the months of hearing about the man from Jaclyn had not only preprogrammed her to dislike him for his womanizing past but to be intrigued as well. The first sight of him had turned from intrigue to love and she was stuck with it whether she approved of him or not. Damn the monster anyway.

"Who am I marrying?" Logan paused before answering. He fondled her back as she leaned into him, knowing she was waiting for his reply.

Lerisa's spine stiffened, despite the pleasure of his wandering fingers as they reached beneath her blouse and stroked her bare skin. She tried to ignore his caress, holding her breath instead, since it was much more important to hear the name of his intended bride.

"Why I'm marrying Ms. Lerisa Forbes, of course," Logan assured him in a pleased voice. "I told you last Christmas I'd close escrow and see the deed was recorded in my name as soon as I found my woman."

Lerisa exhaled with a satisfied smile, considered his high-handed manner in announcing their marriage to someone else before asking if she was agreeable, and decided he needed putting in his place.

Before Logan's wandering fingers left her rib cage and found the sensitive curve of her breast, she pulled away.

Grabbing the receiver from Logan, she spoke sharply into the mouthpiece, "Josh, this is Lerisa. Tell Jaclyn I'll phone her . . . *after* I've dealt with my boss. Apparently he's under the impression that I've flown to California as a subintelligent mail-order bride, not a highly trained, multitalented painter!"

With that parting shot she pulled away from Logan's arms and slammed the receiver down on the phone. Facing him with her firmest glare, she started to speak when he took her back into his arms.

"I love you, Lerisa, you lovely, enticing witch," he laughed tenderly. His eyes shimmered with open amusement at her blunt outpouring to Josh.

"That's absurd. You've known me only a day, which is not nearly long enough for a monumental happening like that to take place."

"The hell it isn't," Logan disputed vehemently. "I fell in love with you the exact moment Jaclyn told me she had a girlfriend as bold as I am. When she described your coalblack hair and said you had eyes the color of expensive emeralds, I was hooked. You sounded like my dream woman come to life."

"That's pretty powerful flattery, Logan." He didn't need to know yet that she'd fallen for him equally as hard. His arrogance needed curbing as it was.

"It's not flattery," he replied huskily, cradling her to his hard chest. "You've been a long time coming to me, honey. For the first time in my memory I felt lonely, yet I hadn't even met you. Now that I have, my life is complete for the first time."

Lerisa returned his glance with a look of wonder. His heady declaration assured her beyond doubt that she was his special woman for all time.

Despite the quivering in her stomach, she leaned back in his arms and expressed her opinion: "That still doesn't give you the right to tell someone we're going to be married before you've even asked me whether or not I'm willing."

"Are you?" Logan asked, bending forward to kiss the tip of her dainty nose.

Her lashes lowered, forming dark crescents above her smooth cheeks. "I'll have to think about it," she managed, breathless at the thought of being Logan's wife.

"Even if I got down on my knees and asked you properly?" Logan questioned. His eyes suddenly darkened, nearly black with his mounting desire to love her.

"Try me and see," Lerisa suggested, her heart melting at the thought that Logan cared enough to appease her displeasure at his audacity. She had had numerous proposals since the age of fifteen, but none had compared with today's. Nor had the men doing the proposing.

Logan gave her a soft kiss, then released her. He knelt on one knee and reached for her left hand. Slowly drawing it to his mouth, he turned it over and placed the tenderest kiss she'd ever received in her life in the middle of her quivering palm.

With a voice that was deadly serious, matching the reverent look in his keen eyes, he asked, "Will you marry me, Lerisa? I love you with all my heart. You're the only woman I could ever want for my wife."

"Oh, Logan," she sighed, barely able to speak she was so overwhelmed with tenderness for the man bowed down before her.

"I do love you, my darling." His solemn glance held her shimmering gaze as he told her truthfully, "I've never said those words to anyone else, Lerisa. Only you."

"Y-you haven't?" Lerisa whispered, too overcome to say more.

"Not once." He turned her hand back over and kissed the finger his gold ring would surround. "You're also the only woman I've ever remotely considered asking to marry me."

"R-really?" she stammered, knowing she sounded like an idiot with a five-word vocabulary.

"Really," he assured her. "I give you my heart for all time."

"I—I can't believe this," she whispered, doubting her own heart would ever beat normally again. It seemed like a fantasy watching the intense features of the dynamic man kneeling in front of her as he laid bare his innermost feelings.

"That's a beautiful proposal, Logan," she praised him gently. "It couldn't be more perfect."

"Is there anything I forgot?" he questioned, caressing her hand as he waited for her reply.

"Let me think a minute," Lerisa whispered back, wondering if her trembling legs would continue to hold her up that long. "Why did you ask?"

"Because"—he smiled, his eyes twinkling with sudden mirth—"I'd like to get off my damned knees while you give me your answer."

"Changing your mind already?"

"No." He grinned. "The floor's hard."

"Hmm . . ." Lerisa paused, devilishly making him wait longer. "I guess there isn't anything else that needs to be decided with you in a cowed position, though it is tempting to keep you there until you've completed fiancé training."

"Fiancé training? It'll be a cold day in . . ." Logan broke off, rising to take her back in his arms before finishing, "a cold day in San Diego before I participate in premarital boot camp. Besides, you haven't agreed to my proposal yet."

Snuggling close, Lerisa thought a moment, then surprised him with a quick reply. "I'll marry you, Logan."

"You will?"

"Yes," Lerisa assured him. "It's a marvelous idea. You're far too old not to have had your wings clipped before now."

"Why you little devil." Logan hugged her to him, wondering if he'd ever be able to curb her impudent tongue.

"Hardly little. I'm five feet eight inches tall."

"You're a wee babe next to me," he told her, resting his chin on her lustrous curly hair as she burrowed her face into his throat.

"Your great size does make me feel fragile and cuddly despite my height." Lerisa nuzzled his throat affectionately. "I like the feeling of protectiveness that seems an inherent part of you. Once I would have given anything for your strength."

"Tell me about it," Logan probed gently, knowing he would lay down his life without question to keep her safe.

"I—I can't. It's a sordid little story and one I forced to the back of my mind years ago." She looked at him with trusting eyes. "Someday I'll share it with you, but not yet. It's something I've never been able to talk about."

"You'll tell me when you're ready," Logan assured her with a compassionate hug, certain Lerisa would confide in him soon. "And I promise to listen with concern and my undivided attention." He placed an understanding kiss on her brow.

"That alone makes you a priceless man," Lerisa confessed, cognizant that in the future she would disclose her most intimate secrets.

"God but I love you, honey," Logan moaned, trembling with the thought of Lerisa being beside him for the rest of his life.

"That's nice to hear," she admitted with a happy smile. "Was my agreement to marry you a surprise?"

"Shock's a better word. I expected you to flail me alive for even daring to ask you to be my wife. Instead you concur without the slightest argument."

"You're not home free yet," Lerisa told him pertly. "There are one or two rules you have to play by and a condition to agree to before we're officially engaged."

"Name them," Logan demanded in a voice that warned her he would make promises only if they suited his purpose and sounded reasonable.

"One"—she leaned back, placing her hands on his tightened biceps—"I expect complete fidelity from this moment on. Absolute, total, positive, unquestionable loyalty to our wedding vows of forsaking all others. There can be no exceptions to this rule."

"Hmm." Logan thought for a while, then threw his head back to stare at the ceiling for a moment. Unaware that his eyes were gleaming with admiration and laughter that belied his grave voice, he challenged, "You plan to cut me off from the rest of the female sex cold-turkey, do you?"

"I most certainly do," Lerisa stormed, not quite certain if he was teasing when he lowered his chin until their eyes met. "I've never taken any commitment lightly. My engagement and upcoming marriage will be the most serious decision of all."

"Mine also," Logan assured her, no longer jesting. "I also believe in fidelity for both of us."

"My loyalty comes without question. Your past life-style might be a bit hard to change."

"I'll never give you cause to worry in the future," Logan vowed.

Lerisa drew back. She raised her chin and gave him a stormy look while confessing her innermost feelings. "I feel confident enough to curtail your future activities, Logan, but frankly I'm not too keen on sleeping in a bed you've spent a good portion of your past sharing with someone else!"

"You're priceless, honey, but there's been no other woman who has slept in that bit of romantic foolishness in the master suite . . . with or without me."

"A-are you sure?" she asked foolishly.

"Definitely," he assured her with a husky laugh. "My wonderful mother shipped that antique monster to me last Christmas with strict instructions that it was to be, *quote* . . . used for the woman I intended making my wife . . . *unquote.* When I phoned to thank her she insisted I promise no one-night stands even see it."

"That's wonderful." Lerisa glowed with pleasure. "Obviously she knows her son well."

"Not well enough," Logan retorted without a qualm, "or she'd know I never bring my partners to my homes."

"Good," Lerisa told him emphatically. "I'd hate to get rid of the most appealing bed I've ever seen in my life."

Logan gripped her shoulders, speaking in a soft, serious voice, "Forget my past, sweetheart, and let's seal your promise to be my wife with a kiss before your overactive mind comes up with a stipulation I can't consent to or explain to your satisfaction."

Shaking her head no, Lerisa surprised him yet again by placing both hands on his chest to stop the intended caress. "I haven't finished yet, Logan. I came here to do a painting and that comes before our marriage."

"The hell it does!" Logan exclaimed, releasing her to pace the paneled room. He stopped, faced her, and declared, "You can paint the rest of your life, but I want you here as my wife now."

"Forget I said yes then." Lerisa spread her fingers, trying

to make him understand her adamant refusal. "I need this opportunity to finish my first commission *after* years of schooling. It's important to me to complete one job before taking on the demanding task of keeping you in line the rest of my years."

"Damn you, woman," Logan complained bitterly over her demand. He wanted her now, not at some distant date in the months ahead. "I'll withdraw my commission."

"You can't," Lerisa threatened defiantly. "I have a signed contract and I intend to see that you honor it."

"I'll tear the damned thing up," Logan warned. "I wrote it and I can damned well break it."

"You're being unreasonable and you know it." Lerisa flopped into a comfortable reading chair, crossed her legs as if she intended to stay there forever, and defied him again. "I'll sue you for breach of contract."

"Go ahead." Logan shrugged as if it didn't bother him in the least what she said or did. "I'll even let you use one of my attorneys and pay the fee, but remember this." He faced her with the assurance of a man used to being in charge. "Before the case gets to court you'll be mine in every sense of the word."

"If that's a threat, it won't work. I've looked forward to you making love to me since I first spotted you on the plane."

"I can't believe this," Logan exclaimed. "You sit there defying me yet openly admit you want me as your lover."

"Yes I do, but I'll abstain now, and so will you after you hear my last condition." She had had a sudden idea that was certain to cause a few gray streaks on his handsome head. A mischievous twinkle shone in her eyes as she thought of the effect of her next words.

"Start talking," he told her, closing his eyes to shut out the sight of her distracting beauty as he listened.

"Are you sure you're ready?"

"Fire away." Logan shrugged one broad shoulder as if he couldn't care less what she came up with.

"When I do paint I lead a celibate life."

"You what?" he roared. How could one slip of a woman be so damned contrary? First she confessed she wanted him to bed her the moment she saw him, then she obstinately stated she didn't have sex while painting.

"You heard me, Logan."

"Yes, I did." He faced her, determined to squelch that idea immediately. "Consider your stupid artistic idiosyncrasy changed as of now."

"I will not! You have to agree to leave me alone until your picture is finished or the marriage is off."

Prepared to end her impossible demands at once, Logan exclaimed forcefully, "If you think I'd ever go along with that harebrained idea, you're nuts. I'm through listening to your rules and your conditions. We'll be married as I planned it."

"I won't!"

"You will!" he stormed back, deliberately crossing his arms across his chest to add emphasis to his firm stance. "I won't put up with a single excuse that will delay that moment one second longer than previously projected."

"When is that moment, Logan, or will Josh and all your other friends hear about it before I do?" Lerisa asked impudently.

She observed Logan's reactions with appreciation. He really was magnificent when aroused, either in anger or in passion. It would take a clever woman to handle his overpowering personality. Her eyes shone with merriment, knowing she was not only willing but equal to the task.

"I asked when you plan to waltz me down the aisle?" Lerisa prompted in a saucy voice.

"The day after tomorrow, you sassy minx," Logan told her calmly, as if there was nothing unusual about a one-day courtship followed by a two-day engagement.

"After spending all your adult life avoiding a lifetime commitment like the plague, why are you in such a hurry to get married?" Lerisa asked suspiciously.

"Because I love you," Logan pointed out, as if she had suddenly grown dense.

"And?" she asked, still not satisfied.

"And," he answered, raising his arrogant chin a notch, "once the word's out how beautiful you are, I don't want to spend my time fighting off all my happily single and *un*-happily married friends everywhere we go. I much prefer enjoying your company . . . not defending my territory."

"Flattering but foolish." Lerisa scoffed at his explanation.

"Wait and see, Miss Temptation," Logan warned her.

"You're crazy, Logan." Lerisa's glance defied him to deny it.

He walked to the chair, grabbed her fingers with both hands, and drew her up. Easily holding her in place when she tried to pull away, he smiled at her ineffective struggles.

"Sunday will be none too soon either, considering how ornery you are, my wife-to-be. A good session in bed would benefit both of us."

"Why the three-day delay then?" she asked with a touch of sarcasm that didn't faze him one bit.

"I thought you might like an extra day to shop for your trousseau and to purchase a fancy dress for tomorrow night's engagement party."

Lerisa stared at him in disbelief. "Are you serious?"

"You wouldn't ask if you knew me better," Logan informed her. "I never joke about things that are this important to my future happiness."

"How can you arrange an engagement party overnight? Even the most important tycoon needs a week or so to reserve a room, hire caterers, and send out his or her invitations."

"It was no problem."

Lerisa thought a moment, then spoke her thoughts aloud. "Oh, I see. Josh and Jaclyn are the only guests and the party will be held here, with my leftover ham and eggs for hors d'oeuvres."

"Hardly," Logan scoffed, refusing to be baited. "There'll be well over a hundred guests in attendance. The details were arranged and taken care of weeks ago by my staff."

"That's a lie!" Lerisa, uncowed, shot back, glowering at him. "Weeks ago I didn't know you."

"It's the truth," Logan rebutted, not the least perturbed. "The party was originally planned before we met so I could introduce you to a few of my friends and some business associates. They're anxious to welcome you to this glorious part of the state."

"I can't comprehend any of this," Lerisa heard herself say. She shook her head in disbelief. "I must be dreaming the whole thing."

Undaunted by Lerisa's stunned expression, Logan continued, "Since you've promised to marry me, it will be our engagement party instead. The only thing that needs changing is the wording on the cake."

Lerisa withdrew from Logan's disturbing hold, walked to the straight-backed chair by the serving cart, and sat down. The man was unbelievable. Nothing she said even fazed him. Given a few minutes' reprieve, she felt confident enough to come up with another scheme to at least delay him. He was far too arrogant to make the kind of acquiescent husband she wanted. Or did she?

Looking at her cold uneaten breakfast, she picked up a muffin filled with plump blueberries, buttered it, and took a bite. She decided to ignore him and eat. With her stomach full she'd be more capable of dealing with it when he threw the next bomb her way.

Logan smiled at her mutinous expression, walked back to his desk, sat down, and pushed a button on the house intercom, asking, "Mrs. Johnson, would you please fix another breakfast? Oh, and bring us a pot of fresh coffee and some additional cups too."

"Thanks," Lerisa mumbled, unintentionally speaking with her mouth full. "I'll need to keep my strength up to deal with you."

"You will," Logan agreed readily. "I can guarantee the upcoming nights and days that we spend in bed will sap all your energies."

"No they won't," Lerisa disputed. "Not mine or yours either." She fluttered her eyelashes, flirting outrageously. "You're forgetting that I never have sex when I work."

"How the hell would you know?" Logan stormed back, refusing to acknowledge her coy actions. "I'm your first damned commission, remember?"

"First or last makes no difference," Lerisa assured him, not looking up as she reached for a honey-bran muffin with a gooey topping. Deciding it would be even better with butter and orange marmalade, she liberally applied both and took a bite.

"Think again, sweetheart," he broke in harshly. "When I decide to have you, you can consider yourself had."

Lerisa ignored his warning and sweetly suggested, "You should have some of these, Logan. They're really delicious." She would deal with his seduction when it happened. In bed or out.

"I know they're good and right now I don't care," he told her gruffly, momentarily irritated by her repeated attempts to place restrictions on their relationship. "My housekeeper's a great cook and a nice old lady when the mood suits her. She'll undoubtedly be eating out of the palm of your hand the moment she meets you."

"If she keeps cooking like this, it'll probably be the other way around," Lerisa chuckled, licking crumbs off her fingers. She leaned back in her chair waiting for Logan to speak. When he didn't look like he was going to, she did.

"Why aren't you working today?"

"Are you already worried about my fortune declining?" Logan queried, going to his desk and sitting down.

"Heavens no," Lerisa assured him with a mischievous twinkle in her eyes. "Private sources have informed me that you're fantastically wealthy."

"Meaning Jaclyn?" Logan mocked, resting his hands on the arms of his high-backed leather chair.

"Her and others," Lerisa expressed without further comment. "She did mention you have homes in Palm Springs, Scottsdale, Aspen, and San Diego, as well as this one in La Jolla. She also said you own a condo in the Hawaiian Islands and a ranch in Oregon."

"The woman should be an investigative reporter instead of a painter," Logan grumbled beneath his breath. His fingers clenched, knuckles taut and visible as he listened further.

"I'll suggest it when we talk," Lerisa agreed, with a soft chuckle at Logan's ill humor. "It seems there are over one hundred real estate offices displaying your name too."

"A hundred and eight to be exact," Logan told her, enunciating each word between clenched teeth.

"Not bad for a man of thirty-four," Lerisa praised him, enjoying his shifting moods and surging temper.

"Anything else you want to know not related by my friend's gossipy wife?"

"How about the exact worth of your stocks and bonds?" Lerisa kidded him.

"What?" Logan exploded, not bothering to control his amazement at her knowledge of his assets.

"I also hear you own a marvelously lucrative portfolio of solid investments."

"Who disclosed that to you, Lerisa?" Logan demanded. "I've always made it a policy never to discuss that part of my life with anyone but my broker."

"No one told me a thing," Lerisa told him smugly. "I guessed as much all on my own."

"Damned brat," he scolded. "I'm getting tired of your impudent tongue. What you need is an introduction to some of the lovemaking you're going to be subjected to when you're my wife."

"Don't bother. I've already experienced as much as I can handle. Both yesterday and this morning."

"Keep talking and you'll never make it to the bedroom. You wouldn't be so much trouble if you were sexually satisfied."

"What a chauvinistic remark." Lerisa grimaced, glaring at him to keep his distance. "I'm going to check out my studio and order supplies so I can start my painting while you cool down."

"Sc— your picture," Logan fumed vulgarly, then added, "which is what I'm going to do to you if you don't shut up!"

"There speaks the typical male," Lerisa giggled, not the least upset. "Every time I voice an opinion you disagree with, you're ready to throw me on my back."

"You're damned right." He rose and started toward her with a look in his eyes that warned she should quit arguing or start running for the nearest exit.

"Stop right there, Logan. You don't intimidate me in the least," she lied, flashing him a glance that belied her trembling stomach. "I'm going to paint your picture before we fool around, and that's final."

"I warned you, witch. We're going to make love now. In this room and this instant. You've had things all your way for too damned long," Logan rasped.

"Me?" she laughed in disbelief. "You're the one making plans and giving orders."-She stopped, unable to meet the desire in his eyes without meeting him halfway. "Don't be so impatient. We have the rest of our lives to indulge our physical whims."

"Think again . . . fiancée. I indulge my whims, as you call them, often, and feel inclined to increase my output more each time you open your smart-talking mouth."

Logan reached her so fast, Lerisa didn't have time to stand. Jerking her up into his arms, he kissed her mouth with such hunger that he doubted if he'd ever stop.

The fire of Logan's mouth brought every last nerve ending bursting to life in Lerisa. She shuddered, responsively parting her lips to accept the intimacy of his tongue. His erotic assault went on and on, leaving her feeling dazed, mindless with pleasure, and eager for fulfillment as her body arched upward into the throbbing pressure of his arousal.

When he finally released her Lerisa clung to his broad shoulders, breathing in great gulps of air. One or two kisses like that each day and she'd do anything he asked. The man was a blasted miracle.

"Delectable mouthy little witch," he scolded, searing her

lips in an earth-shattering kiss that had her clinging to his shoulders to keep from falling to the carpet.

"Hmm," Lerisa murmured unsteadily. "Just how many times a day . . . after I've completed your painting . . . will I be . . . er . . . forced to submit to this type of sexual harassment?" Already she ached for his complete seduction not just the wild kissing they'd indulged in so far.

Logan's laughter was low and intimate. "I can't count that high since . . . *before, during, and after* . . . my painting you'll be subjected to this . . . *morning, noon, and night.*"

"No man's that capable. Not even you," Lerisa scoffed. The idea of trying for a lovemaking record with Logan did sound worth pursuing. Maybe they even had a listing in the *Guiness Book of World Records* to compare scores with.

"You're asking for trouble again," Logan threatened, though his body was still hard from their last kiss. It was unbelievable the way she affected his libido.

"I—I'm not," she stammered, wondering why she bothered to lie.

Logan's body trembled when Lerisa rubbed against him, then kissed his neck with the softest lips he'd ever felt. He shuddered once more, feeling her playfully nibble the taut skin of his throat while stroking his nape with gentle fingers. The vision of her teeth and sweet mouth exploring his body more intimately made him push her away until he gained control of his emotions.

"What's the matter, Mr. West?" Lerisa complained, reaching to draw him back. "Did you already change your mind about seducing me in your office?"

"Hell no. I stopped because I hear Mrs. Johnson in the hall."

Of all the damned times for his housekeeper to intrude!

He felt like locking the door and throwing away the key until Lerisa's temperament was as honey-sweet as her mouth. His frustrations mounted more each second they were together.

"Does the thought of your housekeeper coming in on us bother you?" It surprised her that Logan was concerned about anyone seeing them when he was intent on making love.

"No, but it will bother her. You'd shock the hell out of her if she saw you biting my neck and running your fingers through my hair."

"I doubt that."

"Why?"

"Working for you, she's probably seen everything that Masters and Johnson spent years researching for their sex manuals."

"No way," Logan explained seriously. "I always used hotels in the past. This is my home, and there's never been another woman besides you and her inside it."

Calling out a warning, Mrs. Johnson entered, pushing another cart into the room. "My what a lovely lass you are, my dear." She stopped to return Lerisa's stare. "Logan is a lucky man to have you for his fiancée."

"Th-thank you," Lerisa answered, shaken by the fact that Logan's housekeeper knew they were engaged. Did everyone know before her? "When did you hear the good news, Mrs. Johnson?" she probed, playing along to see what she could uncover. A little subtle interrogation might reveal some further minor details Logan had forgotten to tell her. Like where they were going for their honeymoon and how many children she was expected to have.

"This morning, dearie," the housekeeper answered, beaming at the two of them. "Please call me Maggie."

"I'd like that," Lerisa admitted with a friendly smile.

Despite Logan's giving her waist a warning squeeze to be quiet, she pried in her sweetest voice, "You didn't explain how my"—she leaned into Logan's shoulder with the pretense of affection—"fiancé informed you of our engagement."

Mrs. Johnson's large bosom rose beneath its starched apron. "Mr. West came bursting into my kitchen fit to be tied. Told me to hurry and fix my special homemade muffins and a good big breakfast because his bride-to-be was hungry. When's the wedding, dear?"

"Didn't Logan tell you that too?" Lerisa asked in a honeyed voice that fooled Maggie but not the man standing stiffly beside her.

"How could I, sweetheart?" Logan interrupted with a grin as false as hers. "I was waiting until . . . *we* . . . decided together. It's too important a decision for me to make alone."

"Isn't Logan thoughtful?" Lerisa asked the housekeeper. She lowered her lashes in a pretense of shyness, then gazed into his eyes with a look of such adoration that he was left momentarily speechless.

"Always has been of me," Mrs. Johnson agreed. "You're a lucky lady to catch such a fine man. Mr. Johnson, God rest his soul, was a ne're-do-well and I knowed it when we married. All my good deeds didn't change him one bit either."

"I really am fortunate then, aren't I?" Lerisa continued acting her part as the doting fiancée with complete aplomb. She enjoyed every second of mischief, knowing Logan was seething with annoyance beside her. "Logan's such a darling, he'll need very little guidance at all before he becomes the perfect husband."

Mrs. Johnson gave a hearty laugh that caused both her hips and bosom to shake at the same time. "That's a good one, Miss Lerisa. I know you and me will be friends seein' as how we have the same sense of humor."

"Actually Lerisa's good sense of humor was the first thing I noticed and loved about her," Logan added, giving Lerisa an enamored glance equal to the one she had just given him.

"What was the second thing you loved about me, darling?" Lerisa cooed, deciding to return with a taunt or two of her own.

Logan looked at her. "Why your sweet disposition, of course, my precious *angel face.*"

His comeback was as quick as hers and delivered with such emphatic sincerity that Mrs. Johnson's eyes shone with pleasure. Only Lerisa noticed that his mouth was twitching with amusement. He deserved a sharp kick on the shins and he knew it!

"How many days did you decide it will be before we tie the knot, sweetness?" Logan pushed, taking advantage of his housekeeper's presence. Knowing his hand was out of sight, he let it slide down Lerisa's bottom and intimately fondled the rounded flesh.

Biting back the urge to end the charade with a slap on his handsome roguish face, she smiled instead and repeated his earlier words, "I don't know, *baby cakes.* I can't count that high."

Logan looked at Mrs. Johnson and laughed heartily. "See what I told you about my lady having a great sense of humor? Isn't she the cutest little kidder you ever heard in your life?"

Mrs. Johnson chuckled loudly. "You two are perfect for each other. It'll be a marriage made in heaven."

"What a lovely thing to say, Maggie. I just hope you're right about the area."

His housekeeper didn't understand what she meant but Logan did, and his look warned she was in trouble.

Gathering up the first cart, Mrs. Johnson scolded, "Now quit mooning around you two and get to eating while my food's hot. No need to waste another good breakfast just because you can't keep your hands off each other. There'll be plenty of time for that later." Finished speaking, she bustled her plump motherly body out of the room with her gray head held high.

They both burst out laughing at the same time the door slammed shut.

"Maggie's marvelous," Lerisa chuckled. "I love her already. I certainly didn't expect to find anyone wearing wraparound aprons working for you, much less a lady who's as outspoken as I am."

"She's been in my employ for over ten years now and I'd hate to try and replace her. She's definitely one of a kind. A real independent old gal too."

"Does she live in?"

"Lord no." Logan laughed at the thought.

"Why not?"

"She says I'd be in her way."

"Now I know I love her," Lerisa giggled. She could just imagine Mrs. Johnson telling her aristocratic boss that he'd be in her way, not the other way around.

"She also likes privacy as much as I do. When she mentioned she'd prefer her own home, where she could retire each night and know she wouldn't be disturbed, I bought her one."

"Where does she live?" Lerisa asked curiously. She really was a darling lady, and anyone wealthy enough to afford her would pay well for the privilege.

"About halfway between here and San Diego, which is convenient since I bought this house. She told me the type

93

home she wanted, I found it, and we've had an excellent relationship ever since."

"How does she get back and forth? Does she drive?"

"Like a demolition derby contestant. I purchased a bright red"—he paused to emphasize with good humor—"her choice of color and vehicle type," then continued to explain, "sports car. Now she zips up and down the roads like a Grand Prix driver wanting to self-destruct."

"I can't believe this." Lerisa laughed again. "She really is priceless."

"Hardly priceless," Logan scoffed. "Maggie costs me a hefty bundle every month of my life. And worth every penny," he added with obvious affection.

Lerisa walked to the cart, pulled up a chair, sat down, and began to eat. No one, not even Logan, was going to cause her to miss breakfast the second time.

Logan watched Lerisa take one dainty mouthful after another until her plate was nearly empty. Amused that she showed such obvious appreciation for his housekeeper's cooking, he waited to comment until she leaned back with a contented sigh.

"That was the best breakfast I've had since I left the States ten years ago."

"I'm pleased you enjoyed your meal," Logan told her, leaning his hips against the desk as he slowly sipped a cup of steaming coffee she had poured for him.

Lerisa looked up with a curious expression on her face. She wiped her lips with the soft linen napkin, then relaxed. Logan was in a great mood and had obviously forgotten to retaliate over her verbal outpouring to his housekeeper. That was good, she thought, since she was much too full to argue back.

"Why does it matter to you if I enjoy eating or not?"

"I've heard that a woman who enjoys fine food also enjoys making love."

Lerisa glared at his smug face. Darn the man. She should have known it had something to do with sex. If his remark was true, then he'd better stock up on some vitamin E and powdered rhino horn for an aphrodisiac. He'd need all the help he could get for his own stamina, since she intended to eat three hearty meals a day when in his employ and to enjoy every one of them.

"Is it true?"

Giving Logan a saucy smile, she teased, "Maybe. Maybe not. One fact I do know that is true is—"

"What?" Logan interrupted inquisitively.

"That I enjoyed eating food long before I started fooling around."

"Touché, Ms. Forbes. You definitely won that round."

"As I intend to win all the others," she informed him. Rising, she walked to the door and looked back over one slender shoulder to comment with an impish smile, "It's high time you showed me the studio, Mr. West. The sooner I complete your painting, the sooner I can start your husband-to-be obedience training classes and set the day of our wedding!"

With that shot Lerisa fled the library with Logan in hot pursuit as Mrs. Johnson stood, dustrag in hand, smiling at the foolishness of young lovers.

CHAPTER FIVE

Lerisa rushed into Logan's office just in time to pick up the phone on the sixth ring and reply, "Logan West residence. Ms. Forbes speaking."

Prepared to hang up, Jaclyn greeted her friend enthusiastically. "Hi, Lerisa. I didn't think anyone was going to answer."

Lerisa listened while looking around the high-ceilinged room trying to decide where to sit. She knew the conversation would be a long one and intended to be comfortable.

Too impatient to give Lerisa time to reply, Jaclyn burst out in a laugh-filled voice, "After the outraged way you expressed your feelings to Josh about Logan's high-handed proposal, I was afraid you'd given him a tongue-lashing, packed your bags, and returned to France."

"I threatened to leave," Lerisa chuckled. She gave a big sigh, still regaining her breath after running in from the front porch, where she'd stood to wave good-bye.

"Where's Logan now?"

"He just left, and the first thing I intended to do when I came back inside was phone you. I've been dying to tell you everything that's happened since I arrived."

Lerisa smiled, feeling like a queen as she made her choice of seats and settled down into the comfort of Logan's luxurious desk chair. Why not? She shrugged, thinking he should see her now. She had not only upset the even tenor of his previous life-style but was lording it over his home command center as well. Besides, she excused herself impishly, it was his own fault, since he had told her to make herself at home and she was just taking him at his word.

Not giving Jaclyn time to say another word, Lerisa started speaking rapturously. "You can't believe the studio Logan had built for me. It's the finest I've ever seen. And so's his English Tudor home too. It's really a mansion, with leaded glass windows, Italian marble everywhere, family room, game room with pool table and historic 1850s bar, library office combination, playroom, wine room, and so much more I should pinch myself to see if it's all a dream."

Without taking a breath she continued excitedly, "My bedroom has a king-sized four-poster bed you'll have to see to believe. It will be super to make love on. There're even his and her private dressing rooms, a well-stocked wet bar that's more like a miniature kitchen, a cozy log-burning fireplace, plus the biggest sexiest bathroom, complete with perfume and cosmetics in opulent crystal handmade glass vials, that I've ever seen. My studio's stocked with everything any painter could wish for, has the most fantastic light, vast windows on three sides and—"

"Shush, please," Jaclyn pleaded in mock chagrin. "I didn't call to get a report on Logan's latest house, which I knew would be lovely, or on your studio, which I didn't even know he'd had built."

"Why did you phone then?" Lerisa teased. "As if I need to ask."

"Because I'm dying to find out if the poor man is still in one piece after daring to tell Josh you're going to be married."

"Did your husband tell you what I said to him before hanging up the phone?"

"Oh yes," her friend giggled. "Every vehement word of denial."

"Well, you won't believe this then," Lerisa mentioned smugly. Her eyes twinkled a deep green as she appreciatively scrutinized the numerous book-lined shelves built into the paneled walls. A person could read forever and still have dozens of unread books left.

"After I hung up on Josh I really let Logan have it."

"Don't tell me you boxed his ears, then sent him packing from his own home?" Jaclyn queried, not doubting Lerisa would attempt it if she was angry enough.

"Better than that," Lerisa acknowledged with a soft laugh. "I accepted his proposal instead."

"You what?" Jaclyn screamed into the receiver.

"I said yes, I'd marry him." Lerisa's eyes shone with mirth remembering Logan's stunned features. Her assent had taken him completely by surprise. "I darn near shocked the man to death when I agreed without argument."

"You've shocked me as well," Jaclyn gasped, still not certain she had heard correctly. "I can't believe it's true yet. You always took great care to avoid long-term commitments in the past."

"So did Logan," Lerisa reminded her. "And before he changes his mind I want him locked up." She paused to add seriously, "With me having the only key to his heart, his mind, and his magnificent body."

"That's probably a good idea," Jaclyn agreed in a hushed voice, thinking of Logan's popularity with the feminine sex. "The man's been outwitting women for years."

"Well, this time I outwitted him," Lerisa boasted

proudly. "Wait until you hear one of the minor conditions attached to my proposal."

"Oh lordy," Jaclyn groaned helplessly. "When your voice takes on that self-satisfied tone, I know there's something terrible coming up."

"Have faith in your best friend," Lerisa suggested. "It's only a small condition, though I do admit we haven't quite come to terms on it yet."

"Pray tell." Jaclyn grimaced, wondering what on earth Lerisa had requested. "What unreasonable demand did you insist the poor man concede to?"

"It's not unreasonable at all," Lerisa insisted. "I told him I want to finish his painting before we marry."

"So?" Jaclyn asked, disappointed in Lerisa's mild request. "That's not out of line, considering all the years of schooling you've had."

"Logan thinks it is," Lerisa acknowledged, adding, "He wants to get married in three days. But," she confessed with mischievous confidence, "that's not the condition that made him furious."

"Keep talking," Jaclyn urged impatiently.

"This is the good part." Lerisa chuckled just thinking of Logan's stormy face when she warned him he'd have to abstain. It was equal to the adamant look he gave her when he refused.

She deliberately hesitated in order to emphasize the impact of her next words. "I merely made it perfectly clear to Logan that I never have sex when I paint."

"Good heavens, Lerisa, you're too much," Jaclyn moaned. "Besides, that's a lie and you know it," she contradicted without censure.

"So what? Logan can't expect everything to go as he wishes."

"But this is your first commission so you wouldn't know what you normally do anyway."

"That's the first thing Logan reminded me," Lerisa expressed with devilish humor lighting her eyes.

"Good for him," Jaclyn told her, upholding Logan for his quick comeback. "As I clearly recall during and after art classes, you fooled around all the time."

"I know that, but Logan doesn't." Not the least concerned about her untruth, Lerisa added, "I doubt there was a night during classes that I wasn't out with some handsome student or eager Frenchman."

"Then why deny the man you love? It doesn't make sense."

"To me it does," Lerisa sighed, trying to make her friend understand. "If I give in to Logan on every count now, he'll think he can walk all over me after we're married."

"Don't be ridiculous. The man's no fool when it comes to dealing with people. He does it every day of his life. Anyway, after what I've told him about you he'd never expect you to act like the average tractable female."

"Thanks." Lerisa welcomed her description with pleasure. "You really helped me to convince him that the wild, erratic, bohemian image I project is my true self. Later he'll find out how sweet-dispositioned I really am."

"You're lying again," Jaclyn shot back quickly. "If he did know how independent, self-assured, and offbeat your sense of humor is, he'd run a mile instead of proposing marriage."

"I doubt it," Lerisa disagreed. "Logan seems to delight in controlling my outbursts."

"I'd like to see that," Jaclyn blurted out. "It would be like witnessing the start of World War III."

"Some ally you are," Lerisa accused, confessing her true opinion in a whisper. "Logan's the first man to ever stand up to me, and though I won't admit it to him yet, I love his strength of character."

"You've both acted ridiculously today," Jaclyn pointed out, still stunned by her friend's news.

"I haven't!" Lerisa disputed in a cocky voice. "And there's nothing wrong with Logan's demanding, aggressive personality that a good woman can't control."

"Good woman?" Jaclyn scoffed, correcting her friend immediately. "Are you forgetting that I repeatedly warned you that the man's inclinations have always been toward the other kind?"

"No problem there either," Lerisa promptly replied with complete confidence. "Our few kisses have convinced me it will be pure pleasure on my part to keep this dynamic man entertained."

"Be good, Lerisa," Jaclyn softly scolded.

"I intend to be," Lerisa shot back. "As good and as bad as Logan desires each time we hit the sheets, which I hope is often."

"Your tongue is as outrageous as Logan's, which makes the two of you a perfect pair."

"I think so too," Lerisa told her friend seriously. "For now, though, I intend to keep the man guessing awhile before I set a date to walk up the aisle."

"Don't try that," Jaclyn warned, trying to prevent any future unhappiness from hurting Lerisa. "Your tricks won't work with Logan. The man's shrewd and won't take lightly to being strung along."

"No problem, Jaclyn," Lerisa assured her confidently. "I'm not a fool either. I'll make sure I just dangle the hook a bit . . . not pull it out of the water completely."

"You must be mellowing with age," her friend teased. "Why so cautious?"

"From what you told me there're too many women waiting on the sidelines eager to play games with the man for me to make mischief for over a week or two at the most."

"Be careful, Lerisa. I don't want to see you hurt," Jaclyn cautioned before pursuing the subject of Logan's proposal again. "Are you ever going to tell me the pertinent details about this morning?"

"Make sure you're sitting in a comfortable chair," Lerisa warned her, "as I don't intend to leave out a single thing and it's going to take awhile."

"Good," Jaclyn laughed back, eager to hear everything that had happened. "Let's hear it all."

"First I want to know how you are," Lerisa insisted, knowing that once she started talking about Logan she might not stop until he returned.

"I'm perfect." Jaclyn's voice softened with love. "Thanks to Josh. He spoils me rotten. I—I've never been so content in my life."

"Which translated to plain English means he's a super-stud in bed," Lerisa teased in a nonchalant voice.

"You're impossible," Jaclyn giggled back. "And you're also right. Josh is the most marvelous lover in the world."

"I doubt it," Lerisa contradicted impishly. "No man will best Logan in the sack. He has years of know-how and the appearance of being a virtual sex machine."

"I can see you haven't changed, Lerisa. Each comment you utter still surprises me with its bluntness."

"Surely you've lost some of your reticence now that Josh has clued you in on what you were missing all those years."

"I have," Jaclyn disclosed frankly. "After impetuously playing the part of a hooker when Josh was temporarily blinded, my entire personality changed."

"I can see why." Lerisa teased. "That sounds more like something I'd do." Her voice softened with empathy.

"There never was any need to shyly hide your feelings from your best friend."

"I know that now," Jaclyn assured her truthfully. "I'll never be as bold as you, but I have changed, as you'll see."

"When can we meet?" Lerisa asked, eager to see her friend. "I've really missed you, Jaclyn. Neither Paris nor the art classes were nearly as enjoyable without you to share them with me."

"We'll make plans later," Jaclyn insisted, becoming more impatient by the minute. "Right now I want to hear more about you marrying Logan. Surely it can't be true, despite my wanting to believe you'll be living here permanently."

"It's true." Lerisa gave a smug smile thinking of bursting in on Logan as he calmly told Josh about their wedding plans. She couldn't remember ever being so shocked. Or furious either, she thought, thinking of her outspoken verbal abuse that followed. "Logan's calling his parents tonight."

"Before or after speaking to your father?" Jaclyn asked sweetly.

"I—I'll contact my . . . er . . . father after I set the date," Lerisa spoke without further comment.

"Despite my wanting this to happen from the first moment I met Logan, I still don't see how you can marry a man you've known only a couple of days."

"It's easy," Lerisa told her with a satisfied smile. "I—"

"I met Josh when I was just a young girl," Jaclyn unintentionally cut in, trying to understand her impulsive friend.

"I'm not like you, Jaclyn. I couldn't moon over a man all those years without doing something about it. I'd die of frustration not revealing my thoughts or satisfying my physical needs."

"It was difficult keeping my feeling inside all those

103

years." Jaclyn bared her emotions in a thoughtful whisper. "Most of the time I ached for fulfillment, too, but unlike you, I couldn't give myself to anyone but Josh."

"My gosh, honey," Lerisa sympathized, "why didn't you tell me how you felt?"

"I couldn't. I was too insecure to express myself openly even to you. How I used to envy your poise and confidence with men. Nothing ever seemed to daunt you."

"Oh, Jaclyn," Lerisa whispered. "If you only knew," she added in a serious voice, despite making no further explanation.

Her friend continued, not hearing the plaintive comment. "It was marvelous just watching you foil the many unwanted passes with your quick tongue."

"But you never even dated or you could have learned all the arts necessary for survival as early as I did," Lerisa told her sympathetically.

Unconcerned, Jaclyn admitted, "Maybe, though I never had any desire to go out with other men. It just wasn't my style to fool around until I got up nerve enough to approach the man I love."

"That's sweet," Lerisa told her softly. "Since you two are now living happily ever after like every married couple should, it appears your previous life-style was right for you."

"Enough about Josh and me," Jaclyn said in a bright voice. "I still haven't heard how Logan managed to win your heart."

"Easy," Lerisa sighed. "He walked onto the plane and won me over right then."

"In France?"

"Yes. Can you believe it?"

"Of Logan, yes. He's a very determined man."

Lerisa's brows drew together thinking of Logan's clever

subterfuge. "The imperious devil was my seat partner. All carefully prearranged by him, of course. I didn't have the vaguest suspicion he was also my boss, so with a little clever interrogation he conned me into telling him just what I thought of Mr. Logan West . . . *himself!*"

"That's priceless. What happened next?" Jaclyn insisted, laughing at Logan getting the best of her outspoken friend. "Surely you let him have it when you found out his real identity."

"I did." Lerisa laughed back. "I was so mad I could have killed him."

"I'm surprised you didn't."

"I kissed him back instead. It was love at first fight."

"You're crazy."

"Crazy about my fiancé," she sighed, recalling each passionate caress. "The instant I met the darned man he made any other male I'd known before fade into complete oblivion. Without doubt Logan's the sexiest male in the world."

"Wait until you meet Josh," Jaclyn said with tenderness, unable to keep from teasing Lerisa about her effusive compliments.

"Logan is my Josh," Lerisa told her gently, aware of Jaclyn's meaning.

"With one striking difference," Jaclyn corrected. "Josh was my brother's best friend and I knew him for years before we married. You don't know a single thing about Logan except what I told you."

"Not true," Lerisa disputed quickly. "I spent my last three trust-fund checks prying into his past."

"You didn't?"

"I did. A world-class womanizer and a sexy devil I can handle. But I wasn't about to work for him without finding out if he was a maniacal pervert."

"You're impossible," Jaclyn noted with disbelief.

"No," Lerisa disagreed. "Just cautious. Fortunately his dossier came two days before I left, so I had time to give it a thorough study."

"And what did it tell you that I didn't?"

"Many things that are personal, which I won't repeat without Logan's permission. What I can say is that he's generous to a fault. He totally supports umpteen underprivileged kids here and abroad and anonymously donates vast sums to charity each year."

"If the funds are donated anonymously, how did you find out?"

"I hired the best private investigator I could find. An ex-LAPD officer who knew how to dig and where," Lerisa explained matter-of-factly. Unperturbed at being questioned, she continued, "I can also tell you that Logan has all his own teeth, no communicable diseases, and both parents are alive and well and live in Arizona."

"You're awful," Jaclyn chided. "Logan will have reason to divorce you when he finds out you had him investigated."

"He can't," Lerisa shot back impudently. "We're not married yet." Her voice lowered, soft with caring as she asked, "Were you aware that Logan was an outstanding Marine?"

"Yes. He and his best friend, Brad Lucas, served in the Corp together. Josh said he'd trust either one with his life in any situation."

"I would trust Logan. It's odd really, but I instinctively felt safe and secure when he sat beside me on the plane. He acted wonderfully gentle and protective to me until we parted at LAX."

"Josh makes me feel the same way too. All three men, Josh, Logan, and Brad, act that way toward women. They

106

can handle themselves in any situation, which is nice to know in this day and age. I think that's what gives them the arrogance that sometimes takes getting used to but in turn makes a woman love them so deeply as well."

Lerisa paused, thinking of Logan's strong, charismatic personality, and agreed. "Did you know Logan was assigned to Special Services and worked one dangerous assignment after another?"

"No. He never mentions what he did for Uncle Sam."

"I'm not surprised," Lerisa admitted. "He's not the type to brag, but he has reason to. As his rank increased so did his risk. He has a Purple Heart and a scar on the back of his shoulder to prove it, according to his dossier. I can hardly wait to kiss the wound to let him know I care."

"Good heavens!" Jaclyn exclaimed in amazement. "You sound like you really are in love with the man."

"Of course I am. Completely, totally, helplessly, and forever in love," Lerisa whispered emotionally, as if Jaclyn was foolish to doubt her. "Though Logan doesn't know it yet," she added as an afterthought.

"When are you going to tell him how you feel?"

"Maybe at my engagement party tomorrow."

"That seems appropriate," Jaclyn chuckled, trying hard to understand Lerisa's ability to make such a consequential decision so fast. "You'll get to meet Brad and Brandy Lucas then too. They're driving in from Palm Springs for the gala welcoming fete."

"Wonderful," Lerisa agreed readily. "I can hardly wait. You've told me so much about them and their darling twins, they seem like friends already."

"You'll love them both. They've already said they're going to invite you to spend Christmas with us at their Victoria Point Inn on Vancouver Island, British Columbia."

"I'll be there," Lerisa consented with a teasing smile.

"And this year I'll keep Logan's bed as warm as you made Josh's last year."

"I shouldn't have confessed my devious premarital sex-capades to you," Jaclyn giggled back.

"I loved hearing about them, since I always figured your sweet personality would turn into a hot one when the right man came along."

"I hate to change the subject again, but I originally phoned to invite you to have dinner with us tonight, and if you're coming, I have to thaw the steaks and bake a pie."

"I'm busy tonight," Lerisa explained, hating to refuse. "And so is Logan. When he left he warned me not to make plans for this evening. Since we're going to be alone, I intend it to be a memorable occasion."

"Why don't I pick you up for lunch tomorrow instead?" Jaclyn proposed. "I want to show off the new Porsche that Josh gave me anyway."

"Great idea," Lerisa replied with enthusiasm. "You show me the best place to shop for my combination coming-out-and-engagement-party dress and I'll pick up the tab for our meal."

"That sounds like a fair exchange. Why the new dress though? If I know you, you brought tons of the latest French fashions with you."

"I did," Lerisa admitted, remembering all the clothes neatly hanging in her private dressing-room closet. "I also intend to do Logan proud when he introduces me to his friends, and I want something new and chic to do it in."

"I guarantee you'll make one heck of an impact whatever you wear," Jaclyn laughed, unable to keep from teasing. "At least you will until you express your opinion in disagreement with some of the local less-secure politicians."

"Some friend you are," Lerisa chuckled back. "I remember only two or three occasions where I shocked the guests at a party."

"Two or three per party is more like it," Jaclyn rebutted.

"Hush up, Jaclyn," Lerisa threatened playfully, "or I won't show you my studio or let you tour my new home when you pick me up tomorrow."

"My gosh, Lerisa, you sound like you're already married to the man."

"Well, I am close enough to Logan to know he'd pose as well in the nude as Josh did for your portrait, *Stolen Idyll.* In fact, I've already titled my painting *Bedroom Magic.*"

"Lerisa!" Jaclyn cried out in a shocked voice. "Don't tell me you've already been to bed with the man?"

"Unfortunately not," she complained impishly. "But I'm counting the hours until he decides to seduce me completely, despite what I told him about my remaining celibate all the time I paint."

"Good-bye, Lerisa." Jaclyn moaned in disbelief at what she was hearing.

"See you tomorrow." Lerisa ended the conversation.

She hung up with a sense of satisfaction, feeling decidedly more like an engaged woman after telling Jaclyn about Logan's actions.

Smiling mischievously, she laughed at her friend's stunned reaction during their long phone call. Poor Jaclyn would never get used to her blunt speech.

She swiveled the high-backed chair back and forth, lowering her lashes to think. All thoughts of Jaclyn fled the moment Logan's masculine figure filled her mind. With her vision of him enticingly clear, she trembled, aware that she wanted nothing more than to be in his arms again. She sighed wistfully, not remembering a time in her life when she was ever happier.

Eyeing a bronze sculpture that had intrigued her from

the first moment she stormed into Logan's office, she leaned forward, reached one well-manicured finger out, and touched the cool metal. Compelled by her love of beauty, she stroked the sleek statue of a nude nymph.

Closing her eyes, she decided to let the artist's talent fill her with the tactile pleasure of touching such perfection for a few moments longer before returning to explore her studio once again.

Annoyed by the shrill ringing of the phone, she settled back and let it ring an even ten times in hopes the caller would hang up. Lifting the receiver, she smiled with pleasure, immediately recognizing the deep voice that smoothly inquired:

"Continuing your bad deeds by gossiping with Jaclyn, no doubt?"

"Yes, I was," she told Logan truthfully. "Why?"

"The line's been busy for hours. Then when I do get through you let it ring a dozen times before you answer."

"Ten times," Lerisa corrected him.

"Brat," he scolded in an amused voice. "Why'd you take so long to pick up the receiver?"

"I was stroking the bronze on your desk."

"Do you realize who the sculptor is?"

"Oh yes," Lerisa answered immediately. "A Josh King-man bronze is recognizable worldwide. He's a master."

"As I understand you are as an artist, Lerisa," Logan spoke with husky sincerity.

"Not yet," Lerisa disclaimed. "But I'm striving to be."

"With my commission I'm certain you'll reach your goal," Logan assured her sincerely. "We'll talk in depth about your talent tonight. Now I'd like to know why you had such a long conversation with Jaclyn."

"Because it took me ages and ages to tell her all the

terrible things you've done during the two days I've known you."

"My God, you really are a menace to my peace of mind," Logan groaned, wondering if he'd ever be able to focus his undivided attention on the complicated business problems that cluttered his desk.

He doubted if anything would take his mind off Lerisa for more than a few minutes at a time. Damned if her sassy soft voice didn't send tremors straight from his heart to his groin. His brows furrowed in a deep frown. He already wanted her to the point that it was difficult to concentrate on solving the most simple dilemma. If this kept up he'd be a basket case before he actually got her into his bed.

"Me, a menace?" Lerisa asked in her sweetest, most angelic manner.

"Yes, you!" Logan thundered. "You worry the hell out of me. You're a terror on two shapely legs who has totally destroyed my ability to become engrossed in my work."

"That's wonderful," Lerisa chuckled impudently. "Worrying about me should keep you from thinking about fooling around with other women."

"What other women?" Logan asked with feigned innocence before warning, "All my energies are directed at seducing you as soon as possible. Now shut up. I have something to ask you."

"What?"

"Did you miss me, witch?"

"I've been too busy," Lerisa lied. She missed him terribly and he knew it. Her response to his good-bye kiss should have proved that. They had darned near made love on his bricked entrance at the foot of his elegant front door. "Much, much too busy."

"I've been busy, too, but your beautiful face still comes between me and my work."

"I haven't had time to even think of you at all," Lerisa said, compounding the first untruth with another. She glowed, hearing he thought of her often.

"Take the time then," Logan warned in his deepest voice, "because I miss you like hell and want you to feel exactly as miserable as I do when we're apart."

"You're talking serious again," Lerisa cautioned, loving every intimate word he said.

Logan ignored her and drawled, "I keep thinking about that red underwear I saw you pull out of the dresser drawer this morning."

"So what?"

"So I don't like the skimpy bits of lace being where I want my own hands and mouth to be. I'm dying to taste all of your body, darling, not just the sweetness of your exciting mouth. Would you like that?"

"Why did you call, Logan?" Lerisa insisted, refusing to acknowledge his blunt revelation and the erotic images his question projected.

"Afraid to answer?" he teased huskily.

"No," she stormed back. "I'm afraid to encourage you. You're too oversexed as it is."

"Not for you I'm not," Logan insisted. "You're as passionate as I am, though you seem hesitant to admit it over the phone."

"Why did you call?" Lerisa asked for the second time.

"I've decided to give you a treat and take you out to dinner instead of eating at home."

"You've decided!" Lerisa blasted him, not in the least surprised that he informed her of their plans instead of asking. "Don't I have any rights?"

"For tonight, no. You've got years ahead of you to try to boss me around. For now I'm in charge."

"I can live with that since it'll only be a few hours," Lerisa agreed, overlooking his arrogance for the time being. She wasn't the least surprised that he'd calmly informed her of the latest arrangement instead of inquiring if she was willing first. "Why the change of plans?"

"Because the way I feel now I'm damned sure I'd do more than taste you as soon as I got in the door. My mind is filled with the image of your naked body on my bed quivering with the pleasure I can give you when I—"

"What'll I wear?" Lerisa checked him quickly, not certain she was pleased when he didn't continue with his erotic statement. It would have been interesting to have at least heard what exactly he intended doing to her body.

"Casual or dressy stuff?" she asked sweetly, deciding it best to ignore his audacity for the time being.

"Something special and easily removed."

"Why?"

"It's our first date and I'm as excited as a damned high school kid so we'll probably end up parking somewhere and indulging in some heavy petting."

"Assuming I go." She reminded him of her independence, though already planning what she could wear that would arouse him without seeming too blatant. "I'd better warn you, I don't pet on the first date."

"You will on this one," Logan warned her in his fiercest voice.

"I don't date macho men," she scolded, knowing her eyes were shimmering with excitement over thoughts of their provocative night ahead.

"Me either," he agreed with a laugh. "I'll pick you up at eight o'clock."

"I'll be ready."

Surprised there was no further argument, Logan waited, then asked, "Repeat that?"

"You heard me," Lerisa chuckled. "I said I'll be ready. I adore going out and you should make an excellent escort. All that experience of the past and so forth."

"You're a very unpredictable lady," Logan admitted, "which is probably the third thing I fell in love with about you."

"Don't bring that up. I haven't forgotten your outrageous comments in front of your housekeeper. And if you continue, I'll change my mind."

"You can't," Logan threatened huskily. "It's too late for both of us now." He knew she understood his meaning without further explanation.

"Not for me!" Lerisa declared, telling an outright lie. There was no need to add to his smugness by admitting anything. The darned devil had stolen her heart the moment they met, but that was her secret business.

"Little liar," Logan teased in a mischievous drawl. Thinking ahead, he planned everything he could do to make Lerisa's life the most perfect possible. It still stunned him to realize how quickly he had come to worship her.

After years of only his surface emotions being touched, he never thought he'd find a lasting love like Brad shared with Brandy and Josh with Jaclyn. Lerisa was a miracle and a long time coming into his life, he admitted tenderly, loving her more each time he heard her voice.

"Aren't you, witch?"

"Only to you," Lerisa admitted.

"Like I said, you're very, *very* unpredictable!" Logan emphasized again.

"Remember that," she urged, breaking into his thoughts with a firm recommendation. "It will help you understand my future actions."

"I doubt if I'll ever understand them, but I do intend to curb the more outrageous ones," Logan threatened in a husky voice.

"Fat chance of that," Lerisa teased. "If I didn't find dating a man with a voice like yours irresistible, I'd tell you to forget it. Unfortunately you're also a handsome devil and I've always been intrigued by the perfect male form."

"Keep sassing me and you'll not only be intrigued by my male form before the night's over but under it as well."

"I'm shaking in my bare feet," Lerisa giggled, looking down to see if her bright red toenails needed new polish before they went out. "Your threat doesn't bother me in the least, since I don't think you're the type of man to commit rape."

"You're right," Logan acknowledged in an even voice that did little to assure her of the fact. "But remember that my powers of gentle persuasion have never failed yet."

"Be in for a surprise then, Mr. West. Your days of celibacy are mounting up rapidly and I haven't even started your painting yet."

Lerisa waited, clearly able to hear him inhale with anger. Before he could storm back at her she told him, "I expect you to arrive promptly at eight o'clock, so don't be late. I hate waiting."

"Damned cheeky brat," Logan hurled at her. A wide smile tugged his mouth as he leaned back in his chair. He shut his eyes, not wanting any outside distraction as he imagined her shapely figure and gorgeous little sassy face. His hardened body attested to the sensual path his thoughts traveled after that.

Lerisa gave a rapturous sigh, marveling at the changes in her life that the last forty-eight hours had made.

In a few hours the man she loved would return to take her out for an exciting evening of wining and dining. Afterward he would keep his boyish promise to park and pet awhile. Then, eager to end his frustration, he would speed home and rush her upstairs. And last, in his arrogant manner, he would demand she come to his bedroom to make love the rest of the night.

Of course, Lerisa gave a prankish smile, she had no intention in the world of accepting his offer, but he didn't know it.

She could imagine it all, right down to her surprising refusal. Logan would rant and threaten to seduce her while she casually thanked him for a wonderful evening and walked into her own room alone. Noisily locking him out would be the grand finale and prove her independence once again. A perfect ending to a perfect evening.

CHAPTER SIX

Logan entered his house promptly at eight, as promised. He stood just inside the front door, silently staring up at Lerisa as she gracefully descended the curving stairway to meet him.

She was so beautiful, it took his breath away. From the tip of her dainty high-heeled sandals, up the swirling froth of her chic burgundy dress, to the top of her gleaming raven-black hair she was perfection. A fantasy come to life and she was his. Every last delectable inch.

"You're gorgeous, my wife-to-be," Logan told her, unaware that his voice deepened with uncontrolled yearning. "So damned beautiful I want to keep you hidden for my pleasure alone."

"Tonight I think I'd like that," Lerisa admitted in a breathless whisper before pausing dramatically to add in a lilting change of voice, "Tomorrow I'd probably insist on going shopping in Jaclyn's new Porsche."

"I'll buy you a fleet of Porsches," Logan vowed quickly. "And your own elegant department store if you agree to my first wish to let me keep you cloistered."

"Hmm," Lerisa hesitated, cocking her head as if contemplating what to do. "I'll pass on both lavish presents in favor of our date tonight. It sounds far safer. A gift of expensive sports cars and stores filled with feminine goodies sounds too much like a payment for services rendered."

"Give yourself to me tonight," Logan urged huskily, "and you can have all my wealth."

"If we marry, I'll get it all anyway," she reminded him impishly.

"There's no *if* about our marriage, sweetheart. It's pure fact," he advised with complete seriousness before returning her mischievous grin with a wide smile. "Already you're acting impudent and I haven't been home five minutes."

Lerisa gave him a teasing look and continued down the stairs. After an afternoon spent prowling through the many rooms of his house, her mind occupied with thoughts of starting his painting and preparing for their first date, she wasn't the least surprised to feel her heart beat wildly and her hands tremble with anticipation. The moment he had walked into the entrance hall she had experienced difficulty breathing, she was so filled with excitement.

Normally poised, she found herself swallowing nervously when Logan continued to scrutinize her as he waited below. Unable to take her eyes from his tall, broad-shouldered figure, she returned his tender look with one equally loving.

The sheen of his thick hair, highlighted by the many-prismed chandelier, caught and held her glance. Its burnished color was a potent reminder that he had the temper to control her every outburst. His look was that of a man who wouldn't take the least nonsense from anyone. Especially her, she thought, noticing the strength of his well-shaped, determined chin.

Letting her hand slide along the smooth banister, Lerisa

lowered her lashes, taking one unhurried step after another until she reached the bottom of the stairs.

Her eyes shimmered, a brilliant flash of color between lashes so thick and lustrous they would be the envy of any movie actress, as she looked across to give Logan a devastating smile.

"Cool the woman magic, honey," he scolded in mock anger. "I want you to save those passionate glances and that sexy smile until we get home or I'll have to start fighting off my masculine competition starting tonight."

"No problem there, Logan," Lerisa assured him brightly. "I heard you're fully capable of handling yourself in any situation."

He gave her a knowing look, speaking candidly, "Tonight I prefer to save all my energy for handling you."

"Ah," she acknowledged, quick to understand his implication. "You must mean the parking and petting part of our date."

"I'm not waiting that long," Logan warned her with complete assurance. "You're too stunning for any escort to keep his hands off you until the end of the evening. Much, much too stunning."

Parting her soft, curving lips, Lerisa whispered, "You're pretty awesome yourself tonight, Mr. West. In fact, I'd definitely say you rate a ten."

"You can't be rated, sweetheart," he expressed truthfully. "No other woman could ever come close to being your equal."

"Th-Thank you," Lerisa stammered, overcome by the seriousness of Logan's mood. She'd been flattered often. It seemed part of the game both sexes played when dating. With the man before her it was different. Now she felt as if she truly was the most desirable woman in the world.

Their eyes locked and held as Logan quickly crossed the

space between them to take her in his arms. He was so appealing in his black silk open-necked shirt, silver-gray slacks, and matching sport jacket, that she ached with desire. He was a powerful, dynamic man, handsome enough to capture the heart of any woman.

Without saying another word Logan cradled her close, letting his mouth answer the invitation of glossy lips, parted and willing as they eagerly sought his intimate caress.

Lerisa gave a satisfied sigh as her arms automatically raised to curve around his neck and her supple body relaxed against him.

Logan's muscles tautened, straining her to his hard body as if he never wanted to let her go. Her softness fit perfectly into the arc of his unyielding form when he bent her backward with the hunger of his greeting.

Overcome by Logan's touch, Lerisa's own fervent response soon left her breathless and clinging. A low moan of distress escaped her throat when he started to withdraw. Pulling his head back, she kissed him so ardently that his great body trembled and all thoughts other than her own devastating reaction fled.

"Oooooh . . . *Lo—gan,*" Lerisa dragged out his name in a murmur of exquisite pleasure. It was heaven being wrapped in his strong arms and yielding to the expertise of firm demanding lips as they continued to caress the sensitive skin of her throbbing mouth.

"Oooooh . . . *Lay—risa,*" Logan drawled, equally moved by her response. He lifted his head to observe her flushed cheeks and dreamy expression. "You really are a black-haired witch who has cast me under her spell, aren't you?"

"Not me," she denied in a husky whisper. Openly flirting, she fluttered her eyelashes in hopes that the added

120

feminine wile would keep him spellbound the rest of his life. Annoyed that he seemed unmoved, she stated in a haughty voice, "I'm not a witch, Logan, merely an employee being sexually harassed by her very demanding employer."

"Shut up then, woman," he threatened, ignoring her attempt to put him in his place with a hearty laugh. "And let me get on with my harassing."

"Fine with me," Lerisa barely had time to say before he pressed his lips over hers and she felt the exciting touch of his tongue touching the edge of her teeth. "I . . ."

"Hush," Logan scolded against her trembling lips. Not raising his face, his clean warm breath mingled erotically with hers as she tried to reply. "Just enjoy everything I do to you from now on."

Before she could utter a sound the point of his tongue gently teased her lips farther apart, then lingered to probe the moist inner warmth until she was caught up by the force of his increased intimacy. Pressing her hips and breasts against him, she attempted to get closer as a flood of desire shook her from the tips of her toes to the top of her head.

"Heaven help me," Logan moaned hoarsely when Lerisa began to suck the tip of his tongue. He tore his lips from her ardent mouth to seek the hollow of her throat. "You kiss like every man dreams his fantasy lover would. It's impossible to continue this without wanting to precede our evening out by a passionate bout in the bedroom."

"You'd b-better stop right now then," Lerisa warned softly, taking a deep breath to steady her emotions. "I have no intention of being your appetizer."

"Appetizer, hell!" he scoffed, kissing his way up the side of her neck before giving her earlobe a sharp nip. "When I start nibbling on you in earnest you'll be my whole damned entrée."

With eyes closed Lerisa dreamily continued to caress Logan's nape. The man's lovemaking had her tied in knots it was so perfect. She yearned to let her artistic fingers lower and explore each well-defined masculine feature. It would be marvelous to do a nude sculpture of him as well as a painting, she thought wistfully as she imagined them both holding the place of honor in the master bedroom.

She licked her lips, unconsciously causing Logan's hands to clench on her shoulders when he saw the dainty tip of her tongue.

"What are you trying to do now?" Logan demanded in a throaty exclamation. "Entice me into making you my dessert as well?"

"Definitely not," Lerisa objected, all the time picturing his mouth doing wonderful things to her body. "I was just checking to see if your twenty-minute kiss had removed all my twenty-four-hour lipstick."

"Right now I'd like to get rid of more than your lipstick," Logan moaned, bending forward to place a brief kiss on her forehead. He cocked his head to inspect her tremulous mouth thoroughly before remarking, "I'd like to remove your clothes and your surprising look of innocence."

"Me an innocent?" Lerisa scoffed, lowering her lashes to hide her expressive eyes. "Don't be silly."

"I'm not being," Logan corrected seriously. "I'm rarely wrong about women, and you, my love, have a haunting appearance of purity despite your blunt little tongue and claims of vast experience."

Circling her neck with both hands, he used his thumbs to tilt her chin upward.

Forced to open her eyes, Lerisa returned his questioning look bravely.

"Could it be you lied to me and have somehow managed to remain a virgin these past years?" Logan asked in a roughened voice.

Without telling a direct lie Lerisa countered his query in a steady manner. "If I was virtuous, you wouldn't be interested in me, remember?"

"Why the hell would you think that?" Logan demanded harshly.

"Because," Lerisa reminded him impertinently, "of what you told me on the plane."

"Don't talk foolish. You know damned well I'd be interested in you no matter what you were." Logan kissed her hard on the lips to emphasize his point. "I love you, Lerisa, and my love has no restrictions."

"The heck it doesn't," she chided, ignoring her inner trembling at the force of his declaration. "You audaciously informed me the moment we met that you seek only sophisticates since . . . *quote* . . . the training period, if done right, would take longer than many of your past relationships lasted . . . *unquote.*"

"True," Logan admitted without concern. "Though as a businessman responsible for the livelihood of hundreds of employees, I've learned to be flexible."

"Meaning?" Lerisa questioned, arching one delicate black brow.

"Meaning if you aren't as knowing as you claim, I wouldn't mind tutoring you in the art of love . . . *starting right now.*" He held her glance for a long, tense moment, convincing her beyond doubt that he was deadly serious. "Do you understand what I'm saying?"

"Of course I do," Lerisa answered clearly. "You'd rather seduce me than buy me a dinner."

"I'll do both."

"Forget the seduction. I—I'm more worried now about

my lack of lipstick," Lerisa stammered softly. "Do I have any left or not?"

"You must, since your lips are a lovely shade of deep pink."

"That's me then," she explained, subduing a desire to pull his aristocratic head down and seek lesson number one in the Logan West manual of sensual training. "My lipstick was passion cherry red."

"Let me taste and see," he insisted, giving her mouth the briefest touch as he smacked his lips in an exaggerated manner.

"Well?" she chuckled. "What did you decide?"

"That I didn't get enough the first time. I need another test to judge accurately." His teasing was followed by a kiss so thorough and passionate, she found herself once more clinging to his wide shoulders for balance.

"N-no more samples, please. I can barely stand as it is," she scolded, hoping to break the intense mood between them. Shaking her head no, she drew back. Her fingers splayed across his heaving chest and vainly tried to push him away. The man was strong as an ox and she couldn't budge him an inch.

Ignoring her feeble efforts, Logan's brows drew together as he contemplated out loud, "It's beyond me how you can kiss like a courtesan yet retain a virtuous aura about you." Visibly moved by Lerisa's ardent response, he moaned, "You, my love, are too, *too* much."

"I think the impact of tonight's greeting was definitely a joint cooperation effort," she whispered emotionally.

With Lerisa's upper body arched back, Logan's desire was tautly apparent and a reminder that her merest touch brought him to the point of full arousal so that he could have taken her at any time, any place. It was a heady experience, as she instinctively knew he was a man of vast control.

"Do you feel what you do to me, sweetheart?" Logan asked, sliding his hands from her shoulders to rest on her hips. He held her still, carefully observing her reaction.

"Yes, and it's getting to be a bad habit, Logan," Lerisa whispered, shielding her own heightened senses by lowering her lashes. She knew if their eyes held for even the briefest moment, he'd read she wasn't the least embarrassed by his obvious need.

"I know," he agreed with a note of disgust in his voice. "It seems being in love for the first time is quite an aphrodisiac."

"From what I hear, you're the last man ever to need the use of a sexual stimulant."

"Not with you I'm not!" Logan confessed in a disturbed voice. "It's nearly impossible to repress my emotions when I speak with or look at you, honey. When I touch you I damn near come unglued I'm so stimulated. I've never been this way with another woman before, and it's damned embarrassing to run around in a state of full arousal at the age of thirty-four."

Logan couldn't believe it. He was an experienced man. Very. Had been since the age of fourteen. His emotions in the past had always been easily checked at any time despite the most intimate situation. Unlimited control was one of the things his past lovers had admired the most. Yet he stood holding the woman he loved in his arms and acted like a damned frustrated virgin boy touching the womanly softness of his first girlfriend.

"They tell me thinking of something horrible helps a man," Lerisa smiled sympathetically.

"The only thing horrible I can think of is having to wait so damned long to make love to you."

"I didn't mean that." Lerisa frowned. "I meant a bad job like cleaning bathrooms."

"I have daily household help and office janitorial services that handle that chore."

"What about thinking of working on a dirty car motor?"

"I hire a mechanic."

"What do you do for yourself that you dislike?" she demanded with mock sarcasm.

"Waste time talking about mundane subjects with you instead of fondling your body."

"Forget it." Lerisa gave him a fierce glare. "As I said before, you're oversexed, and at thirty-four that should be wearing off."

"It won't," Logan pointed out calmly. "My dad's still hot for my mom and he's sixty-five."

"Oh lordy." Lerisa gave an exaggerated moan. "You mean you'll act like this from now on?"

"Forever and ever," he admitted with a proud grin.

"That sounds marvelous," she declared pleasantly, reaching up to caress his jaw. "You're a gorgeous hunk and a fantastic kisser and I'll look forward to a spicy marriage."

Surprised by her approving reply, Logan reached out to give her smiling mouth a lingering kiss. "Spice you want," he caressed each rapidly closed eyelid, both satin-smooth cheeks, the middle of her chin, and the tip of her nose, "spice you'll get."

Before she could twist away he possessed her mouth in such a sensuous kiss, she could barely stand it.

"No more, Logan, please," Lerisa cried out, begging him to stop. "Or I'll miss my dinner completely."

"I'll keep you so busy you won't notice."

Lerisa scowled at Logan, removing her hands from his neck to walk to the door. Not because she objected to his obvious desire, but to lessen the intimacy of being alone that threatened their evening out. The light banter had serious undertones she wasn't ready to concede to.

One sideways glance, one wistful word, or the smallest covert action and she knew she'd be in Logan's bed within seconds. The intensity of his mood hadn't wavered from the moment he took her in his arms and was now so strong that the sudden silence between them seemed like a visible force.

"I'm starving, Logan," she lied, hoping to break the heightened awareness until a more appropriate time. Unfortunately, if he did decide to ask her to make the choice, she'd probably beat him up the stairway.

"Our chariot awaits," Logan told her, going along with her subterfuge. He opened the door and motioned for her to move forward. "I'm pretty hungry myself," he concurred untruthfully.

Exhaling with regret, Logan was aware that Lerisa had left the decision to him as to whether to stay home and make love. After months of waiting, a few more days wouldn't hurt, he silently chastised himself. The hell it wouldn't! he corrected his thoughts bitterly. He could already feel the physical pain of sexual frustration increase just watching her shapely body precede him out the door.

In the car Logan reached beneath his seat and withdrew a cellophane-wrapped package. Handing it to her as they eased through the massive wrought-iron, electronically controlled security gates, he grinned.

"A small token of my affection for you to enjoy while we drive to the restaurant."

Lerisa returned his smile and accepted his gift gratefully. She loved receiving surprises, and the single velvety flower somehow seemed more touching than a huge bouquet.

"Thank you, Logan," she whispered, folding back the top of the cellophane.

Inhaling the delightful fragrance of a single rose bud the same deep wine color as her dress, she thought of the many changes in her life-style in the short time she'd been back in the States.

"It's lovely and also my favorite flower," she told him truthfully.

"I'm glad you like it." Logan rested his hand for a brief moment on her thigh before returning it to the steering wheel. He slanted her a sideways glance. "If you look closer, you'll find something else."

With the eager anticipation of a child, Lerisa spread the wrapping to find a pair of delicate earrings hidden beneath the bow.

Logan switched on the overhead light so she could inspect her present. He was filled with intense happiness watching her rising excitement as she closely examined the ruby studs for her dainty ears.

"I—I can't believe this," Lerisa cried out with delight. She held them up, twisting them back and forth so the light could shimmer off their gleaming perfection. "They're so beautiful they look like real stones."

"Now you're insulting me," Logan chided gruffly. "I'd never give my woman anything but the best."

"I didn't mean to imply that I was questioning their value," Lerisa stated apologetically. "I just wanted you to realize how impressed I am by their beauty."

"I understand, honey."

Lerisa eyed each large ruby nestled in a circle of small diamonds and answered in an awed voice, "I'm stunned by your generosity."

"Don't be," Logan explained with a satisfied smile. "I intend to give you many gifts during our life together."

"Saying thank-you doesn't seem enough." She leaned into his shoulder, placing her hand affectionately over his on the steering wheel. "I'm a very fortunate lady and I accept with the utmost pleasure."

"Good." Logan spoke with a sense of achievement. "Continue to do so, since I receive a lot of pleasure in giving gifts to the woman I love."

He gave her a surreptitious glance, pleased that she immediately replaced her small gold studs with his gift.

Preening in the light of the makeup mirror on the visor, Lerisa added lipstick, touched each shimmering earring reverently, and turned to him. "You're really amazing, Logan. The rose and the earrings are both the exact color of my dress."

"That's no coincidence," Logan assured her matter-of-factly. "I called Maggie this afternoon and asked her what you were wearing."

"I suppose if I'd picked out a green dress, you'd have given me a four-leaf clover and some emeralds."

"Yes," he agreed nonchalantly. "And some violets and sapphires if your outfit was blue."

Lerisa glanced at Logan to see if he was telling the truth, decided he was, and smiled. It was no wonder the man was in demand. Any male thoughtful enough to match his extravagant gifts to his date's wardrobe was assured of a lifetime supply of willing female companions.

With the lovely earrings nestled in the lobes of her ears and her flower clasped in her hands as they sped down the highway toward San Diego, Lerisa's mind was overwhelmed by love for the man beside her. It didn't matter where Logan took her to dine, since her happiness was from being with him, not from her surroundings.

"It seems I was right," Lerisa told him without further comment.

"In what way?" Logan asked curiously.

"The moment I saw you I knew you'd be a dynamite escort," she admitted with a chuckle. "I'm already spoiled and I haven't even had my dinner yet. Somehow I don't think it will be a fast-food burger and cola."

"Not tonight," he admitted with a broad grin. "Our first date's special and first class all the way."

"I adore it all!" she exclaimed ecstatically. "But I must warn you, I'm really a connoisseur of all the franchised food establishments."

"I'll see your junk-food cravings are satisfied another day. Tonight, overlooking the bay, we dine on gourmet food and the best wine available."

"Both sound marvelous, and now I really am starving."

"Which means you lied before, the same as I did."

"I had to," Lerisa confessed. "Our greeting was almost out of control."

"Something I intend to see happens often," Logan admitted with a teasing smile.

CHAPTER SEVEN

Lerisa was filled with indecision. The practical side of her wanted Logan to continue toward the restaurant and the sensual part of her, which he had awakened so thoroughly, wanted him to make a U-turn and head straight back to his home.

"How much farther now, Logan?" she asked softly.

Unnoticed, she turned her face to study him critically while waiting for his reply. Admiring the shape of his head and his good-looking, strong profile, she thought what a perfect model he would make for the erotic style of work she specialized in. He wasn't movie-star pretty but forcefully handsome, with the kind of rugged masculine features that appealed not only to her but to most other women as well.

"We're just a few miles away," Logan assured her, excellently maneuvering through the heavy traffic with the ease of a man accustomed to miles of daily driving. "Why?" He gave her a quick glance. "Are you getting impatient?"

"Not me," she scoffed. "You're the one who always acts like an impatient lover."

"My eagerness is not an act." He stopped at a traffic signal and subjected her to a lengthy narrow-eyed scrutiny. "It's a living part of me that only you can sate."

Lerisa met his look with a mischievous smile. "That's

good. Let's see you keep it that way. I kind of like being known as Logan's only woman. The one who finally brought the great man to heel."

"Brat!" he scolded, easing the big car forward the moment the signal changed to green. "For that you don't get dessert."

"Nor do you," she threatened back.

"Oh yes I do," he explained, ignoring her comeback. "Mine comes during our heavy petting session."

"Not tonight it doesn't," Lerisa replied, with her chin tilted at a defiant angle.

"Don't waste your breath arguing, honey." His warm, intimate smile promised it would be useless to resist. "I'd rather you relax and enjoy the view."

Lerisa smiled and outwardly tried to do as he asked. Her mind, though, was busy counting the hours until they would park and make love. She wouldn't deny him a thing and he knew it, but it made her feel better to offer a token objection once in a while anyway.

Intrigued at how much San Diego had prospered since she last visited it, she surveyed the new buildings. When he turned off the main highway her eyes widened at the beauty of the city lights reflected on the calm bay.

Within minutes Logan had pulled up to the entrance of an impressive restaurant, she was standing in the foyer, and the valet had zoomed the Cadillac into the crowded parking lot with reckless abandon.

Not the least surprised that the maître d'hôtel greeted Logan effusively by his last name, Lerisa entered the busy dining room with her back straight and head held high. If any of Logan's ex-women were around, she wanted to make it clearly known that he was no longer available.

She eyed the plush velvet booths, lavish table settings,

132

ornate but discriminate crystal lighting and knew it was going to be a wonderful evening.

Seated in the exact location she would have chosen on her own, Lerisa scanned the room while Logan and the wine steward conferred. There were many women eyeing her escort, but she couldn't tell if they were attracted to his striking looks or were some of his former companions.

The hell with them all, she decided boldly. She was both capable and determined enough to outwit the best or the worst of them, fair means or foul, if they tried to make trouble between her and her fiancé.

"French or California?" Logan asked, unaware that he was interrupting her personal rationalization for keeping him faithful by fending off his ex-women friends.

"Whichever you prefer," Lerisa told him truthfully. She was much more interested in reading the menu than in choosing wines, now that the fate of his future life-style had been decided. It really didn't matter to her what she drank, since she doubted very much if the restaurant had a bad bottle of wine in the house.

"Let's try some Northern California wine," Logan suggested thoughtfully. "You've been drinking French wines for the last couple of years and might enjoy the difference." He turned back to the waiter and ordered before returning his full attention to her again. "Some of the Napa Valley wines now equal any in the world, though I try to stock a few bottles in my cellar from every wine-producing country."

"I noticed how vast it is," Lerisa said brightly. She set the menu down, unfolded the impeccable linen napkin and placed it across her lap, then looked up with a mischievous smile. "Your party could get out of hand if you held it down there."

"Our party," Logan corrected softly. "Have you decided what you'd like me to order for you?"

"You can pick the appetizer, but Roquefort dressing for my salad is a must." She looked up and met his waiting glance with a smile. "Since I don't see any Texas-style barbecue beef and pinto beans on the menu, I'll settle for broiled salmon filets with lime-ginger sauce and a crusty stuffed baked potato."

Logan returned her smile indulgently before ordering with the poise of a man long accustomed to dining at the finest restaurants. "We'll start with the house specialty plate plus duck *pâté en croute.*" He turned back to Lerisa, explaining, "You can chose the one you want, darling, or we'll share." Speaking to the waiter, who had already written down Lerisa's request, he added, "I'll have roast rack of lamb Madeira with asparagus hollandaise."

The moment they were alone Logan took her hand across the table and held it, getting her full attention. "Now, my evasive little witch, we're going to settle once and for all any differences that might arise about the painting I commissioned."

"What's the problem?" Lerisa asked, perplexed. "You wanted a nude and I intend to paint you one."

"I don't want just any nude." His keen eyes pinned hers until she lowered her lashes to avoid the intensity of his expression. "I want you."

"Do you mean me nude in your bed or nude in a painting?"

"Both," he informed her in a deepened voice. "I hired you to paint an unclothed self-portrait in oils. You in all your naked glory I desire as the woman I love."

"That's ridiculous," Lerisa objected, vainly attempting to withdraw her fingers when his grip tightened to under-

134

score his point. "I can't do a nude painting of myself. It's just not done."

"Why not?" Logan tossed back. "I know you have the talent."

"How could you? You've never seen any of my work."

"I've seen all of your more important works," Logan contradicted readily.

Too surprised to give a sensible answer, Lerisa asked, "How? When? Where?"

"What I could arrange flown to me, I looked at here. What I couldn't, I saw after my flight to Paris before meeting you."

"You haven't seen all of my works then," she corrected him. "I've illustrated dozens of medical textbooks, did a frieze for a gay bathhouse in France, and painted several nudes for an extremely wealthy, lecherous old patron of the arts in Cannes."

"I have each of the medical books with your talented imprint in my library, was given a royal tour of the bathhouse in Paris, and was introduced through mutual friends to your senior-citizen count in Cannes."

"Stop!" Lerisa threw up her hands in surrender. "I'm speechless at your thoroughness."

"Never underestimate me," Logan warned. "When I want something bad enough I pursue it with meticulous detail. As an example"—he leaned forward, pinning her shimmering eyes to emphasize his point—"I had color prints made of every available work you've ever done. They're under lock and key in my office."

Logan watched with interest, knowing his statement had thrown her off guard even more than his continued scrutiny did.

Lerisa gave a relieved sigh when the waiter served their attractively arranged first course. Impressed by the perfection of sliced lobster tail, red and black caviar, smoked salmon, scallops, and jumbo prawns arranged on Bibb lettuce leaves between slices of kiwi fruit, prosciutto, and ripe melon, she hesitated before deciding what to try first. Dipping a generous portion of chilled lobster into a tiny fluted dish of seasoned mayonnaise, she took a bite, chewed slowly to savor each delicious morsel, and wondered if there was anything Logan didn't know about her. She'd definitely miscalculated his interest in her career.

"I'm extremely flattered that you were concerned enough to be so thorough," she finally told him. "But I would never even consider doing a nude self-portrait for any Tom, Dick, or Harry to leer at."

"I didn't ask you to," Logan declared in an affronted tone. "The painting will be for my eyes alone."

Lerisa mused over the idea, not the least adverse to Logan staring at either the real thing or a likeness of her without clothes.

"You're sure you wouldn't put it on display in one of your offices?" she questioned uncertainly.

"Of course not!" Logan promised. "I intend to hang it in my master suite to gaze at when you're not in my bed. You must have observed the empty frame above the fireplace."

"I noticed it," Lerisa acknowledged, knowing the nude that would hang there would be the exalted Mr. West, not herself. Hoping Logan didn't have a telepathic mind, she admitted their thoughts did seem to run along the same sensual lines.

"Will you do it?" Logan probed, squeezing her hand to gain her full attention.

"It would certainly be a challenge," Lerisa admitted. She withdrew her fingers, tapping her nails on the tablecloth while she thought it over.

"Then there's no problem," Logan pointed out with confidence.

"There isn't if you agree to me choosing the background." Lerisa's eyes shone, thinking what she could do to guarantee that he wasn't totally getting his own way.

"I'll agree to that." He pinned her with his eyes. "Since you wouldn't dare depict anything inappropriate. Right, Lerisa?"

"Actually I do have a suitable idea in mind already," she enthused, hiding her thoughts behind lowered lashes.

"Something that will enhance your voluptuous curves, I assume."

"Certainly." Lerisa held her features straight. "I can guarantee the background will be a perfect contrast to my feminine form."

"Good." Logan smiled. His voice was pleased as he leaned forward to praise her decision. "You're not only a beautiful, intelligent lady, but a talented one too. I have tremendous admiration for your artistic ability since I have none, nor have any of my family."

He spread some butter-smooth pâté on two bread crusts, handed one to her, then held his in his fingers while asking, "Who did you inherit your talent from? Your mother or father?"

"I don't know," Lerisa explained thoughtfully. "No one on either side of my family, past or present, even dabbled in watercolors as a baby. My father, to this day, isn't even remotely interested in art. I guess that makes me a mutant."

"How fortunate for me." Logan's praise was sincere. "I'd be proud to display your art in any of my homes." He offered her another serving of pâté, and when she took it he smiled. "Filling that order should keep you happily painting for years to come."

"I think I could live with that." Lerisa gave him a dazzling smile in return. Wanting to share, she handed him the remainder of her appetizer, then took a sip of the white wine. As expected, it was delicious.

"Speaking of parents," Logan interjected in a loving voice, "mine are cruising the South Pacific. I put a call in to their ship from the office but they were spending the day sightseeing the island of Moorea. Knowing how excited Mom and Dad will be to find out I'm going to be married, I can expect a return call anytime day or night."

"That's marvelous," Lerisa told him wistfully. "You sound like you love your parents very much."

"I do," Logan assured her with a tender smile. "As does every good son or daughter. Jaclyn told me your mother died years ago, honey, but I'd like the honor of contacting your father first thing tomorrow."

Lerisa avoided Logan's knowing eyes. "I—I'll notify my father after the wedding."

"But I don't understand." Logan reached across to hold her hand. "Surely you want me to tell him about us now?"

Withdrawing her fingers, Lerisa met his look and stated evasively, "I don't know where to reach my father now. He travels most of the year and I leave it to him to get in touch with me when he's in one place for over a few days. After we're married, when he calls, I'll tell him the good news."

Realizing Lerisa was ill at ease, Logan decided not to press the issue until he knew more of her background. He changed the subject so smoothly, she was visibly relaxed in seconds.

Time passed in a glow as Lerisa listened spellbound to Logan. He made her feel like a precious jewel with his undivided attention. As an escort she couldn't fault the man. He conversed easily and knowledgeably on a broad range of subjects and everything he said or did seemed designed to please her. She was totally captivated by his charisma and didn't care if he knew it.

After each had finished their crispy fresh, mixed green salad, Lerisa asked, "I've been curious as to why you were so tired during the flight from Paris to LA. Was it because of all the running around you did looking at my artwork?"

"That, plus the fact that I was there only long enough to see your paintings, shower, shave, and reboard. I've also been working night and day so I'd be able to take time off for our honeymoon."

"But you hadn't met me yet and didn't know if you'd even like me, much less want to marry me."

"It was destined to happen, Lerisa. I knew it from the first moment Jaclyn described you to me."

"Are you psychic?"

"In business, a little I think. I seem to always intuitively sense what property to invest in and what not to." He leaned back as the dishes were removed and the entrées placed on the table. "With you I think I'm very psychic. Right now I know you're in love with me, yet you're hesitant to tell me so because we've known each other such a short time."

"That's true," Lerisa divulged, amazed he could read her thoughts so accurately.

"You're also going to attempt to lead me a merry chase once or twice before you concede we were meant for each other and settle down to being my lover and my wife."

"Does that bother you?" she asked, admitting nothing despite the impish twinkle in her eyes.

"Not in the least," he laughed. "I'm looking forward to quelling your more outrageous ideas and enjoying the rest. In my arms you're always so responsive, I don't foresee any problems that can't be peacefully solved."

"You're not only arrogant but you're more outspoken than I am."

"Possibly," he laughed. "Which makes us a perfect pair."

Chin tilted upward, she warily glanced across the table. She tried hard not to reveal her thoughts to Logan while inwardly admitting that he was the only man capable of keeping her in line and making her like it.

Amused by the momentary touch of belligerence that crossed Lerisa's face, Logan grinned. When she boldly continued to hold his gaze he returned her look with passionate interest. He deliberately lowered his eyes, letting them linger on the enticing curve of her full breasts for a long tense moment before lifting them to meet her expressive features with a loving smile.

"You're beautiful, sweetheart. I'll never get my fill of looking at you."

Lerisa glanced at a group of women dining alone who hadn't taken their eyes off Logan long enough to eat their dinner and hissed between lips shaped in a forced smile. "The trouble with you, Mr. West, is that you're too damned sexy, too powerful, and too rich for your own good."

He threw his head back, laughing at her unexpected condemnation. "Not for you I'm not," he countered, pleased by her jealous outburst. "Now eat that overpriced canned peach half or we'll leave for the petting part of our date immediately."

His eyes lowered once again to the beauty of her full breasts, making her physically aware that he was no longer joking.

Obviously her feminine curves incited him as much as his broad chest and masculine form did her. Lord knows, the man literally exuded leashed virility. Even across the table he made her feel aware that he was only biding his time until they were alone.

After Lerisa had taken the last exquisite bite of raspberries, creamy vanilla ice cream, and fresh peach in her peach melba, she continued her interrogation.

"One more thing has bothered me, Logan."

"What is it?" he asked, raising his brow in concern.

"I've been puzzled how you managed to get to San Diego before I did. The chauffeur you hired for me exceeded the speed limit all the way from LAX to your office."

"I flew," Logan told her calmly, as if it was the most natural thing in the world.

"Flew what?" Lerisa demanded, still curious about many things in his life.

"My plane."

"Your plane?"

"Yes." He took a sip of wine and laughed at her stunned expression. "Didn't Jaclyn tell you I had one?"

"Heavens no." Lerisa's look grew serious as she contemplated the impact of his wealth. "I can't believe your possessions." She met his glance squarely and inquired, "I suppose you have a yacht too?"

"Fifty-five feet of sleek-hulled beauty with a king-sized bed in the main cabin and all the amenities of the average home."

"Aren't you worried I might be marrying you for your wealth?"

"Are you?"

"No," Lerisa whispered, reaching across to place her hand over his. "I'm not that kind of woman."

"Why are you marrying me?" Logan insisted quickly, holding her glance with his keen eyes.

Lerisa cocked her head, contemplated a moment, then

141

spoke in mock seriousness. "Because you need protection from your past life-style and an excess of women. The way you're going you'll get . . . *mid-life burnout* . . . soon and I hate to see a lucrative commission ended before I've collected my full fee."

"You damned brat," Logan swore beneath his breath. "I was going to take you dancing, but now we're cutting out of here and going directly to the heavy-petting part of our date."

"That's fine with me," Lerisa chuckled. "You're a devastating kisser and it stands to reason you're not too bad in the petting department either."

Motioning for the check, Logan laughed at her quick comeback. He laid several bills on the table, stood up, gently took her arm, and escorted her from the restaurant before she could complain.

"I had really looked forward to dancing," Lerisa insisted while Logan waited for the valet to bring his Cadillac.

"You can dance at our engagement party." Logan looked her up and down, thinking her the most appealing woman he'd ever known. Beautiful, impudent, and trouble with a capital *T*.

"Who with?"

"Me."

"Big deal," Lerisa scoffed. "For all I know you have two left feet."

"If I do, you're liable to find both of them in your bed when you wake up in the morning."

"If you dare, I'll—"

"Shush, sweetheart," Logan warned. "I've had enough of your lip tonight and am quick coming to the conclusion that the only way to keep your sharp little tongue quiet is to kiss you breathless."

Lerisa refused to comment, inwardly pleased at his declaration. Little did he know, she wasn't the least bothered by his threats. She was in the mood to be kissed senseless, and finding him in her bed in the morning didn't sound too bad either.

In a pleasure-filled haze, Lerisa watched the city slide by as Logan drove north from the restaurant. Barely able to contain her curiosity, she kept quiet, waiting for him to pull off the road and park.

Acute disappointment filled her as he drove straight from the restaurant to his home. Not one darned detour, she complained in silence. She could hardly wait to feel his lips on hers and he beelined home as if he could hardly wait to get rid of her.

Entering through the massive gates, Logan pulled around to the left of his sprawling house rather than parking in one of the vast garages on the opposite side.

Lerisa watched in silence, wondering what on earth he was up to now.

Driving along a mere path, barely wide enough to allow the car to squeeze past the lush landscaping, he drew up to the western edge of the property and stopped.

"We've arrived."

"Why here?" Lerisa asked in amazement as she glanced out the front windshield to the moon-washed waves gently breaking on the sandy beach below.

"I warned you we'd park after our dinner and do some heavy petting." He turned to her and smiled. "It's much safer inside my locked gates. There're too many nuts prowling around at night to take a chance on parking with you in lovers' lane."

"Who ever heard of two adults necking in a car parked in their own yard?"

"Who cares?" Logan countered. "Besides, the good parking places are probably filled with teenagers and I'd

143

hate to embarrass the boys in front of their girlfriends with their lack of finesse versus my expert lovemaking."

"Fool!" Lerisa admonished with a smile. "Though I wouldn't brag about my abilities if I were you."

"Why not?" Logan asked, tilting his arrogant chin in the air.

"Because you'd have to be an idiot not to have learned a little something about pleasing a woman in twenty years of acting a notorious rake."

"I warned you your tongue needs curbing," Logan scolded, placing his finger over her lips when she opened her mouth to protest. "It's a damned good thing we're assured of not being bothered by anyone here because as soon as I quiet your shrewish mouth I'm going to show you just how I go about pleasing the woman I'm interested in enough to marry."

"According to Ann Landers a girl shouldn't pet on her first date." She took his hand and nuzzled it affectionately. "What do you think of that?"

"Not much."

Logan stared at her a moment as she smiled up at him, totally enthralled by her captivating, outspoken personality. Her eyes shone like rare jewels in the moonlit interior of the car, and he thought her the most beautiful woman in the world.

"I didn't figure you'd be easily convinced Ms. Landers was right," Lerisa taunted saucily.

"Forget the lady's advice tonight, brat," Logan demanded, moving his hand beneath her hair to stroke the sensitive skin of her nape. "If you get carried away and seduce me later, you can make an honest man out of me on Sunday."

"Me seduce you?" Lerisa chuckled happily. "And make an honest man out of you? What conceit!" Her eyes shone with merriment as she glanced at his smug expression. "There's not a chance in the world of either happening now, since forewarned is forearmed."

She playfully crossed her arms over her breasts and forced the curve of her lips into as straight a line as possible considering their feminine fullness.

"Another thing you're forgetting, Mr. West."

"What's that, honey?" Logan asked, never taking his eyes from her face.

"That *I* set the date of our marriage, which is determined by the week *I* finish your painting!"

"Whatever you say, sweetheart," he agreed, shrugging one broad shoulder noncommittally. Ignoring the obvious keep-off signs, he continued to fondle her nape. He watched her unconscious reaction as she laid her head back against his hand. A wide smile played across his mouth as he leaned forward.

"Like that stuff, do you, witch?"

Lerisa stiffened. "Of course I do, though you're a beast to comment on my reaction." She looked him square in the eye. "Damned cocky monster. Maybe I should hide how I feel from now on."

"You can't," he warned, then quickly admitted, "nor can I. Now shut up and let's get to the good stuff."

"You're far, *far* too impatient," she scolded, giving him a fierce glare.

"Impatient am I? If I hadn't had the control of a saint the day we met, you'd now be a member of the Mile High Club."

"I don't fool around in airplanes," Lerisa stated saucily, trying hard not to laugh at the vision of Logan making love in the cramped seat of a 747.

"You would have if I'd set my mind to taking you after the attendant dimmed the lights."

"Hardly." Lerisa smiled, reaching up to outline his mouth with her index finger. "You're much too big to ever make out in a plane even if it's a jumbo jet."

"Don't you believe it," he scoffed. "As I'll prove soon in my own jet."

"You have a jet?"

"Yes."

"My gosh," Lerisa exhaled breathlessly. She touched his chest, spreading her fingers across the warmth of his skin, penetrating the thin material of his shirt. "I thought you just had a regular little one-engine propeller-type plane." Meeting his glance squarely, she asked, "What don't you have?"

"You," he answered smoothly. "And I intend to remedy that now."

Logan captured her hand, took each finger into his mouth one at a time, and sucked the tips so erotically that she could feel her senses flame to life. It was unbelievable the way the smallest physical contact made her heart pound out of control.

"No more," she moaned softly when Logan trailed a series of kisses from her fingers across her sensitive palm, then up to her wrist. She could feel her pulse beating unsteadily beneath the fine skin of her wrist as she tried unsuccessfully to pull away.

"Please, Logan." When he refused to stop she glanced up to see if he was listening.

"Do you like it?" Logan asked, unconcerned by her sudden desire for him to quit. "Do you like my mouth on you?"

"I love it." She couldn't help but imagine the intimacies he would seek.

"Good." He reached out, gently drawing her arm forward to nibble a path of fire along the satiny skin of her inner elbow. As he slowly caressed the sensitive hollow she soon strained against her seat belt to get closer.

Logan released his buckle, then hers, before drawing her fully into his arms. Making them both comfortable on the plush leather seat, he gently began to caress her. Deliberately taking his time, he rubbed her back, stroked back and forth across her shoulders, fondled the lobe of each dainty ear, probed the hollow of her throat, the arch of her chin, and her smooth cheeks. He touched everywhere but her trembling mouth until she was so aroused that she squirmed restlessly in his arms.

"Kiss me properly, Logan," Lerisa demanded in a broken whisper. Clinging to the tightened muscles of his shoulders, she pressed her breasts against his broad chest and passionately declared, "If you don't kiss me this instant, I think I'll die of frustration."

"Who's impatient now?" Logan suggested, laughter breaking deep in his throat. Cradling her face in both hands, he tilted her chin upward to give her a tender smile. "Answer me, woman."

Unable to speak without admitting he had every right to tease her, Lerisa kissed him instead. She sighed with exquisite pleasure when he instantly responded to the touch of her mouth. No man could ever compare with Logan's way of kissing and she hoped he never stopped.

It really was a miracle how he seemed to know instinctively what roused a raging hunger in her. In turn she was intuitively aware that when the time came he could sate that same hunger over and over again.

Breathless, Lerisa drew back, giving Logan a tremulous smile. Beneath his narrowed lids she observed his eyes. In the moonlight they appeared black. She knew it wasn't the dimly lit interior of the car that made them that way but that the dilation of his pupils was caused by his rising urge to possess her completely. And she imagined hers were equally dark with the desire to be possessed.

Something of Lerisa's thoughts flashed across her expressive face . . . an awareness, a need that deepened his own yearning to please her.

"Oh, baby," Logan drawled in a shaken voice, "I can't believe my luck in finding you. Will you always be so responsive to me or are you just a dream?"

"I'll never change," Lerisa vowed. She burrowed her face into the warmth of his chest, adjusting her weight in order to rest her body more fully against his. "Whatever you do to me, I can't seem to get enough."

"My God, sweetheart," Logan drawled. "Are you aware of the implication of that statement?" Both hands slid to cup her bottom, fondling the soft flesh as he pressed her over the aching hardness of his arousal.

"I th-think so," she admitted in a breathless whisper. The heat of his desire was a heady experience and she moved restlessly, causing his body to tremble beneath her.

"I'm glad," Logan returned huskily, trying to keep a semblance of control over his emotions. He eased Lerisa away a fraction in order to gain some control. "I'd hate to shock you when we do go to bed if I decide never to leave it."

"I heard from a reliable source that a man can't survive on love alone, even though one tried to do it."

"Knowing Josh, I'd say it was him, and that Jaclyn shared some intimate secrets of her nights at Victoria Point Inn."

"It was and she did," Lerisa chuckled. "She told me that despite Josh's intentions to keep her in bed for a week, they both got hungry after one love-filled night."

"That won't be a problem with us," Logan claimed boldly. "My master suite's bar has a good-sized refrigerator with an ice-maker, a built-in microwave oven, and a well-stocked cupboard. A year or two in isolation should be about right before we decide to emerge and face the world again."

Lerisa lifted her face, chuckling at his impossible threat. "Your cupboards don't hold that much food."

"Maggie can sneak in any extra supplies we need."

She clasped his neck, holding him steady while she kissed the end of his hard chin. "Like powdered rhino horn?"

"Never use the stuff."

"Oysters and avocados?" She kissed him again.

"Don't need them."

"Extra-strength vitamins?" She moved her abdomen against his hips.

"I'll order a case," he moaned, holding her motionless as he shuddered with frustration one more time.

Suddenly overcome by a wave of tiredness, Lerisa yawned sleepily. "Quit bragging about your stamina and take me inside, Logan." She checked her wristwatch. "Midnight's long past and I'm ready for bed."

"Me too," Logan shot back, giving her a gentle hug as he sympathized with her need for sleep. "You're probably still suffering from jet lag."

Releasing her, Logan started the car and backed it away from the bluff edge of his yard until he reached the driveway. He parked it underneath a broad carport and took her hand.

"How about a midnight swim? That should wake you up."

"It's much too dangerous," Lerisa objected. "I suspect you never wear a swimsuit."

"Only when decency insists," Logan admitted truthfully.

"I thought as much. I'll swim with you when there are old folks and young children about."

"Until we're married you will," he warned, adding beneath his breath, "If I decide to wait that long."

"I heard that," Lerisa pointed out, yawning again.

"Come on, honey. It's been a long night and I can hardly wait to spend the rest of it close to you."

Lerisa smiled without comment. She had prepared all day for the moment Logan got to his room and tried to usher her inside. What a shock he'd get when she refused. Especially after the wanton way she'd responded each time he took her in his arms.

With her hand still in his grip, they entered through the service area, walked across the mammoth kitchen, past the formal dining hall, and up the stairs.

Lerisa counted each step, hiding her impish smile as she anticipated Logan's outrage. Five more steps and forty feet or so down the hall to his bedroom door and she would say "Thank you for a wonderful evening, Mr. West, but no more loving for you tonight."

At his door Logan stopped and turned her into his arms.

Bracing for her surprising coup de grace, Lerisa tilted her chin upward and prepared to speak.

"Thank you for a wonderful evening, darling," Logan interjected before she could say a single word. Planting a lingering kiss on her surprised mouth, he released her, entered his room, and closed the door firmly between them.

While she stood in the hall, hands on hips, thinking him the worst monster in the world and Jaclyn her worst friend for arranging their meeting, he purposely and noisily secured the lock.

"Run along to bed, honey. You should sleep well knowing I'll be close by to protect you from any prowling perverts."

"The only prowler I need protection from is you!" She was furious with him for outwitting her again.

"Darn you, Logan," she stormed, unable to control her volatile temper. Still stunned by his actions, she reacted childishly but didn't care. "If you're supposed to be such an experienced lover, how come you don't even know how to pet?"

"Did I leave something out?" Logan's voice answered with false meekness.

"Yes!" Lerisa blasted back.

"What's that, Ms. Experienced Lady?"

"Upper body contact," she blurted out, waiting for him to reply. When he didn't she pointed out with candid emphasis, "Not once did you make any attempt to touch my breasts."

Before Lerisa could rush off to the much-needed privacy of her own room, she heard Logan's deep voice tease.

"Well, I'll be damned," he observed incredulously. "I knew I forgot something, but it's been so long since I necked in a car, I forgot what it was. Since you're such a capable, knowledgeable date, I'm surprised you didn't show me what to do."

Lerisa heard Logan's rumbling laughter with rising irritation as she turned away to flee down the hall. His strong voice was clearly audible despite the heavy door tightly closed between them.

Spinning back around, Lerisa rattled his door handle noisily and raged, "You're lucky you locked me out of your damned room, Mr. Ex-fiancé, or I'd come inside and really show you what I'm capable of when my temper's roused."

"Sweet dreams, *angel face,*" Logan called out, having the last word once again as she stormed off to her room.

CHAPTER EIGHT

Late in the morning Lerisa sat up in bed to find Benjamin Franklin's face staring at her from the center of a hundred-dollar bill. There were five images, to be exact, all neatly lined up on her nightstand. If she hadn't spent a restless night locked . . . *out* . . . of Logan's room, she would have felt like a call girl being paid for services rendered.

Ready to continue her tirade where she had left off, she showered and dressed in record time but with the utmost care. It was time she put a stop to his lock-picking, early-morning forays into her bedroom.

Storming down the hall, Lerisa burst into Logan's room unannounced, only to find it already tidy and her adversary nowhere in sight. She threw his money on top of the neatly made bed and proceeded on her way.

Unfortunately, as she quickly surveyed each room on the way to his office, they were all empty. Deciding he must be at the breakfast table enjoying a hot cup of coffee or eating brunch, her chin automatically tilted to a defensive angle and her eyes flashed brilliant sparks of temper.

Confidently prepared to make a grand entrance, she reached out with steady fingers to turn the doorknob. Poised and impeccably groomed, she had practiced her cool greeting well. Much to her annoyance when she entered the sunlit room, she was calmly informed he wasn't even in the house.

"When did you say Logan would return?" Lerisa asked Maggie once again. She accepted a frosty glass of pineapple juice with pleasure, declined coffee or a full breakfast, and picked up a warm slice of buttered whole-grain toast to nibble on.

"Like I said before, Miss Lerisa"—the housekeeper paused to give her an indulgent glance—"Mr. West took off early to do some special shopping." She observed the dark circles beneath the young girl's eyes and smiled sympathetically. "He never had no need to let me know when he'd be back, but being such a thoughtful man, and your intended, I'm surprised you don't recall not only what business it is he's taking care of this morning but where he's doing it as well."

"I forgot," Lerisa lied with a nonchalant shrug of one slender shoulder. No need telling the woman that her . . . *thoughtful intended* . . . had rarely clued her in on his future actions.

She picked up another piece of toast and chewed it thoughtfully while studying Maggie's complacent face.

The woman thinks I'm hopelessly in love, Lerisa chuckled inwardly as the housekeeper clucked over her like a mother hen. She boldly met the clear brown eyes probing her features and smiled. She also suspects that I've lost my brain power in addition to my heart if I can't even remember where my fiancé went, she mused between bites.

"I put some money on Logan's bed, Maggie. It apparently fell out of his wallet when he came in to see if I was awake. Could you put it in a safe place until he returns?"

"I'll do it, but I'll bet Mr. West will be back before you know it, dearie."

"It doesn't matter when Logan arrives," Lerisa assured

the older woman in her best couldn't-care-less voice. She wanted Maggie to know right off how independent she was and that she not only had better friends than the woman's arrogant boss but had wonderful plans for a full afternoon without him as well.

"You won't have to bother with lunch for me today. I'll be out browsing through the better dress shops all morning and most of the afternoon too. In fact"—she emphasized the words with a coy smile—"I have a date for a lavish meal with a . . . *very dear* . . . friend."

Lerisa hoped Maggie thought her escort was a sexy man and relayed the message back to Logan. It wouldn't hurt him to think there was a little competition for his affections even if there wasn't. Unfortunately he had a memory like a computer and would know darn well she was spending the hours gossiping with Jaclyn.

"It's a good thing you're leaving, Ms. Forbes," Maggie told her bluntly. "You and the master of the house would just be in the way when the caterer and his staff get here and start setting up for tonight's big party."

"When are most of the workers expected to arrive?" Lerisa asked curiously. It would be interesting to see what Logan had in mind for an engagement party. Somehow she couldn't picture him having anything less than the best.

It didn't matter to her if it was a keg of beer, a bowl of pretzels, and taped music instead of something really snazzy. She fully intended to have the most fantastic time of her life and to make a lasting impression on each guest as well.

"The whole lot of 'em are due in here anytime now. No doubt they'll try an' act like they own the place," Maggie gruffly interrupted Lerisa's thoughts. "Which means I best get busy right now. I'm still in charge here even if Mr.

West did hire himself some persnickety uptown professional staff. One of 'em already had the nerve to tell me he wouldn't be needin' any of my chocolate cream pies for the dessert table. Mr. West won't like that much 'cause he's partial to my flaky pastry and dark chocolate pie filling."

"Do you really make mouth-watering cream pie?" Lerisa asked, attempting to soothe the housekeeper's ruffled feelings.

"The best in the country," Maggie snorted, raising her double chins with pride. "Won me a batch of blue ribbons for 'em at the county fairs when I was younger. Be glad to fix you one if you like."

"Would you?" Lerisa's eyes shone with pleasure at the abrupt change in Maggie's expression. She hated to see anyone get their feelings hurt. "I'll look forward to having a thick slice for a midnight snack."

"It'll be waiting," the housekeeper assured her pleasantly. "You and Mr. West can enjoy a piece in your room last thing tonight."

"We will," Lerisa laughed, glad Logan wasn't there to make a lewd comment on his employee's innocent remark.

"Good." Maggie's bosom swelled with pride. "I'd better get the ingredients ready. Knowing you'll have one tasty thing to eat after your fancy catered meal makes me feel better. Think I'll make up some roast beef sandwiches too. Mr. Logan's a big man and needs to keep his strength up."

"For what?" Lerisa asked in an innocent voice.

"You know perfectly well what," Maggie shot back, bustling out of the room with her ample bottom stiffly corseted and as unyielding as her straight back. Before closing the door she called over one plump shoulder, "And the same applies to you, too, young lady."

The last was added with a decided twinkle in her eyes

and intended to let Lerisa know she was perfectly aware that her fiancé was a demanding lover.

Lerisa smiled thoughtfully, wondering if Logan had the vaguest idea that his housekeeper was jealous over his hired staff as well as being aware of his libidinous inclinations. Purchasing Maggie a frivolous gift in town should at least soothe her hurt feelings.

Lerisa looked with approval at the healthy bright green leaves of the potted plants sitting on each side of a colorful chintz-covered window seat. Wistfully imagining all the happy meals she would enjoy with her husband in the room's pleasant surroundings, she found it difficult even to remember why she was mad at Logan in the first place.

Standing, she checked the time, pleased that Jaclyn was due to arrive in a matter of minutes. She was eager to show off her studio and new home before they went shopping. When they returned time would be limited and her friend would be as anxious to drive on to her Laguna Beach home and prepare for the party as Lerisa was.

Leaving the breakfast area, Lerisa walked into the living room and impatiently paced back and forth across the deep-piled carpeting. In between peeking out the leaded glass windows to see if Jaclyn had arrived, she unnecessarily plumped and replumped the numerous velvet pillows. Not satisfied with the color arrangement, she switched the already perfectly placed pillows along the entire length of the vast modular couch.

Clutching a satin-edged pillow to her breast, she looked around. It was such a beautiful room, immense but so exquisitely furnished that she had felt welcome the first moment she'd entered.

Too unsettled to appreciate the decor for very long, Lerisa's brows drew together in a scowl. She was unnaturally restless and knew the cause. It was Logan's fault for leaving her so physically aroused the night before. The least he could have done, she fumed inwardly, was to pacify her with a lingering departure and repeated promises of his everlasting love. Instead he had left her a bundle of irate nerves from his abrupt good-bye.

Lerisa ignored her strong conscience, which kept reminding that she had fully intended giving Logan the cold shoulder first by saying good night in an equally hasty manner.

"That was different," she rationalized beneath her breath, arguing out loud with her moral sense of fair play. "No one in the world would expect a renowned rake to lock his bedroom door with a female on the outside of the room."

Crossing the rug once more, Lerisa inspected an intriguing collection of pewter mugs displayed on a wide windowsill as she thought over her tumultuous relationship with Logan.

It alternated between heaven and sudden outrage. On her part anyway, she admitted truthfully, since Logan seemed to be surprisingly even-tempered for a man with bronze highlights in his hair.

Everything that had upset her from the moment she returned to the States she could directly blame on the man. Everything sensually exciting and lovingly tender that had happened in her entire life she could credit him with also. It wasn't fair that one man could hold so much power over her emotions.

Glancing up as a powerful silver-gray Porsche was driven up the circular bricked drive and braked to a stop, Lerisa made a wild cry of greeting and rushed from the house to welcome her friend.

* * *

One hour later Lerisa was seated in the low-slung front seat of Jaclyn's sports car and being driven down the highway. Momentarily quiet, her thoughts were filled with visions of the perfect engagement dress for that night's occasion when a red-haired man drove alongside, tooted his horn, and gave her a wide-toothed, leering smile.

"Darn fool!" Lerisa glared at the stranger angrily. All set to ignore his actions, she eyed the man's bright hair, immediately thought of Logan, and became even more irate.

"You always did attract men's glances, Lerisa," Jaclyn, unperturbed, told her. "Why get so upset when you get honked at today?"

"Because the creep's vibrant mop of hair reminded me of Logan and what happened last night. Plus this morning too."

"Tell me about today first," Jaclyn insisted. "So far you've done nothing but listen to me rave about being married to Josh. I'm dying to hear about you and Logan."

"Get set for a long tirade then."

"Good," Jaclyn laughed. "I love extended romance stories."

"Some romance," Lerisa scoffed. "This morning I found five hundred dollars beside my bed."

"That's bad?" Jaclyn slanted her friend an amused glance.

"It is when Logan picks the lock . . . *for the second time* . . . to get inside my bedroom to give it to me."

"What's the money for?"

"Not payment for services rendered!" Lerisa informed her in no uncertain terms.

"What'd you do with all that cash?" Jaclyn asked, enjoying Lerisa's lightning-fast mood changes.

"Threw it on his mattress. For all I know it might be the

158

great man's loose change that fell out of his pocket when he came in to take another lecherous peek at me sleeping in the buff."

"You're ridiculous," Jaclyn told her. "Maybe I'd better hear about yesterday's trauma before we run out of daylight and we're both late for your party."

"Good idea," Lerisa agreed, continuing without pause. "The moment last night's date ended I was all set to verbally knock my fiancé-to-be on his elegant behind and he outsmarted me."

"Don't stop talking just as the story gets really intriguing," Jaclyn urged when Lerisa paused. "I want to know how and why."

"Why is because the man is psychic. After I spent the evening passionately responding to each caress Logan gave me, I figured he'd think it would be a cinch to bed me."

"Weren't you?"

"Yes and no," Lerisa admitted without guilt.

"That makes Logan psychic?"

"Yes." Lerisa held Jaclyn's glance briefly. "He knew darned well I wanted to sleep with him, yet must have sensed I didn't intend to, so he never gave me the chance to refuse."

"Logan didn't even try once to tempt you into his bed despite you two sleeping in the same house alone?" Jaclyn exclaimed, giving Lerisa a stunned look.

"Not once." Lerisa gritted her teeth, becoming upset just thinking about the man.

"What a switch," Jaclyn laughed softly, slanting Lerisa an amused look as she maneuvered through the heavy downtown traffic. "During the entire two years we studied art together in Paris all I heard was complaints about your boyfriends trying to rush you to bed the moment you met. Now you're even more furious because Logan didn't."

"You'd be mad, too, if a man who claims you turn him on so much that he's in a semipermanent state of arousal didn't give you a chance to refuse getting it on with him."

"Maybe," Jaclyn admitted, chuckling at Lerisa's blunt rhetoric. "But I really don't think I've ever been so amused in my life. You should see your peeved expression."

"You're some friend," Lerisa chided, giving Jaclyn a sharp frown before turning back to watch the local sights.

"Your best one," Jaclyn agreed in an amused voice, smiling softly.

"It doesn't sound like it," Lerisa rebuked. "You just can't imagine how Logan surprised me. He's the sexiest man I've ever met in my life, and at the bedroom door he acted like a wimp."

"I wish I'd been there," Jaclyn declared curiously. "I can't imagine anything more entertaining than your stunned expression when Logan pulled an about-face on you." She gave Lerisa a serious look. "Other than not trying to seduce you, what did the man do that was so upsetting anyway?"

"He gave me a chaste kiss."

"That's upsetting?" Jaclyn asked incredulously. "I've seen women look at Logan like they'd die for the slightest sign of affection, however brief."

"Bully for them," Lerisa scowled. "I prefer a lot heavier lovemaking when I'm in a man's arms."

"I'm not surprised," Jaclyn proclaimed pointedly. "Though I imagine Logan's chaste kisses are more sensual than the average man's best are. He looks like a great lover to me."

"Why would you notice?" Lerisa responded in sudden ill humor. "I thought you were in love with Josh."

"I am," Jaclyn admitted with a telling sigh. "But loving and being loved in return, plus having an extremely sensual relationship with Josh, has made me appreciate for the first time how few really passionate men there are around. Josh is one, Logan another, and also Brandy's husband, Brad."

Lerisa's narrow brows drew together in a brief frown. She was annoyed with herself for feeling a momentary twinge of jealousy because Logan's appeal was so universal that even Jaclyn noticed he was a sexy beast.

"That's a good sign you're in love," Jaclyn broke in on her thoughts.

"What?" Lerisa feigned innocence.

"Jealousy." Jaclyn pointed out matter-of-factly. "You're miffed at my remarks yet aware I love Josh dearly."

"That's true." Lerisa observed the purity of her friend's profile and smiled. "You're really a dark horse, Jaclyn. I still can't believe you loved Josh since you were fourteen yet conducted yourself like a nun while eating your heart out with fantasies as erotic as mine."

"I guess we have the same yearnings but go about getting them satisfied in different ways. You're much more impetuous than I am." Jaclyn thought a moment, then laughed. "Or you used to be. I've changed drastically in the last few months, thanks to Josh's loving."

"Since your husband is such an excellent lover you should understand why I was furious when Logan merely gave me a hurried peck on the lips, thanked me for a . . . _wonderful time_ . . . then said good night."

"That doesn't seem like enough to make you sit there with your hands clenched together like you wish they were around his neck," Jaclyn mentioned with concern.

"That wasn't all the man did."

"I have a feeling that now we're getting to the heart of the story," Jaclyn exclaimed, weaving around a driver who suddenly double-parked his truck to deliver a package.

"What did Logan really do that made you mad? Force you out of his bedroom before the seduction was complete?"

Ignoring the fact that Jaclyn's intuitive guess was nearly accurate, Lerisa informed her haughtily, "I never got inside his damned room. He entered alone and then had the nerve to shut the door and lock me out while I stood gaping in the hall!"

"Good heavens!" Jaclyn exclaimed. Her eyes were bright with mirth as she pulled her Porsche into the parking lot of a well-known department store. "That's a priceless story." She switched off the motor and turned to Lerisa with an amused smile. "I told you Logan was your perfect match."

"Perfect, hah!" Lerisa scoffed. "Our relationship definitely has flaws. In fact, I wouldn't think of marrying the man if I didn't love him so much."

"Forget the traumatic good night and tell me what you two did on the rest of the date."

"We parked and necked."

"Quit joking, Lerisa. I asked a serious question."

"It's no joke." Lerisa shrugged calmly. She gathered her purse from the floor after undoing her seat belt and added, "We really did neck. Logan promised to pet but didn't and that also made me mad."

"Why?" Jaclyn asked, pushing back a wayward strand of silvery blond hair from her forehead.

"Why?" Lerisa retorted in a huff. "I'll tell you why. In the afternoon Logan called from work and asked me to wear something on our date that was easy to remove. I naturally assumed he'd get down to some serious lovemaking after our dinner."

"Didn't he?" Jaclyn inquired incredulously. She was dying to find out every detail of Lerisa's sudden and serious romance with Logan.

"No!" Lerisa complained bitterly. "My French, barely-there bra . . ." She looked at Jaclyn to explain. "A new one that handily unclips in the front that I just purchased in Paris at Belligne's, where you bought your sexy underwear for Josh . . . never even got a peek."

"Knowing Logan's reputation, I'm surprised," Jaclyn spoke thoughtfully.

"I'm not only surprised but darned disappointed too," Lerisa informed her in a peeved voice. "I go out with the sexiest man I've ever known, who's a reputed make-out artist that gets it on with any willing female, and he makes no attempt to fondle my breasts. Plus, he ends the date with me standing in the hall, heart beating a mile a minute, panting for more."

"Hmm," Jaclyn mused, trying to think of a probable cause. "That doesn't sound like the Logan Josh told me about."

"Like I said earlier, if I wasn't so crazy in love with Logan, I'd detest the man."

"Did it ever occur to you that Logan held back because he's afraid of losing control around you?"

"Logan afraid of that? Phooey!" Lerisa rebuked. "He's got the control of a computerized robot. The only reason the man abstained last night was he somehow knew I intended to reject him and beat me to it."

"Possibly," Jaclyn agreed, aware of Logan's astute mind. "And if so you deserved it." Jaclyn's brows drew together as she contemplated Logan's unusual behavior. "Or maybe he wants to wait to make love until after you're married."

"You're way off base. He's much too impatient to wait for anything he wants," Lerisa contradicted firmly, then thought a moment. "If there is even a remote possibility that you're right, it makes him kind of sweet. Don't you think?"

"I've always thought of Logan as a handsome hunk, actually," Jaclyn teased, expecting a sharp reaction.

Lerisa overlooked Jaclyn's baiting comment and smiled. Her eyes grew soft with love, wondering if her worldly, sophisticated fiancé really did have a reason for not making love to her other than being just plain irritating by outwitting her at her own game. Jaclyn's comment gave her a whole new perspective to consider. Also a new idea on how to tempt the man.

"I'll find out tonight what Logan's problem is as I intend to test his willpower to the limit," Lerisa promised, filled with confidence that her latest scheme would succeed.

"How?"

"By wearing the most daring dress of my life. One that reveals nearly my entire bosom."

"I wouldn't if I were you," Jaclyn suggested seriously. Her advice was given with the insight of a woman married to an equally strong-minded male. "Most men act very different with their one-night stands than they do with the woman they love. I don't imagine Logan would like it one bit if he observed other men gawking at your upper torso."

"I hope Logan does object." Lerisa gave Jaclyn an impish smile. "I'd like to make him jealous as hell."

"Logan jealous might be more than you can handle," Jaclyn pointed out astutely.

"No problem," Lerisa assured her, checking her reflection in a cosmetic mirror to see if she needed additional makeup. Deciding she didn't, she dropped it back in her purse and sighed, "It's ironic really."

"What is?" Jaclyn asked, opening the driver's door to get out.

"The fact that I've spent years slapping men's hands off the two parts of my body Logan ignores." She looked Jaclyn in the eye and confessed, "I even squirmed and wig-

164

gled all over his chest last night, aching for him to touch my breasts. The man has yet to react like a normal male other than bluntly telling me to stand up straight that first night in his office because my nipples were hard and they aroused him."

"You haven't changed a bit," Jaclyn chuckled. "You're as outspoken as ever and I've missed you. It's going to be great having you close by."

"I'm pretty thrilled about the idea myself," Lerisa admitted with a pleased smile. "Let's forget my timid-acting fiancé and start shopping. I can clue Logan in on the proper way to treat a hot-blooded bride-to-be later."

"Poor Logan," Jaclyn sympathized with a mischievous giggle. "He's really in for a hard time when you get started."

"Agreed," Lerisa chuckled. "We may not finish the pre-honeymoon test trial in time for the wedding if I have my way with him tonight."

"You're crazy," Jaclyn laughed, stepping gracefully out of her car, then turning to wait for Lerisa.

"Crazy in love with the man," Lerisa admitted easily before sliding off the passenger seat to join her friend on the concrete parking lot. She gave Jaclyn a wide smile. "I owe it all to you too."

"Remember that when you pick your matron of honor," Jaclyn chuckled.

"I wouldn't consider anyone else and you know it." Lerisa's features glowed with love. "Meeting Logan is the most wonderful thing that ever happened in my life. When I get him properly housebroken and husband-trained, no man in the world will compare."

"That I'd like to see," Jaclyn returned with a doubtful look. "Logan's his own man, as you've already found out."

Lerisa hitched the thin strap of her purse over one

shoulder and urged impatiently, "Forget Logan and let's get going. I'm dying to see what the States has to offer that beats the tons of new clothes I brought from France."

Side by side, Lerisa and Jaclyn walked toward the department-store entrance. With Logan temporarily pushed aside in her mind, she entered through the gilt-trimmed glass doors, chatting nonstop about the type of dress she intended to buy.

Lerisa and Jaclyn were in and out of shops for the next two hours until each had found the perfect dress.

"Now that you've purchased that slinky emerald-green topless nightgown . . ." Jaclyn taunted.

"Hardly a nightgown, since it has long sleeves," Lerisa interrupted with a mischievous laugh. "It's an evening dress guaranteed to raise the pulse beat of any red-blooded male interested in the opposite sex."

"My description's better," Jaclyn disputed. "Your gown is as near nothing as decency will allow. A nonexistent bodice and nonexistent back barely held together by a designer belt are bound to get you just what you want. And maybe more," she added with a knowing smile.

"You have no right to complain about my dress after purchasing a decidedly skimpy froth of black lace to entice Josh." Lerisa tried hard to keep her voice expressionless. "Which is also indecently suggestive, considering you're an old married lady."

"*Old married lady!*" Jaclyn objected, noticing the mischievous smile that Lerisa failed to conceal. "We're practically the same age, sweets, or have you forgotten?"

"Not in the least," Lerisa laughed, unperturbed by the comparison. "I have one more thing to accomplish, then I can buy you lunch."

"What?" Jaclyn asked inquisitively.

"I want to buy Logan's housekeeper a bottle of outrageously expensive perfume."

"That's sweet." Jaclyn wasn't the least surprised by Lerisa's generosity. She'd always been that way with people she cared about.

"Do you happen to have Frank Smith's phone number? I heard he still lives in Costa Mesa."

"I have it," Jaclyn replied, giving Lerisa a questioning glance. "He's been to the gallery a couple of times lately looking for some seascapes."

"Good. I need to contact him."

"Why?" Jaclyn was curious. Frank was a young golden-haired Adonis who had modeled for Lerisa's life classes many times. He and Josh hadn't hit it off at all, and she knew Logan would feel the same animosity.

"You'll find out the end of next week if all goes according to plan."

"Oh no," Jaclyn moaned. "Not another scheme to try and deceive Logan!"

"This one's a cinch," Lerisa told her smugly. "According to my plan, about the middle of next week Mr. Logan West will be begging me to let him pose naked."

"Oh lordy," Jaclyn moaned. "I don't think I want to even hear how you intend to accomplish that."

"I wouldn't tell you if you asked," Lerisa teased back. "Just to whet your curiosity I'll confess that my fingers are itching to start making preliminary sketches for *Bedroom Magic.*"

"What about the nude Logan commissioned you to paint for him?" Jaclyn asked seriously. "After all, that's the original reason for you being here, remember?"

"Don't worry, I'll do the thing," Lerisa promised with a devilish gleam in her eyes. "But I'll do it after I've finished my painting."

"Won't Logan object?"

"Loudly, furiously, and continuously if he finds out," Lerisa agreed, laughing as she planned ahead. "Since I don't intend to tell him I'm not working on his painting, and you won't either if you really are my friend, there can't possibly be anything that can go wrong."

"I wouldn't count on it, considering Logan's keen mind. He's no dummy, as you've already found out."

"Let me worry about the man's intelligence," Lerisa prompted with confidence. "I may not be a Rhodes scholar but I was always in the top ten percent of my classes, which should give me the intellectual capability of out-smarting Logan if I set my mind to it. If you keep quiet, this time next week I'll have him jumping through hoops if I want."

"Now you're dreaming," Jaclyn returned in disbelief. "I won't say a word to Josh," she promised, doubting the wisdom of Lerisa's scheme, whatever it was. "But I will be the first to comment . . . *when* . . . it backfires like last night's plan did."

"I don't care what you say . . . *after* . . . Logan willingly poses in all his naked glory long enough for me to capture his likeness on canvas."

"I'm surprised you don't just ask him to take his clothes off. I'm sure he'd eagerly strip for you in a minute."

"He probably would," Lerisa concurred. "But I want Logan to pose, not come charging at me like a stallion after a mare in heat."

"That isn't what you said earlier," Jaclyn reminded Lerisa, ignoring her wild comparison. "You blasted the poor man for not trying to seduce you."

"Last night had nothing to do with art and you know it. You've got your painting *Stolen Idyll* to look at whenever

Josh isn't around and I've yet to see Logan's magnificent body in the buff."

"If you haven't seen it, how do you know it's magnificent?" Jaclyn giggled. "Logan might be bowlegged, have lily-white skinny thighs, a flabby belly, and a flat behind."

"Don't be silly," Lerisa scolded her friend in a miffed voice. "I'm the expert on nudes, and I can guarantee that Logan will look like a bronze God undressed. If you're nice, I'll let you have a quick peek at my finished painting. I assure you Logan will match Josh in every way, if you get what I mean."

"Don't be more explicit." Jaclyn broke into amused laughter as she added, "I clearly remember your unladylike comments on Josh's . . . er—"

"Manly proportions," Lerisa interrupted her friend with a playful chuckle.

"Shush, Lerisa."

"Don't shush me, Jaclyn. You're the one who painted your lover in a semiaroused state, not me."

"I hate to think how you'll pose Logan."

Lerisa contemplated a moment, then suggested, "How about a side view? Hmm," she calculated with a knowing giggle before adding, "Maybe not. If Logan was aroused, I'd probably have to turn the canvas sideways just to get all of him on it."

"Logan should hear you now," Jaclyn interjected in a vain attempt to be serious. "He'd run a mile and with good reason."

"I doubt it," Lerisa contradicted. Her eyes shone with humor. "I've heard some pretty wild tales of locker-room exchanges between males."

"It's time we changed the subject or I'm liable to rush home and seduce Josh," Jaclyn teased, trying her best to imitate Mae West's throaty come-up-and-see-me-some-time drawl.

Lerisa raised her hand to her brow as if overcome. "I can't believe what I'm hearing. Your speech is becoming downright lewd."

"Hardly," Jaclyn corrected quickly, giving Lerisa a wide smile. "No one could ever hope to match your rhetoric when you get started."

"Maybe so," she admitted without remorse. "Do you know anywhere close to purchase perfume?"

"When you finish I'll take you to a small shop that sells most brand-name perfume at discount prices."

"Good, then I can get me a vial too." Lerisa checked the time. "No wonder I'm starving. It's after one and I didn't have breakfast. Besides, spending money always gives me an appetite."

"I'm hungry too," Jaclyn acknowledged, casually making a suggestion. "How about Mexican food? You used to complain that no one in France knew how to cook it like the California Mexicans did."

"I'd love it," Lerisa enthused. "We can drink jumbo strawberry margaritas and eat tortilla chips heaped with guacamole dip while we contemplate what scandal I can create tonight."

"Don't worry. All you have to do is act natural and trouble will seek you out," Jaclyn added matter-of-factly. Without sounding obvious she recommended, "There's a very good restaurant right in La Jolla. Would you like to try it today?"

"Sure," Lerisa agreed pleasantly. "You're the chauffeur, so any place you pick will be okay."

CHAPTER NINE

Thirty minutes later Lerisa was seated across from Jaclyn in a comfortable padded booth constructed of a dark stained wood identical to the heavy beams traversing the ceiling. While waiting for their drinks she scanned the picturesque Mexican restaurant, noting it was filled equally with authentic Hispanic decor and satisfied-looking customers.

She watched, intrigued, as their uniformed waiter placed a frosty glass before each of them. Before she could do more than take a sip of her vivid pink cocktail she looked up and spotted Logan entering with a man she recognized from Jaclyn's painting as Josh.

"Don't look now, Jaclyn," Lerisa warned with a teasing smile, "but I think we're about to be picked up by two of the most handsome men I've ever seen."

She watched with envy as Jaclyn twisted around, her eyes glowing with love for the dark-haired man who scooted in beside her. Without embarrassment her husband cradled her face in his palms and gave her a breathtaking greeting full on the lips.

Before Lerisa could comment Logan settled his long limbs beneath the table and she was being drawn without resistance into the arms of the man she had berated all morning.

"Good morning, witch," Logan breathed against her lips just before he gave her a kiss so long and devastating that she completely forgot she'd ever been mad at the man in the first place.

"It—it's afternoon," Lerisa contradicted softly, giving him a tremulous smile. She was too overcome by his presence to notice the amused look of the interested couple across the booth.

"Good afternoon then, witch," Logan added, taking her mouth in another sensuous kiss that far surpassed the potency of her drink. "Hmm"—he licked his lips—"you taste of strawberry margarita. Your mouth is salty and sweet at the same time." His eyes gleamed with rising interest. "I think I'll have another serving now." Reaching down to caress her mouth, he was interrupted by Josh.

"Lay off, amigo. You haven't introduced me to your fiancée yet."

Lerisa turned to face Jaclyn and Josh, tenderly leaning into Logan's broad shoulder as she did so. Her eyes glowed with happiness as she boldly teased her best friend, "There's no need to introduce me to Josh. I'd recognize your husband anywhere, though he does look a little less erotic with all his clothes on."

"That statement could only come from Jaclyn's friend Lerisa," Josh laughed, not the least embarrassed by her outspoken remark. He reached across to grab her hand and comment, "Welcome to Southern California. Jazzy's raved so much about the nudes you do, I'd like to see them. It's possible I could hold an exhibit for you in my gallery after you complete Logan's commission."

"I have color prints of most of Lerisa's works," Logan spoke up. His voice was filled with pride as he told his friend, "I'd be happy to show them to you if I can manage to sneak into my office during tonight's party."

"I'll see you get away," Josh insisted, always eager to see quality paintings. Turning back to Lerisa, he smiled, "I'm pleased to see Logan has met his match. No married man likes a wealthy single guy in the crowd. It's too threatening to his peace of mind."

Logan placed his arm around Lerisa's shoulder, squeezing it while his eyes met hers in a tender look. "Consider your problem solved, Josh. I've found my lady and forgotten all the others. One like Lerisa is all any man can handle."

Reminded of their traumatic last meeting, Lerisa turned to Logan and frowned. Surreptitiously she tried to scoot away, becoming more annoyed when he calmly moved his thigh until it touched hers. The intimate pressure caused such an impact on her equilibrium, her hands started to tremble and she seriously doubted if she could finish her drink.

"Having troubles, honey?" Logan whispered into her ear when she set the fine-stemmed glass down with a decided thump.

"Only since you arrived," she turned to hiss back between tightly clenched teeth. When he tilted her chin upward, preparing to give her another kiss, she gave him her fiercest glare. "Monster."

"Ah," he murmured softly, immediately aware of her thoughts. "Did I displease you last night, sweetheart?"

"Not a bit," Lerisa dissembled, trying hard to ignore Logan's thumb as it tantalized the sensitive skin of her lower lip with its insistent probing.

"Little liar," Logan whispered, seeing through her untruth immediately. "Your gorgeous eyes are shooting sparks of temper at me again."

"They're not," Lerisa denied beneath her breath so she wouldn't disturb Jaclyn and Josh's deep conversation.

"Will this help?" Logan reached beneath the seat and withdrew a package.

Accepting the large bag without comment, Lerisa cautiously peeked inside. Unable to contain her instant happiness, she exclaimed excitedly, "Oh, Logan, he's darling!"

She took out a life-sized floppy-eared toy puppy the same color as Logan's hair. It had big black sad eyes, one of which was leaking a solitary tear.

"Here's a substitute pet to keep close until we pet," he told her with barely concealed humor.

"One kind of pet is all I need," Lerisa shot back, trying desperately to keep her voice down. "And after last night I prefer a stuffed pet."

"I thought you might," Logan laughed, unconcerned that Josh and Jaclyn were watching them curiously. "What a temper you have, my sweets."

"Only with you," she stormed, giving him her brightest smile, though it was as false as the waiter's teeth.

"Cut the private conversation and let me see your gift. . . . Oh, he's precious," Jaclyn cried out in delight when Lerisa handed it across the table. "I'd forgive a man anything who gave me that cutie to love."

"I was hoping you'd say that," Josh replied huskily, returning the toy before giving his wife a bag the same size as the one Logan had had.

Lerisa watched with interest as Jaclyn withdrew an identical-type toy puppy except that its fur was as dark as the raven-black color of Josh's hair.

Cuddling her soft present close, Lerisa gave Logan a swift kiss on the jaw. She met his glance squarely, knowing whatever mischief he pulled, her love would never lessen.

"What's his name?" Lerisa asked, noticing with amusement that Jaclyn kissed Josh on the jaw also.

"I thought Baby Cakes might be good," Logan said with

a straight face, though he reached beneath the table and gave her leg a slight pinch before lowering his fingers to stroke her shapely knee. Not satisfied, he slid beneath her dress and, under cover of the booth, lovingly fondled the satiny skin of her thigh. "I'm glad you didn't wear nylons today," he whispered in her ear.

"Quit playing with Lerisa's leg, Logan, and let's order lunch," Josh teased, overhearing the remark and knowing what was happening.

"You take care of Jazzy and I'll keep my woman occupied," Logan scowled before asking Lerisa, "Have you ordered yet?"

"Only margaritas and the guacamole dip for our tortilla chips." Lerisa offered her drink to Logan, wanting to share more than her margarita with him. His fingers were playing havoc with her pulse rate as she tried to concentrate on what to order for lunch.

"Let's both have the combination plate of taco, chili relleno, and enchilada," Logan suggested without glancing at the menu.

"Are you buying?" Lerisa taunted devilishly.

"Naturally. Why?"

"Then I'll have that as well as another drink and dessert." Lerisa thought a moment, then suggested with a devilish taunt, "You'd better order dessert also, Logan. As I recall, you didn't have any last night."

"I knew I hadn't heard the last of that," Logan laughed, looking across at Josh. "Didn't I tell you Lerisa would be trouble with a capital *T*?"

"You did," Josh agreed, watching them curiously, then turning to Jaclyn. "Do you want to make that four orders, honey?"

"Sounds excellent." Jaclyn piled a chip with dip and reached up to place it in Josh's mouth.

"Where's mine?" Logan asked in a throaty whisper.

"In the bowl," Lerisa answered with feigned sweetness. When he gave her a rejected look she fixed him a chip, giggling as a large blob of avocado dropped off when she raised it to his lips.

"I'd better feed you," Logan suggested grimly. "You're too sloppy." When his chip also lost a portion of dip, he threw up his hands in defeat. "Let's each fix our own or we won't finish in time for tonight's party."

"Excellent idea," all four agreed in unison.

"Where'd you buy this scarf, Jazzy?" Josh asked, fingering the pure silk square attractively draped around his wife's neck. "It looks hand-screened. The design especially intrigues me."

"Lerisa gave it to me," Jaclyn explained.

She took it off and watched in silence as Josh inspected it with the keen eye of an artist. "This is an exceptional use of color. If you can find the artist, I'd like to place some in the gallery. I think they'd be a big seller during the summer tourist season."

"How about it, Lerisa?" Jaclyn asked as she listened to the interplay. "Would you like to do scarves instead of nudes for a few months?"

"You did this?" Josh questioned. His voice became businesslike as he continued before she could reply, "Do you have any more?"

"Yes and yes." Lerisa smiled at his keen interest in her work. "It was only a hobby started when I couldn't find head scarves to purchase in the vivid, jewel-toned colors I preferred."

"Would you like me to sell them for you? They'd command top price."

"I might be interested. I have dozens of new ones in my Paris flat."

Logan had remained silent through the interchange, though Lerisa knew his mind was filing everything away for future use.

"We can pick the ones already made up on our honeymoon," Logan informed Josh, then added with emphatic certainty, "In the future I intend to keep Lerisa so occupied in the bedroom that the only thing she can make as a hobby will be me."

"Idiot," Lerisa scoffed, trying hard not to laugh at Logan's sensual teasing. It amazed her to listen as he sat there calmly telling Josh what he planned for her and also talking about jetting off to France as if it was no more of a problem then flying to Los Angeles.

"Josh wants them for the summer crowd," Lerisa reminded Logan with complete disregard for his arrogantly telling her that he intended they get married the day after they became engaged. "Which will be no problem since I haven't decided the month, much less the day, of the wedding."

"I understand your implication." Logan smiled indulgently. "And you, sweetheart, should understand that I haven't agreed to a single idea you've had yet."

"Meaning?" Lerisa demanded in a low hiss.

"Meaning that by the end of this summer you'll be long married and undoubtedly pregnant as well."

"Oh my gosh," Lerisa exclaimed in disbelief. "Did you hear that chauvinistic remark, Jaclyn and Josh?" She looked across the table, then back at Logan and asked sweetly, "With my first or second child?"

"Our first," Logan gave her a smug smile. "Why?"

"You're such a fast worker, Mr. West, I presumed you might have single-handedly figured out a way to speed up the normal term of pregnancy."

"Do I detect a touch of sarcasm?" Logan gave a hearty

177

laugh, not the least perturbed that Lerisa wasn't clear if he was serious or not.

"Me, sarcastic?" Lerisa asked in her sweetest voice. "Never," she vowed, "especially to my . . . *thoughtful intended* . . . as your housekeeper refers to you when we're alone."

"Bless Maggie." Logan grinned, changing the subject abruptly. "Did you purchase a sexy dress for tonight's party?"

"She sure did," Jaclyn broke in. "Wait until you see what there is of it, Logan. You'll realize why all the men in France were hot on Lerisa's trail."

"I can hardly wait." Logan looked at Josh. "I suppose Jazzy had to have a new gown also?"

"Did you find one, honey?" Josh asked tenderly.

"She bought a little bit of black lace and will look beautiful as always," Lerisa broke in, pleased to observe how happy Jaclyn and Josh appeared together.

"Did you spend the money I left on your nightstand?" Logan whispered when the waiter served Jaclyn.

"No," Lerisa murmured beneath her breath. "I'm not your mistress, only your fiancée-to-be."

"What'd you do with it?"

"I threw it on your bed in hopes Maggie would think you left her a big tip."

"Insolent female," Logan scolded, moving back as a delicious-looking plate of food was placed in front of Lerisa.

For the next ninety minutes Lerisa enjoyed the bright company and casual talk. As she became better acquainted with Josh it was obvious why Jaclyn loved the man. He was intelligent, a talented, dedicated artist, and strikingly handsome as well.

Logan, though, was her dream come true. His ready sense of humor was endless and kept them all laughing as he recounted tale after hysterical tale of true occurrences that happened while selling real estate.

Sitting close, Lerisa listened attentively. She was filled with pride knowing that the charismatic man beside her had chosen her to be his wife. He was everything she had ever fantasized about and she loved him with all her heart.

"Are you happy, sweetheart?" Logan asked, meeting her bemused glance with eyes glowing with tenderness.

"Very," she admitted lazily. "And full too."

"Aren't we all?" Jaclyn sighed with satisfaction as she glanced at Josh for affirmation.

Replete after the tasty lunch had been consumed, along with a large pitcher of margaritas and dishes of tangy orange sherbert, Lerisa turned to Logan and asked, "How did you know Jaclyn and I would eat here today?"

"I told you I was psychic," Logan explained, trying to hold a straight face. When Lerisa frowned doubtfully he admitted, "I planned our lunch with Josh and Jaclyn when I went to the office yesterday."

"But Jaclyn never said a thing!" Lerisa blurted out, eyeing her friend in disbelief.

"You'll have to admit it's a pleasant surprise for you," Jaclyn insisted, snuggling close to her husband's wide shoulder affectionately.

"A marvelous one," Lerisa agreed happily.

"Because of me?" Logan asked innocently, though his eyes were sparkling with mischief.

"No," Lerisa taunted. "Because I don't have to pick up the meal tab and I have Baby Cakes to cuddle."

"You can cuddle me," Logan scowled, eyeing the toy puppy with sudden disfavor. He laid down several bills to pay for their lunch and tip the waiter, who had given them excellent service. "Starting as soon as we get home."

"Jaclyn's driving me home," Lerisa reminded him in a saucy voice.

"Jaclyn and Josh are taking the Porsche to their own home. You're coming with me to ours."

Before Lerisa had time to say much more than a quick good-bye she found herself seated in the Cadillac with Logan driving the short distance to his house.

"Lunch was really nice," Lerisa said softly as she played with the plushly piled puppy. "Jaclyn and Josh are so much in love, it's wonderful to watch them together."

"Brad and Brandy act the same way about each other, as you'll notice tonight. Both men are very lucky to be married to women they're passionately devoted to and who return their love equally."

"Are you envious?" Lerisa asked, holding her breath until he answered.

"Not in the least," Logan returned seriously. He pulled through the opened gates and past a flower-bordered drive to park his gleaming Cadillac in a garage big enough to stall five cars the same size.

"Why not?" Lerisa inquired softly, hoping he'd declare his love again. She couldn't hear the words enough and he knew it.

Ignoring the numerous vans lined up in rows along the wide drive, plus the many people working outside, Logan drew her into his arms and tenderly whispered, "Because I have you, sweetheart." His voice was deep and filled with emotion as he continued, "And nothing in the world matters to me but keeping you securely by my side . . . happy, satisfied, and forever in love with your husband."

"Wow," Lerisa exclaimed breathlessly, giving him a lingering kiss on his sensuous mouth. "That's a lot for one man to live up to."

"I'll manage, honey," Logan assured her between one

breathtaking caress after another. "You can bet money on it."

"Speaking of money." Lerisa withdrew long enough to give him a curious glance. "What was the reason for all that money on my nightstand this morning?"

"It was to buy your engagement-party dress." Logan pulled her back into his arms. "Why? Did you think I had an ulterior motive of some kind?"

Boldly meeting his keen eyes, Lerisa explained, "I naturally presumed you were so used to paying for your dates' illicit favors after each evening out that you automatically gave me the usual . . . *stipend* . . . before you crept out of the house."

Logan threw his head back, shaking with laughter before pinning her furious look. Enjoying her open display of temper, he mocked, "That's pretty high-priced loving considering what I got from you last night."

"As I recall, Mr. West," Lerisa corrected him quickly, "you locked . . . *me* . . . out of . . . *your* . . . room before I even had a chance to earn a fee!"

"You're just mad because I beat you at your own game. Your eyes are extremely revealing, my bad-tempered beauty, and expressed beyond all doubt that you were biding your time to give me the old heave-ho . . . should I have asked to share your bed."

When Lerisa lowered her head and refused to answer, Logan asked, "Am I right?"

"Yes, darn it." She faced him, giggling softly in good humor. "I'm warning you now, Mr. Know-It-All, that I don't give up easily and you're still due for a setdown. Several, in fact."

"You scare me to death," Logan chuckled as his head lowered to give Lerisa another unhurried passionate kiss.

When he finally drew back he had to inhale deep gulps

of air to regain his breath. "Here we are in broad daylight making love in my damned garage. No telling where you'll try to have your way with me next."

"Who cares?" Lerisa teased, giving his firm chin a quick kiss.

"I sure as hell don't," Logan agreed, "though when I bed you for the first time I guarantee we'll be completely alone and have the whole night to enjoy it."

"I suppose you'll want to be completely undisturbed too?" Lerisa asked, barely able to whisper as she hurriedly smoothed her skirt down in preparation for getting out.

"Hell no," Logan scoffed. "I want you to disturb me in all the ways your experienced little body and creative mind can dream up."

"Forget I asked," Lerisa chided, though she loved it when Logan talked sexy to her. "Before I lock myself in the bedroom to prepare for tonight's gala event I want you to give me a guided tour and brief outline of the setup. I'd hate to act a nitwit at my own coming-out party."

"Okay, Mistress of the Manor," Logan teased, grabbing her hand as they strode toward the nearest group of workers, who were busily carrying tables around the back toward the landscaped area surrounding the swimming pool.

CHAPTER TEN

Freshly bathed, perfumed, and powdered, Lerisa felt like a million dollars as she walked from the bathroom into her bedroom. Her makeup was complete and she had little to do before putting on her new dress. Excitement made her fingers fumble as she hurriedly cinched the sash of a vivid scarlet-silk kimono.

Standing in front of a full-length mirror, she twisted and turned, trying to determine if her hair would look better worn loose around her shoulders or up off her nape with casual curls pulled down around her face and ears.

Still undecided, she turned toward the door as a sharp rap disturbed her concentration.

"Come in," Lerisa called, knowing it would be Maggie. She had asked her to come to her room at six-thirty and she was right on time.

"Oh, my stars," the housekeeper exclaimed, stepping inside the room. She clasped both hands over her bosom. "Aren't you the lovely one tonight?" Walking to the bed, she picked up Lerisa's dress and eyed it with dreams of her long-past youth. "Why I daresay Mr. West will bust his seams with pride when he sees you in your pretty green gown."

"I hope he likes it." Lerisa smiled, thinking of Logan's

shocked eyes when he first saw that it revealed most of her bosom and all of her back.

She walked to the bedside table and picked up a beautifully wrapped package. "This is yours, Maggie."

"What on earth for?" the older woman asked in a surprised but pleased voice.

"For being so nice to me and also for baking that scrumptious-looking chocolate pie I saw in the refrigerator when I came home from shopping. I'm really looking forward to tasting it after tonight's party."

"Why I do declare," Maggie gushed, "aren't you the thoughtful one?" She eagerly tore off the gold bow and gift wrapping to reveal an ornate glass vial containing the latest perfume sensation, Sinfully Sexy. "Oh my, Miss Lerisa, what on earth will I ever do with this naughty-titled scent?"

"You can wear it the next time Frank comes to do the lawn," Lerisa suggested with a knowing twinkle in her eyes. "I saw him leering at you with wicked intent this morning when I left with my friend Jaclyn."

Lerisa watched a deep flush color Maggie's cheeks and knew she had sensed right when she thought there was a developing romance between Logan's two employees.

"I don't know if I'd have the nerve." The older woman flushed an even deeper pink.

"You do," Lerisa assured her. "Put some on right now and see how nice it smells." When Maggie hesitated she reached for the bottle and softly suggested, "Here, let me help you."

Lerisa removed the stopper and dabbed a drop on the housekeeper's wrists and behind each ear. "Hmm, you smell sexy. Frank will fall like a brick when he gets a whiff."

"Well, maybe I could dab on a tiny drop now and then,"

Maggie promised. Her cheeks were flushed as she preened in front of the dresser mirror for a moment before turning back to Lerisa. "You'd think it was my birthday, all the presents I'm gettin'," she added in a pride-filled voice.

"What do you mean, Maggie?" Lerisa asked curiously, having a suspicion she'd underestimated Logan again.

"First Mr. West sneaks into my kitchen and hands me a box from one of those fancy Beverly Hills dress shops I never been inside of, then you—"

"What did Logan get you?" Lerisa interrupted, amazed that despite his heavy work schedule Logan cared enough to be concerned with his employees' feelings and soothed them thoughtfully and generously. The man continued to amaze her with his perception.

"Well," Maggie looked at Lerisa and confessed shyly, "Mr. West knows I like to read murder mysteries late at night and says he didn't want me gettin' a cold in my shoulder." She raised one hand to rub the top of her right arm. "I've got a touch of bursitis that starts actin' up when I get chilled so the dear soul bought me a quilted satin bed jacket."

"How considerate," Lerisa told her truthfully, though it was hard not to laugh at hearing Logan called a dear soul. "Your gift sounds beautiful. What color did he buy?"

"Black." Maggie dropped her skimpy lashes shyly. "As wicked a color as that scent is you got me." Her eyes raised to meet Lerisa's squarely. "Why I'll feel like a regular movie star." She smiled, speaking from the heart, "I'll tell you, love, these are the two most pretty, ladylike gifts I ever got in my life. Mr. Johnson never so much as got me a card all the years we were wed."

"Remind me tomorrow and I'll pick you out a nice silk scarf with colors that will make your brown eyes shine like cat's-eye gems."

"You best be keeping those nice scarves I unpacked and get yourself dressed or the guests will be here before you're ready."

"I've got plenty of time, Maggie," Lerisa pointed out with a mischievous smile. "It would be a shame to waste that elegant curved stairway by not making a grand entrance and arriving late at my own party."

"Why, Miss Lerisa, you really are a kidder," the housekeeper scolded with a knowing smile. "But aren't you the perfect one for Mr. West!"

"I hope so," Lerisa chuckled as she laid out the garter belt and stockings she intended to wear.

"I hate to admit it but those fancy caterers and their staff made it look like a fairyland downstairs with all the flowers and candles sparkling like magic. That Mr. West even had them switch the red tableclothes for emerald green when he heard the color of your gown."

"It is beautiful," Lerisa admitted, nearly overcome by the thought of Logan ordering a last-minute change of table linen just to complement her gown. "They weren't even finished when I got back from shopping and I was stunned by the beauty of everything. Eating around the pool will be lovely."

"It's a good thing the weather's behavin' by being warm or you'd all be messin' up Mr. West's fine home something terrible. Sometimes it can blow real wild here on the coast."

"I'm sure it can," Lerisa agreed, smiling as she watched Maggie leave with her perfume clutched in both hands as if it would disappear if she let go.

Lerisa had turned back to the mirror, reaching for a hairpin to hold her hair up, when she heard the sound of the door opening. Not turning around, she called, "Did you forget something, Maggie?"

"Yes I did, Miss Lerisa," Logan answered in a teasing falsetto imitation of his housekeeper's voice as he stepped inside the room.

Closing the door firmly behind him, he stood speechless, staring in awe at the beauty of his fiancée as she spun around.

Lerisa faced him, one hand clutching the lapel of her kimono and the other over her breast in hopes it would stop the wild beating of her heart. It was always the same. The moment she saw Logan her heart pounded out of control.

Her eyes surveyed his partially dressed form starting with the unbuttoned, white ruffled shirt that exposed a tantalizing glimpse of dark, hair-covered chest. They continued down his long limbs clad in black formal trousers that fit to perfection. She stopped to stare in amazement at the sight of his large bare feet covered in black silk stockings.

Obviously fresh from the shower, glints of moisture were still visible in his wavy hair. All told, Logan looked so handsome that Lerisa wanted to rush into his arms and stay there forever.

Instead she calmly asked, "What do you want, Logan? I haven't finished getting dressed yet."

"I want you," he told her bluntly. "And not being dressed will save me time getting you."

"You can't be serious?" Lerisa questioned, raising her brows as if he had lost his mind. "Over one hundred guests are due to arrive in a matter of minutes."

"Who gives a damn?" Logan asked, shrugging one broad shoulder as he started across the carpet. "I sure don't."

"Are you forgetting my celibacy clause?"

"Hell no," he scoffed, pausing one step away to give her

a look that glinted a warning to take him seriously. "I'm ignoring it."

"You can't!" Eyeing him warily, Lerisa lifted her hands outward.

"Think again, witch," Logan argued, moving one step forward as Lerisa retreated the equal distance back. "I never had any intention of keeping my hands off you."

"You're the man who insists we be totally undisturbed the first time we make love. Remember?"

"Certainly," he answered without concern. "I also told you earlier that as a businessman I've learned to be flexible."

"But I've already put my makeup on."

"You look gorgeous without any."

"I spent a half hour just brushing my hair smooth."

"I prefer it a mass of raven-black curls spread across my pillow."

"I just got out of the bathtub."

"Aren't I the lucky one. You smell as exquisite as you look."

Lerisa clenched her teeth, refusing to say another word as she looked toward the bathroom as an avenue of escape. When determined, Logan was impossible. Surely no other woman had been forced to miss her own engagement party because she was locked in the bathroom trying to escape an imperious fiancé's untimely loving.

"Don't attempt it," Logan intervened smoothly, reading her mind. "I'd have you in my arms before you started to move."

"Darn you, Logan," she broke her vow of silence. Endeavoring unsuccessfully to keep her temper in check, she denounced his actions. "I'm about to—"

"Get the devil kissed out of you," Logan interrupted,

covering the space between them before Lerisa could voice a further objection.

"I came in here to tell you how much I love you, sweetheart. I just want to enjoy the warmth of you in my arms for a few minutes before we get swallowed up in the throng due below."

"Why didn't you tell me that in the first place then?" Lerisa asked eloquently. "Instead of charging at me like a-a—"

"Shush," Logan interposed. With both hands on Lerisa's shoulders he cradled her close. His voice deepened, harsh with his bluntly spoken need. "I really ache for you. I've been a damned long time without a woman."

"Go hire one," Lerisa pulled back to flare jealously, despite knowing she'd kill him if he took one step away from her to do as she demanded. Just as she conceded that he was the most romantic man in the world, he had to break her dreamy mood by mentioning his sordid affairs. "Your bank balance can obviously stand the expense."

His disgusted look warned her against making another foolish outburst.

"I'm interested only in you, Lerisa. I don't want just any woman. I want you." His grip tightened until she raised her face upward. "And you I'll have!"

Drawing Lerisa fully into his arms before the cutting reply trembling on her lips could be uttered, Logan continued, "I'm damned tired of you arguing with everything I say. So be forewarned, woman. The longer your impertinent tongue goes uncurbed the sooner we'll be in bed and the sooner my frustration ends."

"Your timing is atrocious," Lerisa berated Logan with total lack of concern for his adamant advice. Summoning up all the courage she could, she raged on, "I don't have time to set you straight on what I will and will not allow,

189

Mr. West, but let me make this one point perfectly clear." Her chin raised belligerently. "Before I meet your guests there will be no—"

"I warned you, honey," Logan growled deep in his throat before plundering her mouth in a long devastating kiss that asserted beyond all doubt that she should have heeded his admonition.

At the limits of his patience, he ignored Lerisa's gasp of outrage as she was swept off her feet. Carrying her to the wide bed, he dumped her squirming form unceremoniously in the middle. Quick as lightning, he followed her down on the satin spread, holding her still with the strength of his greater size.

"Now listen and listen good, my love. *I'll hold you when I want . . . I'll kiss you when I want . . .* and *I'll damned well make love to you when I want!*"

Staring in silence at the mixture of defiance and sensual interest that played back and forth across Lerisa's face, Logan imprinted her tempestuous beauty in his mind forever.

Lerisa returned his intent look uncowed. Just the intimacy of being on a bed with the man for the first time was almost more than she could bear. Her eyes grew dreamy and her lips softened, parting in anticipation of his possession. With a soft moan of entreaty she twined her arms around his neck and pulled him close.

"The heck with a little bit of makeup, your lavish party, and my celibacy clause, you arrogantly sexy monster," Lerisa groaned against Logan's mouth. "Kiss me now and I'll forgive every damned sneaky, deceptive, terrible, horrendous deed you've ever—"

Her startling retort was broken off mid-sentence as Logan laughed deep in his throat before taking the sweetness offered with a hunger that was long denied.

On and on he kissed her, caressing her with such thorough and lingering expertise, she didn't care if they ever left the bedroom.

When he gently stroked the length of each shapely leg, rested for a long traumatic moment at the top of her thighs, then moved upward across her quivering abdomen to finally stop when he cupped the fullness of one breast in his long fingers, she thought she'd explode with the pleasure it invoked.

"Oh, Logan," Lerisa confessed in a soft murmur, "each time you touch me I think I'll die it feels so good."

"It's supposed to feel that way, sweetheart," Logan whispered, drawing back so he could part her gown and glimpse the exquisite beauty of her breasts.

"Is this what you expected me to do when we parked last night?"

"Yes. Oh yes!" Lerisa cried out, feeling her nipples become taut buds beneath his heated gaze.

Logan's eyes darkened with desire as he viewed the rise and fall of her satiny bosom beneath him. Repeated shock waves rushing through his veins flooded him with such excitement that his body tautened to a rock hardness he never recalled the likes of before.

"Heaven help me," he moaned, resisting the impulse to plunder the rosy peaks a moment longer just so he could explain how he felt. "I've never seen anything so erotic in my life as watching your beautiful pink nipples harden beneath my gaze. I want to suck and lick them so bad I'm damned near ready to explode just thinking about it."

Lerisa squirmed beneath Logan's intent stare, unaware how enticing she looked as her voluptuous breasts swayed with the motion. The hunger in his expressive eyes and bold entreaty had equally heightened her senses. Without thought of the consequences she drew his head down to her breasts at the same moment she arched upward to enable his parted lips to reach their goal.

Pulsations of pleasure stabbed through her body from head to toe. It was the most sensual moment in her life, superseding all thoughts in her mind other than the sweet tugging motions that continued without cessation. When she thought she couldn't stand another moment he moved to the other breast, anointing it with all the reverence of a man in love with the woman he pleasured.

"I—I love what you're doing to me," Lerisa moaned, knowing Logan was the man she had been dreaming about all her life. Each abrasive stroke of his tongue licking around the aureole, then laving the sensitive tip over and over, increased her passionate response. A response that threatened any moment to get out of control.

"Oh, Logan," she whimpered helplessly. "It feels so wonderful."

"Doesn't it though?" he agreed in a roughened voice barely recognizable as his own.

"Do you really enjoy it too?" Lerisa entreated in a soft, foolish query.

Logan drew the entire peak of one breast into his mouth, then the other, sucking each reverently before withdrawing to implore her silence, "Hush, woman. Since I was taught not to talk with my mouth full I can't answer you now."

Unable to acknowledge his foolish remark sensibly, Lerisa wiggled beneath him. It was hopeless trying to pull away from his demanding mouth, but the continued ministrations on her sensitive nipples was driving her wild and she couldn't lie still.

Having Lerisa in his complete control, Logan's fingers cupped her burgeoning flesh. Nibbling his way around the entire fullness of each breast, he ground out a hoarse demand against the creamy skin. "Quit squirming, you tempting witch! I have no intention of ending this delightful petting for a long while yet."

"F-fool," Lerisa chided, barely able to speak as she began to explore beneath Logan's shirt. She ached with a sudden, unequivocal need to place her hands against his hair-roughened chest before exploring the rest of his hard male physique.

It was heaven what he was doing to her body. The most beautiful moment of her life, and she knew there would be others to follow. Despite his erotic warnings, she hadn't been prepared for the wondrous pleasure of his touch. It was magic, and as his body trembled beneath her inquisitive fingers she knew the urgency for release was equally shared.

As her fingers sought the scar she'd been told crossed the back of his shoulder, she had an uncontrollable urge to caress it with her lips. It couldn't help ease any pain, since the accident was long past, but it would let him know she cared.

Eagerly nuzzling deep into her scented cleavage, Logan lifted his head the moment Lerisa pushed his shirt aside to bare his right shoulder. He remained motionless, startled by her intent as she raised up and unerringly placed a series of kisses along the flat wound.

Drawing back, he looked at her with questioning eyes. "You went to my old injury as if you knew it was there."

"I did," Lerisa admitted, pushing him back on the bed so she could kiss his wide, muscular chest. The intriguing pattern of curly hair, thick across his pectoral muscles and trailing in a narrow line down his flat abdomen, drew her like a magnet. She wanted to investigate, not talk.

"How?" Logan asked, quick to question. "Jaclyn has never seen me without a shirt on."

"I'll tell you later," Lerisa shrugged noncommittally. She had the most passionate lover of her life on a bed and didn't want to waste time being quizzed.

Before Logan could say another word her mouth was on his dusky, flat nipple and she was gently tugging the hardened bud. Loving the taste of his skin, she became bolder, licking and exploring with moist lips through the dark brown hair on his chest. When she trailed down the line of hair leading to his trousers, he immediately reached out to push her away.

"No more for you now, sweetheart. I've damned near climaxed a dozen times already tonight. One touch of your hands or your lips on that part of my anatomy and I'll need a change of clothes as well as a shower."

Ignoring his warning, Lerisa teased by pushing his belt aside and nuzzling the taut skin of his flat abdomen before placing her tongue gently into his indented navel.

When her fingers, of their own volition, moved to the evident rise threatening to burst his slack zipper and prepared to stroke the pulsating flesh inside, she found herself suddenly pushed beneath him with her hands pinned high over her head.

"You just never listen do you, witch?" Logan moaned, growling deep in his throat as he desperately fought for control. "I think it's time to see how much . . . *heavy petting* . . . you can stand before we party."

"No more, please," Lerisa implored, helplessly trying to pull her hands free. "You already made me completely forget you have guests arriving soon."

"I intend to see you forget it again," Logan threatened. "You're an experienced lady and know it's dangerous to tease a man the way you did after he asks you to quit. To see we share tonight's frustration equally, I'll show you a

194

couple of erotic tricks guaranteed to leave a woman begging for more."

Dangerously close to that point already, Lerisa closed her eyes, waiting with rapidly beating heart for the promise of his experienced love play.

Kneeling while straddled each side of her hips, Logan never took his eyes from Lerisa's face. He watched each vacillating expression while making certain she felt the full pressure of his stimulated body until her tentative pushing upward changed to the instinctive motions of a female demanding to be loved.

When he could stand no more he released her hands and kissed her full on the mouth until she responded with all the passion in her being.

As Logan lingered over the erratic pulse beating in Lerisa's throat before slowly, expertly, and thoroughly licking the throbbing peak of each breast, she bit back the urge to cry out that he'd won. She was his . . . however, whenever, and wherever he wanted her.

When she was certain her erotic chastisement was finished, the man above her soon showed her how very wrong she was. With her rumpled kimono pushed aside he lazily tongued his way the entire length of her body from breast to toe. The return journey left her gasping for breath as he intimately explored each silken inch of inner thigh.

"N-no more. *Pleeease* . . ." she implored, trembling convulsively when he parted her limbs, placed his face between her thighs, and kissed the silk crotch of her teeny lace panties as if he was deep-kissing her sweet mouth.

"My beautiful, beautiful love," Logan moaned, briefly raising his face. "Open your eyes and look at me, Lerisa."

Barely able to do as he demanded, she observed his handsome face through slumberous, dazed eyes. His well-cut mouth was wholly sensual, wholly masculine, and wholly intent on her complete capitulation.

Playfully running the edge of his teeth back and forth over the center of the silk, he cupped her bottom in both hands, then lifted his head to confess:

"I adore you, my wife-to-be." His husky drawl was filled with so much passion, he could feel her entire body tremble from head to toe.

Too overcome by the wild sensations consuming her, Lerisa tossed her head back and forth, unaware that Logan observed her seductive actions. With her hair spread in a glossy black sheen across the satin pillow, he thought her the most beautiful woman he'd ever seen.

In one fluid movement his mouth settled back to its original goal. On and on he caressed her, always over and never under the silk barrier that separated him from penetrating deep inside her feminine warmth.

Lerisa moaned, dying by degrees as he continued his sensual teasing. The thin material seemed like the most impenetrable obstacle in the world as she yearned to feel his mouth on her nakedness.

Writhing beneath him, she cried out, pleading for him to stop while her body and dilated eyes beseeched him to continue.

"Please, Logan," she panted, reaching up to cling to his shoulders. *"I can't stand any more."*

"Nor can I," Logan admitted with a shudder.

He eased up, deftly rolled her onto her stomach, and pulled her kimono high above her shapely bottom. With nimble fingers he eased her panties down until the smooth flesh was completely exposed to his view. Before she had time to protest he had pulled the wispy bit of black silk back up after calmly taking a sharp nip, followed by a lingering kiss, on each pink globe.

Lerisa spun around, jerking into a sitting position before bounding off the bed. She stood on the floor, legs braced while she rubbed her bottom.

"Darn you, Logan," she berated him. Not knowing if she was more furious that he broke her passionate mood or took a bite out of her bottom, she glared. "That hurt."

"Are you sure?" Logan contradicted with a knowing smile. He got off the bed, straightened his trousers, then casually proceeded to button his shirt. "I enjoyed it immensely, you tasty wench."

"Well." Lerisa lowered her lashes briefly to admit, "It actually felt darned good." She held his amused look boldly. "But it could have hurt if you had closed your damned teeth on me."

"I may make love to you in many, many ways but I'll never cause you pain, sweetheart," Logan assured her softly. "That's not my style, nor is it yours."

"We still haven't made love fully yet so how can you tell my preferences?" Lerisa asked with an impish smile.

"It's easy," Logan assured her, trying hard to hold back a grin. "You wear silk instead of leather panties, dainty bracelets rather than heavy bands with metal spikes, and you carry a handbag instead of a braided whip."

"I'm not surprised you're an expert on kinky sex. Now get out, you fool," Lerisa demanded, trying hard not to giggle. "Don't come back for a full thirty minutes, since I have to completely redo my makeup and get dressed."

"See you at eight sharp and don't wear any jewelry."

Lerisa stared in amazement as Logan strolled from the room, casually closing the door behind him as if the last emotionally shocking hour had never happened.

She looked at her shaking hands, observed the tips of her breasts, still hard and overly sensitized from his intimate touch, felt the aching deep in the recesses of her femininity, and knew that even though it felt like a dream, it had been the most potent reality of her life.

Surely the wonder of her response to his passionate expertise was a fantasy come to life. It was as if her past had never been and meeting Logan was fate, predestined by powers stronger than their casual introduction through a best friend.

After a quick check of the time she returned to the luxurious bathroom and carefully remade her face. A smile drew her lips into a knowing smile as she witnessed the heightened color in her eyes. They really did have the same sheen as emeralds, she admitted without conceit. Expensive emeralds, she added with a chuckle, remembering Jaclyn's description to Logan.

Twenty minutes later Lerisa's hair was brushed into a mass of gleaming curls sweeping across her bare shoulders as she slipped her arms into the tightly banded full sleeves of her dress.

She had added a wispy garter belt that matched the lacy briefs to hold up nylon hose so sheer it was a miracle she had slipped them up her long legs without getting a run. She stepped into spike-heeled sandals held to her feet by diamenté straps as delicate as those on the belt around her dress.

Adjusting the material so that it clung to the point of her shoulder, she stood up straight and frowned at her reflection. The top of the gown was slit right down to the waist both front and back. Taking a deep breath, she prayed that nothing more than her cleavage was exposed during the evening ahead.

Twisting back and forth in front of the mirror, she knew it was definitely the most revealing dress she had ever worn. Impossible to wear with a bra, it seemed much more daring now that Logan was due to come bounding through the door any second than it did in the sedate atmosphere of the dress shop.

"Oh well." Lerisa shrugged. "Why not?"

"Why not *what?*" Logan asked, entering the door in his usual unannounced manner.

Hesitant for him to see the revealing bodice, Lerisa continued to stand with her back to him, looking over her shoulder to ask, "Why not knock before you enter?"

"I'm certain that isn't what you were asking yourself in the mirror," Logan interjected perceptively.

He stepped forward, touched her shoulder, and slowly turned her around as a whistle of shock broke through his even white teeth.

"Now that I see this frontless-backless wonder that Jaclyn warned me about I imagine the . . . *why not?* . . . referred to why not shock the hell out of Logan?"

"You're too damned perceptive for your own good." Lerisa met his stunned glance boldly. "I have far more clothing on than women wear at the beach now."

"At the average California public beach, you mean," Logan corrected. "In France, at Cannes or Lyon, you'd fit right in."

"I would not," Lerisa stormed. "I wouldn't get a second glance."

"You'd get a second glance whatever you wore," Logan contradicted. "That's the sexiest damned dress I've ever seen." He ran one finger down the deep décolletage, asking, "What, pray tell, keeps the front from spreading apart more than it does?"

"My breasts."

"Well, lucky for you there's plenty of flesh each side to keep you decent all night or you'd damn well be wearing something else. I intend to enjoy a party, not try to stop a riot."

Refusing to answer, Lerisa slapped his hand away when the fingers started to explore beyond the silky skin visible to his interested glance.

Unperturbed, Logan slowly turned her around, eyeing her gown as the connoisseur of feminine beauty that he was.

"Decidedly designed to entrap a man," he told her as he fingered the jewel-toned folds of material. "It's soft and slinky, yet with enough fullness in the bodice so that it manages to reveal your gorgeous shape without clinging unduly. You'll drive all the men wild tonight."

"Does that include you?" Lerisa asked, giving him a heady dose of flirting with her outrageously thick eyelashes.

"I'm already wild," Logan returned, drawing her forward as he placed a lingering caress up the side of her neck. "Wild with the scent of you in my nostrils, wild with the feel of you close to my body, and wild with the intimate taste of you still on my tongue."

"And wild with an overabundance of hormones," Lerisa teased. She drew back, giving him as thorough a scrutiny as he was still giving her. "It certainly pays you to dress," she announced, figuring it safer to lead the conversation away from her outfit. "I never knew a red-haired man in a tuxedo could look so handsome."

"Quit changing the subject, sweetheart," Logan chided, ignoring her compliment to let his eyes trail once more over each inch of exposed skin. "Enjoy your gown tonight, witch," he warned her in a no-nonsense voice, "because from now on if you want to reveal that luscious figure, it will be only to me."

Deciding it was safe to taunt Logan since his guests were undoubtedly already arriving, Lerisa withdrew, slowly and gracefully twirled around to give him the full effect of her dress, then went back into his arms with a devastating smile aimed at soothing his growing scowl.

"Do you really think it's sexy?"

"You're sexy. The dress is nothing without the body beneath it," Logan pointed out wisely. "It makes your eyes appear greener, your waist smaller, your hips inciting, and your breasts the most exciting feminine temptation I've ever observed."

"That's all the approval I need for tonight," Lerisa said impudently, slipping from his arms to add another spray of her favorite perfume behind each ear. If the scent worked as guaranteed, he'd be enslaved for life.

"It's really an amazing style," Logan admitted reluctantly as he observed the material move around her body in easy fluid motions. "It promises to entirely expose your flawless breasts, yet hides nearly every delectable inch except the enticing cleavage."

"That's what it's supposed to do," Lerisa explained as she checked to see if Logan's tie was straight. It was. As was every impeccable inch of his tailored suit. He looked stunning. Sexually magnetic and compelling enough to get any woman he wanted. Thankfully it was her.

"Every man will envy me tonight," Logan huskily interrupted, unaware of Lerisa's deep musings about his masculine appeal.

"And what will you be thinking while they do that?" Lerisa asked curiously.

"I'll be thinking I'd rather be tasting your heavenly soft breasts than looking at them."

"I should never have asked," Lerisa moaned, though her eyes were bright with remembered delights. "Are you ready to make a grand appearance now?"

"No." Logan removed a small box from a jacket pocket.

"It doesn't seem right for a man to present his fiancée to his friends and not have his ring on her finger."

"Oh, Logan," Lerisa whispered, overcome by his continued ability to plan ahead on a moment's notice. Trying to act sophisticated, despite the rapid beating of her heart, she met his tender look head-on.

Tears gathered in her eyes as she accepted the box and opened it to catch her first glimpse of the exquisite stone. A large perfect emerald set between two equally perfect diamonds sparkled in the light of the room. Set in gold, it was the most beautiful ring she had ever seen in her life.

Lerisa looked up at Logan and whispered, "It's gorgeous, Logan. I love it already." She held out her finger for him to place it on, asking, "When did you have time to shop for this beauty?"

"Today. I flew to LAX this morning, drove to Beverly Hills, and picked what I wanted from the stones waiting on my arrival."

"You did all this alone today?"

"No," Logan assured her nonchalantly, as if it was nothing to call ahead and have a jeweler display his best wares on a moment's notice, "Josh went with me. In fact, he bought a gorgeous necklace for Jaclyn."

"This is all pretty hard to believe," Lerisa admitted, holding her hand up to twist it back and forth. The weight of the expensive stone would take getting used to, but she knew she'd never want to remove it, it was so gorgeous.

Logan drew her hand to his bowed head, placed a kiss reverently over the ring, then turned her palm over to place an equally loving caress in her hand.

"I love you, Lerisa." His voice was deep and serious. "This ring is as binding to me as the matching wedding band I'll place next to it tomorrow."

Lerisa's expression grew somber as she informed Logan

202

in an even voice, "I was serious when I told you that you could name the date for our engagement if I could set the day for our wedding."

She met Logan's narrowed glance with her chin tilted at its most determined angle. "Six weeks sounds like an appropriate number of days to prepare myself for a lifetime of living with you."

"Six weeks, hell." Logan shook his head firmly no. "I'm not waiting that long for you, Lerisa, especially after the painful trauma of nearly consummating our relationship a matter of minutes ago."

"Six weeks or nothing," Lerisa answered, resolved to settle their difference of opinion before she went downstairs.

"I'll delay one week," Logan agreed reluctantly, taking her chin in his hand as he held her stubborn glance with one even more strong-minded. "Seven days and seven days only."

"Four weeks?" she insisted in a wavering voice.

"I refuse to cool my heels for an entire month while you paint a picture," Logan told her adamantly. "Especially one that I commissioned."

"Then consider our engagement the shortest on record," Lerisa declared, refusing to give in only because she liked the way he handled her impetuous outbursts. If he accepted her rejection, she'd do the fastest about-face on record.

Logan stared into Lerisa's eyes, reading her as easily as an open book. She was determined to defy him and he knew it, but he loved her all the more because of her courage. He had had a surfeit of willing females the past few years and the woman in his arms was an exciting change.

"One week from Sunday you'll be my wife," Logan insisted, brooking no argument as he continued, "And I'm warning you right now that if you give me the slightest runaround, or try any more playful tricks, we'll begin the honeymoon whether we're married or not!"

"I can live with that." Jaclyn gave him her most devastating smile. "You'd be surprised how much I can accomplish in a week if I can work undisturbed."

"I presume you're going to bring up your idiotic celibacy clause again?" Logan reminded with disgust.

"After your attack on my innocence earlier you obviously need reminding." Lerisa reached up to smooth some unruly waves over each ear. It was only an excuse to touch him and he knew it, but she loved the feel of his thick shiny hair against her fingertips.

"Before I supposedly attacked you, my hot-blooded little fiancée, you were handling a part of my body guaranteed to get you in trouble fast."

"It's time to change the subject, Logan. I want to admire your generous gift."

"I'm not through yet," Logan told her agreeably before leading her to the mirror. "Now turn around and let me see how you like this."

Lerisa stared at her reflection, silently watching as Logan removed a necklace from another box. With deft fingers he pushed her hair aside and fastened the clasp over her nape.

She watched speechless as an emerald, nearly equal in size to the one on her finger, fell on its gold chain to rest at the top of her cleavage. It was the perfect touch to her outfit, and she was awestruck at how it seemed made for the dress.

Raising a hand, she fingered the stone nestled in a circle of small diamonds, then turned back into Logan's arms. Unconcerned that she would smear her lipstick, she drew his head down and gave him such a long passionate kiss that it left her trembling and him gasping for air.

"After that enthusiastic thank-you I hate to tell you I have matching earrings." Logan inhaled deeply. "You'll probably seduce me right now if I give you the whole set."

Lerisa's eyes shone as she sassed, "You're over twenty-one and will have to take your chances." She held her hand out, mischievously waiting for her next gift.

"Greedy female." Logan handed her the earrings, explaining, "You'd better put these on without my help. They're for pierced ears and I'd hate to hurt you."

Lerisa took them, slipping each one into her ear and attaching the lock behind her lobe to ensure they didn't come out. She turned back to the mirror, twisting back and forth as she glanced at her new jewelry.

Their eyes met and held in the mirror as Logan spoke, "Jaclyn said we'd make a striking couple. Do you agree?"

"Most definitely." Lerisa returned his smile, turning around to give him a loving look.

Holding her at arm's length so he could imprint her beauty in the deepest recesses of his mind, Logan knew the days ahead would pass with torturous slowness.

Lerisa tore her glance away as a sudden, disturbing thought came to mind. "Did you pick me for your wife because we look good together?"

"Of course not," Logan denied as if she were losing her mind. "I've taken out too many beautiful women to remember. You"—he kissed her on her smooth shoulder before continuing in a solemn voice—"have much, much more than your stunning looks to offer a man."

"What?" Lerisa insisted, filled with feminine curiosity.

"Your independent spirit and fiery uncurbed tongue. I knew the moment I met you that, once given, your heart would be totally mine. I want fidelity in my woman."

"I demand fidelity in my man," Lerisa reminded him emphatically. "Are you really certain you can live with that, Logan?"

"I already have."

"Since when?" Lerisa asked in a mocking voice as he unconsciously fondled her shoulders with both hands.

"Since I first heard about you last Christmas. After Jazzy described you to me I found I couldn't even think of another woman."

"That's hard to believe," Lerisa admitted, though well pleased with his reply. She tilted her chin impudently before twisting back to face the mirror.

"Keep up the good work, Logan. I hear purity is good for the soul. And especially yours."

Logan moved up behind her, crossed his hands over her abdomen, and pulled her tight to his body. "I'd rather be seduced than be pure. I'm also ready, if you haven't noticed."

"I noticed," Lerisa assured him as she leaned over to apply lipstick for the second time and unintentionally thrust her buttocks hard against his aroused flesh.

"God, honey." Logan held her hips still as he pushed forward. "Don't keep squirming into me like that or I'll take you right here and without turning you around."

Lerisa spun to face him, leaning back to glare at his serious face. "I refuse to redo my makeup for the fourth time, so behave. As I said before, for an . . . *old man* . . . you're awfully frisky."

"You make me sound like a horse." Logan scowled at her wording.

"A stud horse," Lerisa hurled at him, heading toward the door with her bared back straight and head held high.

"Brat," Logan called out, catching up with her in two strides as she reached for the doorknob. "We make our grand entrance together if you don't mind, Ms. Independence."

"Then come on, slow poke," Lerisa prodded in a teasing voice. "I'm anxious to let your former lady friends know that you're truly hooked and I don't share my goodies with anyone."

"Goodies!" Logan recoiled at her rhetoric. "First I get called Baby Cakes, then a frisky stud horse, and now I'm placed in the category of a bag of goodies."

"Actually that's wrong," Lerisa assured him. "Goodies is a synonym that should never be used with you, considering your reputation. I should have said I never share my toys."

"Toys, goodies, whatever." Logan scowled, taking her arm as he closed her bedroom door behind them. "I'm your lover, your—"

"You're not my lover yet," Lerisa insisted, slanting him a wide-eyed, teasing look.

"I came close enough to being your lover today that I know what you taste like," Logan insisted, running his hand along the swell of her bottom to emphasize the intimacies he had taken earlier.

"Beast," Lerisa chastised, rubbing her behind with one hand. "If I have bruises tomorrow, I—I'll—"

"I'll kiss them well," Logan whispered, raising his chin as he quietly closed her bedroom door behind them.

CHAPTER ELEVEN

A sudden and horrendous thought struck Lerisa before she had taken a single step down the hall. Gripping Logan's arm, she raised her face to his questioning gaze.

"Please tell me if you've made love to any of the women invited here tonight."

With her heart in her eyes she implored him to be completely honest.

"Of course I haven't, honey," he assured her with a gentle embrace. Drawing away, his look was compassionate as he scolded softly, "Give me credit for having some sensitivity."

"B-but you've known so many women."

Understanding her inner turmoil, he bent to console her with a tender touch of his lips on the forehead.

"I have, but I'll never knowingly subject you to meeting any of them. If it's in my power to do so, I'll see you're neither hurt nor forced to endure any petty jealousy because of a life-style that occurred before I knew of your existence."

"Won't that be a hopeless task, considering your past?"

"Perhaps," Logan admitted truthfully. Cradling Lerisa's face in both hands, he met her concerned look head-on. "The women in my past are just that, honey . . . *past* . . . *and long forgotten.*"

"What about former lovers that are friends or wives of your friends?" Lerisa continued to question in a soft, plaintive whisper. "There must be lots of them around, considering you know over one hundred people who you're close enough to to invite them here tonight."

"Don't worry, baby," Logan replied sympathetically. He hugged her close to reaffirm his love. "Two rules I learned while still a young man were . . . never to mix business with pleasure . . . or get involved with women an acquaintance tried to set me up with. Both actions can be deadly to a friendship. My past liaisons were rarely close to home."

Feeling happier after Logan's explanation, Lerisa cocked him an impudent look. "Have you forgotten that Jaclyn not only introduced us but I'm also a paid employee who lives in your home as well? It appears, Mr. West, that our relationship has broken all your rules."

"And look what happened to my freedom when I got careless." Logan returned her saucy glance with an indulgent smile. "I told you before you were trouble with a capital *T.*"

"None of this was my idea," Lerisa reminded him pertly. "Either the party or the engagement."

"True," Logan admitted, stroking her satin-smooth back as he bent to kiss the tip of her nose. "Which just proves how much I love you since I'm impatiently marking time until I lose my previously guarded bachelorhood too."

"Keep talking, fiancé. A woman could get addicted to hearing words like that." She fluttered her lashes, flirting boldly just to observe his response.

Holding up her left hand, she stared in wonder at her ring finger. The flawless stones flashed brilliant fire beneath the overhead lighting. "I feel like royalty tonight."

Logan cast Lerisa a loving glance, awestruck once again

by her stunning beauty. "You look better than any blue-blooded lady I've met."

Lerisa let one finger outline Logan's firmly chiseled jaw with an oval-tipped nail before touching his compressed lips in a teasing caress.

"Quit the woman magic, sweetheart," Logan warned, taking Lerisa's hand in his to continue along the hall. "I'm a very frustrated man tonight."

"You wouldn't be if you hadn't come prowling inside my bedroom before I was dressed."

"Point taken," he admitted with a low chuckle. He lowered his head to gently nip the side of her neck.

"Damned brute!" Abruptly stopping, Lerisa stood on tiptoe to return his nip, less gently, on the lobe of his ear. With deliberate intent to arouse she slowly brushed her breasts across his chest as she pulled away.

Giving her a teasing swat on her shapely bottom, he warned, "Since we're on our way to go *down* the stairs and not *up* them, you'd better cool down those heated glances and inciting little tricks until after the party. Then I can reciprocate in an appropriate manner, as you should have learned earlier."

"I'll try to behave," she announced brightly. "But you're a very sensual man and a devastating lover, so if I get carried away you'll have to take my newly engaged status into account."

"Meaning I should forgive everything you do tonight?"

"I think it might be a good idea to at least be tolerant. Just in case something traumatic happens . . . such as a former mistress crashing our party."

"Thank heavens . . . *for her sake* . . . I've never had a mistress," Logan returned with a knowing sigh. "I'd hate to think what you'd do to the poor woman if you ever met."

"Nothing too terrible," Lerisa slanted him a devilish smile. "Before we're married I'd just throw her out of your home."

"And afterward?" Logan asked, enjoying Lerisa's outspoken temerity.

"I'd scratch her eyes out first, then I'd toss her out on her b—"

"Back," Logan intervened, finishing her threat with a deep laugh.

She stared at him with a gleam of mischief in her eyes. "Actually I meant derriere."

"Behave, witch," Logan warned out of the corner of his mouth as they reached the top of the dramatically curved stairway.

"Yes, sir!" Lerisa snapped in a pretense of bowing to a higher authority.

She removed her hand from Logan's firm clasp, lifted her head to a regal angle, took his outstretched arm, and prompted in a lilting voice, "It's late enough now that our grand entrance, as promised Maggie, should make a memorable impact. So move it, Mr. West."

"You really are a menace," Logan ground out through lips formed into a perfect smile. "And for God's sake keep your back straight. That damned dress is enough to incite a violent uprising."

"Then it will be worth every dollar it cost."

Lerisa's eyes shimmered with delight, noting Logan's forehead crease in a quick, censorious frown.

As they descended in perfect step toward the interested gaze of the waiting guests, he informed her through tightly clenched teeth, "I have a feeling you're not only going to raise a few eyebrows tonight but my male friends' blood pressure as well."

"I'll be a perfect angel," Lerisa promised, giving Logan a

211

dazzling smile that nearly rocked him on his heels. "Wearing a king's ransom in jewels, I'll have to be good or the king might take them all back."

"That is something to consider," Logan agreed, slanting her another all-encompassing glance. She was so beautiful, he found it nearly impossible to tear his eyes from the flawless perfection of her profile. Filled with pride, he nodded to the welcoming crowd below.

For the next hour Lerisa smiled her way through one exciting greeting after another, always keeping an eye out for Jaclyn and Josh.

From diplomat to landscape artist, professor to mayor, polo captain to councilman, restaurateur to broker, TV anchorman to contractor, she was welcomed effusively by them all. They were a marvelous blending of ages, personalities, nationalities, occupations, wealth, and background and she found each to be equally interesting.

Normally gregarious, Lerisa was right in her element as she was swept on Logan's arm from one flower-bedecked room to another inside the house, outside among the beautifully set tables surrounding the sparkling aquamarine pool with its sprinkling of gardenia and camellia blossoms, then back in again.

With Lerisa's genuine interest in Logan's elegantly groomed guests, her inherent beauty and poise, she capably managed to charm each one as her fiancé, with darkened, possessive eyes, looked on entranced.

Cases of fine champagne were emptied along with silver platters filled with mouth-watering hors d'oeuvres carried by young waiters wearing impeccable black uniforms with green cummerbunds. Her eyes twinkled, wondering if Logan had insisted that the vivid sashes also be changed to match the tableclothes, which in turn had been switched to match her gown.

A nine-piece band played a medley of songs from their vantage point inside a charming gazebo set up near the opened glass doors leading from the game room to the pool.

As Maggie had exclaimed earlier, everything looked like a veritable fairyland. To think she was the guest of honor seemed impossible until she glanced at her engagement ring or looked into Logan's love-filled eyes.

"Lerisa!"

She turned when her name was called, ecstatic to see Jaclyn's smiling face as she arrived along with a lovely, petite brunette whose minuscule waist was firmly clasped by a towering man as devastatingly good-looking as Jaclyn had said he would be.

Greeting Jaclyn with a quick hug, Lerisa was introduced to Brandy and Brad. Giving them as well as Josh a welcoming smile, she knew instantly why Logan considered them his best friends.

Lerisa spent the next few minutes proudly displaying her engagement ring, necklace, and earrings. After they had been properly oohed and aahed over, she admired Jaclyn's exquisite new necklace as well as Brandy's flawless rubies with equal enthusiasm.

The men merely exchanged indulgent smiles and looked as if they wished they were somewhere else.

"Why are you all so late?" Lerisa asked, noticing by her watch that it was nearly ten o'clock.

A knowing glance was exchanged between Josh and Brad, who laughed as Jaclyn and Brandy said in unison, "We'll tell you later."

"Tell us *now*," Logan insisted drolly, aware that the two

men had been as sensually entranced earlier by their enticing wives as he was by his fiancée.

"Forget it, amigo," Brad told him. "I came here to meet
your bride-to-be, not to be questioned about my private
life."

"I'm here to check out the contents of the bar and the
sooner the better," Josh observed. "I've been thirsty ever
since that Mexican hot sauce ate out my stomach lining at
the lunch you bought me today."

"Let's go then," Logan said enthusiastically. "We'll down
a bottle of champagne while Lerisa gives Jazzy and Brandy
a tour of her new home."

"Excellent idea," Jaclyn agreed readily. She gave Logan a
happy smile. "I inspected your elegant home this morning,
but Brandy hasn't seen it yet. Besides, we need a breather
from you three."

The men left, already absorbed in talking about mutual
interests as they headed for the game room with its boun-
tifully stocked, extremely busy 1850s bar.

The elegantly groomed women formed a startling contrast as they swept from the room. Lerisa, exotically dark
in her sensual emerald gown, looked like a vivid painting.
Jaclyn, fair and lovely with ash-blond hair that shimmered
across the shoulders of a black lace designer dress, had a
secretive smile on her soft lips. Brandy, as petite as the
others were tall, wore an eye-catching wine-colored gown
that highlighted her gleaming chestnut-brown hair to
perfection.

As Lerisa skillfully maneuvered the two women through
guests happily settled into conversing groups, she had one
intent in mind . . . sneaking upstairs to the quiet sanctu-
ary of her own bedroom.

"I'm dying to see Logan's four-poster bed," Brandy told

her curiously. "Jaclyn said it was a present from his mother to encourage him to marry."

"Apparently it worked," Jaclyn chuckled, following Lerisa's straight back upstairs.

With a sigh of relief Lerisa opened the heavily paneled door to the master suite, stepped aside so Jaclyn and Brandy could enter, and motioned to her left.

"There's the beauty in all its gleaming glory."

"Good heavens," Brandy gushed. "It really is a romantic piece of antiquity. I love it."

"I'm pretty keen on it already myself," Lerisa admitted. Closing the door behind them, she walked to a fireside chair and flopped down, giving each a pleased, conspiratorial smile. "This brief respite is really a relief. My head's spinning trying to remember everyone's name."

"Don't even attempt it," Jaclyn advised with understanding. "They'll all sort themselves out later. It took me at least a month to greet Josh's clients and friends by the correct name."

Brandy continued to survey the plush bedroom with interest before stopping to stare once again at the unique bed dominating most of one wall.

Noticing Brandy's undivided attention, Jaclyn joined her to also give the bed a thorough once-over. "Tell me, Lerisa," she asked impishly, "why's the pillow crumpled and the bedspread all messed up?"

"Logan gave me my engagement ring," Lerisa explained without further comment.

"What else did the man give you?" Jaclyn insisted in a laughter-filled voice.

"Nothing."

"It looks like it," Jaclyn teased as she and Brandy giggled at Lerisa's evasive comment.

"Well, we did have a discussion too."

"Josh and my . . . er . . . *discussion* . . . was what made us late picking up Brandy and Brad."

"Oh no!" Brandy laughed in amazement. "You too? It looks like all three of us were had by our lovers tonight."

"Just two of you," Lerisa told them emphatically. "I was only an . . . *almost* . . . had."

"So," Jaclyn continued with a knowing smile, "that's why Logan was glaring at a group of his male friends leering at you when we arrived. He's not only jealous, he's frustrated as well."

"By the way, Lerisa, who won the discussion you . . . er . . . almost had?" Brandy interjected curiously. She knew Logan well, and the man had never lost a discussion with a woman that she'd heard of, whether it was a physical or a verbal one.

"I'm not certain," Lerisa admitted with a cheeky smile. She rose to check her reflection in the dresser mirror. Deciding she didn't need to apply another layer of lip gloss, she turned around to add, "At the time, though, I readily granted the victory to my arrogant fiancé."

"That's not surprising," Jaclyn agreed. "Our men seem to come out on top every single time."

"As I vividly and pleasantly recall, Logan was definitely in that position," Lerisa conceded with a playful chuckle.

"I told you my friend was blunt," Jaclyn announced to Brandy, shaking her head in dismay.

"Come on, you two," Lerisa encouraged. "Let's go up to my studio. It should be gorgeous at night with Logan's estate lit up like a three-ring circus."

Chattering nonstop after they had given each upper room a cursory inspection, Lerisa was descending the stairs side by side with Jaclyn and Brandy when she was stopped by a sharp tug on her right sleeve.

"See that horrible little man staring up at the woman with blond hair?"

"Do you mean the old blonde with enough gold around her neck to stock Fort Knox or the young blonde in the froth of red chiffon?"

There were so many people mingling in the broad foyer, Lerisa wasn't quite sure who Jaclyn meant.

"Fort Knox," Brandy interjected barely above a whisper, "who incidentally happens to be this area's leading politician's wife."

"I remember her telling me that at least twice." Lerisa smiled. "What about the man?"

"Avoid him like the plague. His name is Knickerpepper and he obviously crashed your party, because Logan detests him as much as Josh does."

"Brad hates him too," Brandy added. "The man invades Palm Springs two or three times a year." She turned to explain further to Lerisa. "He's a reporter who never prints anything but dirt . . . whether true or not."

"That's right," Jaclyn agreed. "He's also extremely clever and has managed to avoid the threat of libel action like someone charmed. I've never read a single nice thing about anyone in his gossip column. Unfortunately he's been spreading his slime for so many years that he has a large and devoted following of readers."

"Lucky for you he didn't look up," Brandy said. "He's heading for the bar now, where he'll prop up his puny little elbows until Logan throws him out or the caterer runs out of liquor."

"His power and vicious tongue scare me to death," Jaclyn said.

"Me too." Brandy shuddered.

"He sounds intriguing," Lerisa insisted, not the least cowed. Her eyes sparkled with the thought of doing battle.

217

Before the night was over she'd make certain she had introduced herself to the notorious Mr. Knickerpepper. If he was as bad as reputed, she'd delight in having Logan toss him out on his ear.

Continuing down the stairs, Lerisa boldly explained, "Come on, you two. Logan has been on his own long enough. He promised to dance with me tonight and I'm dying to see if he's as good on the dance floor as he is on the bed."

"Can you believe my friend, Brandy?"

"Yes and I love her already." She turned to Lerisa with a tender smile. "You really are perfect for Logan. I love the man dearly and couldn't be happier that he's found you to make his life complete. We six will have a ball running around together."

"I'm looking forward to it," Lerisa assured Brandy sincerely. As Jaclyn had promised, she liked her on sight.

Laughing together, they entered the game room, which had been cleared and its oak floor polished to a high shine.

Spotting Lerisa the moment she entered the vast room, Logan walked forward, clasped her fingers in his, and gallantly bowed low as he kissed the back of her hand. "Come to me, my lovely bride-to-be," he insisted, cradling her close.

"My turn, I believe," Josh announced, tapping his friend on the shoulder. "I owe you a big one for driving me wild with jealousy last Christmas." He looked at Lerisa's interested gaze and explained, "While I was recuperating from my eye injury on Vancouver Island, and couldn't see to accurately punch Logan in the face, he did his best to cause trouble between Jazzy and me."

Josh ignored Logan's possessive attitude and asked, "Would you dance with me, Lerisa? I have a lot to tell you about this man you've hastily agreed to marry."

"Peddle your wares elsewhere, Josh." Logan frowned, slapping his hand away from Lerisa's shoulder. "No one dances with my woman tonight but me."

"Actually I should take Lerisa for a twirl or two around the floor," Brad teased his best friend. "I've known you a hell of a lot longer than Josh. When I'm through cluing Lerisa in on all your bad habits, there probably won't be any wedding."

As Jaclyn and Brandy listened to the interplay with amused smiles they observed Logan's face. His jealousy was not an act. The man was crazy in love with Lerisa and even resented his best friends' wanting to share her attention for the brief period of one dance number.

Sweeping Lerisa back into his arms, Logan gave Josh and Brad a stormy look before twirling his fiancée away as the band played a rhythmic ballad of the 1950s.

"It's about time you asked me to dance." Lerisa leaned back in his strong arms, giving him a dazzling smile. She had never felt so cherished in her life.

"Missed me, did you?" Logan asked, returning her greeting with equal enthusiasm as he maneuvered her expertly around the crowded floor.

"A little," Lerisa admitted, pleased when Logan motioned for the band to switch to a slow romantic tune. Snuggling comfortably when Logan drew her tight into his arms, she raised her face to whisper against his throat, "You dance as well as you do everything else."

"Hmm, woman," he drawled suggestively, "you haven't experienced anything yet."

"Enough to know I'm already addicted to wealthy red-haired realtors."

"Keep talking like that and your slightest request is my command."

"I was hoping you'd say that," Lerisa told him. "I have something to ask you."

"Fire away." Logan nuzzled her neck, whispering love words in her ear as one hand stroked up and down her spine.

Trying not to be distracted by his persuasive lovemaking, Lerisa blurted out, "Will you pose for me in the nude?"

Logan raised his face, pinning her with narrowed eyes. "What the hell did you ask?"

"I want you to pose nude."

"Are you forgetting . . . *I* . . . commissioned . . . *you* . . . to paint a self-portrait of yourself? I'm damned if I'll parade around in the buff so you can paint me."

"You said I could pick the background."

"Yes I did," Logan acknowledged with a frown.

"Well, I want you in it . . . *unclothed."*

"Heaven help me," Logan moaned in despair. "Was it too much to assume you'd chose something normal like the beach, mountains, or meadows? Me posing naked is the dumbest idea I've ever heard."

As they continued to dance Lerisa persisted, "Are you going to pose nude for me?"

"Hell no." Logan pulled her close, drawing her head into his chest in hopes she would be quiet.

"Is that definite?"

"Absolutely," he hissed over the top of her head. "You couldn't force me into posing without my clothes on. If you want me to strip and play a little slap and tickle in private, let's go to the bedroom right now. In fact, it's a damned good idea." He started maneuvering her toward the edge of the floor.

"Forget it," Lerisa fumed, dragging her feet until Logan

was forced to stop. "I'm darned if I'll be subjected to your . . . *nip* and tickle play . . . again tonight."

Resuming his steps, Logan slowly moved his feet in time to the music. "Get to painting my picture then or we'll do nothing else but . . . *play* . . . starting now," he warned fiercely.

"I intend to start on . . . *your* . . . picture immediately."

Lerisa reached up to kiss the corner of his determined jaw. Without the least touch of conscience she knew her interpretation of his wording was the direct opposite.

"That's more like it." Pleased the argument was ended, Logan brushed his lips across her mouth in a brief caress.

"You'll soon wish you had agreed to pose for me," Lerisa whispered daringly.

"I doubt that very much." Logan gave her a sharp squeeze to make her behave.

"Tell me who that handsome, bronze-skinned man is." She nodded to the side of the room. "The big one with the pitch-black hair and piercing eyes who's standing alone by the bar. I don't remember being introduced to him."

Logan turned his head, grinding out an answer between tightly clenched teeth. "That's Sasq O'Brien. A friend of mine from Northern California. Apparently he just arrived. Why do you want to meet him?"

"Because I imagine he'd pose beautifully without his clothes on." She slanted Logan a twinkling smile. "Maybe even better than you."

"One thing for damned sure is that you'll never find out," Logan declared emphatically. "Sasq has been looking for a wife for a long time now and until we're married he can keep searching in his own neck of the woods. Like me, he's damned particular who he selects and you're a very special lady."

"Is he rich?" Lerisa teased. She could feel Logan's muscles tighten as her continued curiosity began to rankle.

"Very," he admitted with resentment. "Why don't you forget Sasq and keep your sexy mouth shut for a while? I'd like to hold you close without having to hear about how handsome you think my woodsman friend is."

"That's fine with me," Lerisa sighed with pleasure.

Logan's eyes scanned the room, noticing there were now several groups of his single male friends staring at the beauty of the woman in his arms. "Damn it!"

"Now what?" Lerisa asked dreamily, refusing to raise her cheek from Logan's lapel. She didn't want to do anything that might make him stop the heavenly stroking of her sensitive spine. Just as her fiancé had woven a magic spell around her, the music had too.

"What are you thinking, Logan?"

"The same as my frustrated friends watching you with feverish eyes. We're all dreaming about how good you'd be in bed."

"You're insane," she scolded beneath her breath.

Continuing unabated, Logan drawled huskily, "They're also standing on the sidelines speculating how many times I got it on with you the first night I took you to my bed."

"But you haven't!" Lerisa drew back to glare at Logan with stormy eyes.

"Don't you think I know it," Logan moaned, pulling her back into his arms until she lay her face on his chest again. "Not one man here tonight would believe that of me. They'd assume I'd lost my touch if I hadn't bedded you the first day we met."

"Why didn't you?" Lerisa taunted.

"Damned if I know now," Logan told her bluntly. "You sure as hell need it."

"Be quiet and dance or I'll find me a different partner," Lerisa threatened with a soft chuckle.

"Not tonight you won't," Logan informed her with possessive arrogance.

Lerisa smiled at Logan, in complete accord with his admonition. They danced song after song. Some held close in his strong arms and others apart when the band switched to rock. All were marvelous because of her partner. His attention never veered, the warmth in his eyes possessively letting everyone know she was his. It was a heady experience she could relive in her mind over and over again.

After the third fast number in a row, Lerisa clung to Logan's shoulders and beseeched him to have mercy. "I need a drink and an hour or two away from your big feet."

With his arm around her waist Logan guided her to a private dimly lit niche overlooking the far end of his swimming pool. "Wait here for me, honey. I'll be right back with our drinks."

Lerisa watched Logan, towering head and shoulders above everyone else, weave his way smoothly through the tables until lost from sight. Within seconds, it seemed, he had returned carrying a large frosty glass of orange juice, which was what she preferred to quench her thirst.

"Do you mind if I leave you alone for a little while, sweetheart?" Logan asked after checking to make certain Lerisa was comfortable.

"Of course not. It's beautiful here, hidden from everyone else by the massive ferns. Why?"

"I saw Josh at the bar and he wants to see my color prints of your works. Brad's coming too. On my word alone he'd like to display your nudes in his Palm Springs resort if you're interested."

"I can't believe this," Lerisa said excitedly.

"It's true," Logan assured her. "During our honeymoon

we'll crate the originals you have in Paris, then air-freight them back to the house. After we return to the States you can decide what you want to do."

"You sound too good to be true," Lerisa told Logan. "I love to paint but hate taking time to sell my work. Would you like to be my agent?"

"You don't need one," Logan told her proudly. "Josh and Brad both will be excellent help and all the contact you need. They each have clients with unlimited wealth who take delight in discovering new artists and outbidding each other if they think the work will appreciate. Since Josh held Jazzy's exhibit her work is in such demand that she can't fill the need."

"Don't waste time talking to me then," Lerisa told him. "I need all the help I can get."

"The hell you do." Logan gave her his most arrogant look. "Your talent equals the best. My interest in displaying your art is in being able to brag about the good choice I made in picking my mate. I doubt very much I'll allow a single work to be sold to anyone other than myself."

"Fool," Lerisa chuckled, loving him more each impetuous thing he said.

With Logan gone she leaned back to relax in the comfort of the padded patio chair. Taking a third sip of her refreshing citrus juice, she set the drink on the glass-topped table beside her and listened to the muted sounds of the band. It was heaven to relax a moment alone before the late supper was served.

"Ah, there you are."

Lerisa's happy musings were interrupted by the fronds of a feathery fern being pushed aside and the grating voice of the man she had been waiting to cross words with all night. Sitting upright, she met his challenging look straight on.

"Hello, Mr. Knickerpepper." She extended her perfectly manicured fingers in a friendly welcome. "I'm Lerisa Forbes, Mr. West's fiancée."

"I know who you are," the little man told her bluntly. His eyes ran avidly over her face and gown. "I watched you dancing earlier."

Not bothering to wait until invited, he sat down across from her, placed his drink on the table, and crossed one black-clad leg over the other. His glance was as cold as the hand that had touched hers during the introduction.

"Apparently you've heard all about me." His voice was filled with conceit.

"I hope not," Lerisa told him.

"Why?" he asked curiously.

"Because everything that I heard was bad. Your reputation is that of a horrible, vindictive, small-minded man whose only power lies in the readership of his newspaper."

Lerisa watched, intrigued, as the blood left his face and he spluttered in a terrible rage. He looked like a cocky penguin with his pudgy body clad in a tuxedo.

Completely taken aback by her blunt honesty, he spoke spitefully. "To get a gold band on your finger the great man must have made a mistake. Are you pregnant?"

Totally poised, Lerisa looked at him and parried smoothly, "Why on earth would you consider that's any of your business?"

"I'm a reporter."

"Being a newspaperman doesn't give you license to be insulting," she told him with a sweet smile.

"It gives me license, as you say, to ask any question I feel my readers will be interested in," he said in a huff.

"You're also an uninvited guest tonight, and if I so much as move an eyebrow wrong, my fiancé will remove you from . . . *our home* . . . before you can write down one word that I've said."

Lerisa gracefully stood, holding her shoulders straight as she towered over the man trying desperately to understand the first woman who'd ever spoken back to him in his life.

Drawing himself up to his full five-feet-five-inch height, he stared upward with pale blue myopic eyes. "You'd better watch out, young lady! Your fiancé isn't known for being faithful to women. He's this area's most notorious bachelor."

"Aren't I lucky then that Mr. West chose to make our relationship legal and marry me," Lerisa told the man in front of her. She gave him a dazzling smile. "Being so experienced, he'll make a dream of a husband."

"I wouldn't think so," the reporter spluttered. "He's known for loving them and leaving them."

"Leaving them what?" Lerisa countered with a mischievous twinkle in her eyes. She was enjoying every minute of the altercation.

"What's the matter with you?" The man observed her startling composure with awe. "Doesn't anything I say make an impact?"

"Not if the intent is to demean my fiancé." She paused to give him her most regal look. "I love Logan. While you, Mr. Knickerpepper, are merely a temporary irritation." Adding insult to injury, she added, "You may quote me if you like."

Utterly speechless, he was trying to gather his wits in order to blast the daring young lady with a flood of vindictive words when she stunned him yet again:

"Don't waste your breath trying to think up an insult. I could care less what you think about me."

Lerisa's expressive eyes held his and she asked in a

bright voice, "What I can't understand is why a man with such a gorgeous head of wavy blond hair and lovely white teeth should be so objectionable."

She watched with amusement as her personal comments sank in. He was a vain man and as stunned by her flattery as he had been by her sharp retorts.

"In fact," she added as a coup de grace, "if I thought you'd be interested, I'd ask you to dance. They're just starting a tango"—she gave him a wistful glance and lied without a qualm—"which is my favorite"—another lie—"and one Logan can't do at all."

Within seconds Lerisa was in Mr. Knickerpepper's arms and giving the exhibition of her life. To her surprise the man was a miniature Fred Astaire and it took all her ability to play the part of Ginger Rogers.

By the time the band had finished playing the guests were standing around the dance area to stare in stunned disbelief at Mr. Knickerpepper, who glowed happily, just as if he was the guest of honor. None were more surprised than Logan, Josh, Brandy, and Brad. Jaclyn merely smiled, knowing Lerisa had made a male conquest once again.

Logan's eyes narrowed warily as Lerisa was escorted like a queen to his side. He made no comment as her escort bowed, thanked her for the most delightful time of his life, then left with head held high, like he owned the place.

"I must need glasses," Logan told her. "That damned cocky little bastard even had a smile on his face."

"Why not?" Lerisa countered. "He dances the tango like a dream."

"So do I," Logan grumbled jealously. He hadn't wanted anyone holding Lerisa close but himself. Instead he had walked from his library with Josh and Brad only to find his guests enjoying the exciting sight of his fiancée floating around the dance floor in the arms of the nastiest man he'd ever met. "In fact, I'm damned good at doing the tango."

"Mr. Knickerpepper doesn't think so." Lerisa beamed at him with mischievous eyes. "I told him you didn't know how to dance it at all."

With Lerisa's hand in a firm clasp that boded ill for her later, Logan pulled her with him to the bandstand. He grabbed the microphone and announced, "Since nothing can top the sight of my lovely fiancée dancing, I suggest we eat."

Motioning with his head to Brad and Josh to follow, he grated beneath his breath, "Show-off!"

"Aren't I though," Lerisa admitted with a chuckle.

The six of them were soon standing in front of long tables heaped with hot and cold delicacies so elaborate that they resembled a midnight buffet on a luxury liner.

After everyone had consumed all the lobster tail and prime rib of beef they could eat, the outside lights were dimmed. The silence of the moment was broken by caterers flamboyantly wheeling a three-tiered cake, topped with lit sparklers shooting flashes of brilliant color, across the patio to stop in front of Lerisa.

"Oh, Logan," Lerisa whispered, looking at him with her heart in her eyes. "You planned all this for me?"

Turning in his chair, Logan took her in his arms and possessed the softness of her lips with all the yearning he'd been holding back the past few hours.

"Every bit, sweetheart," he whispered against her mouth. "Welcome to my life, my friends, and my city."

Tears blurred Lerisa's vision as she clung to Logan's shoulders. Surely no other woman had ever been so lucky in her life.

"I love you, Logan," she told him, unable to keep her feelings inside any longer.

"It's about time you confessed how you felt." Turning to Brad and Josh, Logan groaned in disbelief. "I spend a fortune on jewels for my woman and she doesn't tell me she loves me until they bring in a damned cake lit up like the Fourth of July."

"It's much too pretty to cut." Lerisa eyed the elaborate frosting formed into fat pink cupids nestled between rosebuds and leaves so perfect that they looked like real flowers circling the cake.

Logan drew Lerisa out of her chair and walked proudly around to his pièce de résistance. The two of them held center stage for the next hour, smiling happily as they received congratulations ranging from the formal to the ribald.

Presenting each guest with a slice of the cake, Logan announced, "The buffet, the bar, and the band will all be going full blast until three o'clock. Enjoy it now, because I'm damned if I'm going to repeat this when Lerisa and I get married."

At four in the morning Lerisa sat curled up in the corner of a comfortable leather couch in Logan's office. She had kicked her shoes off and was wiggling her toes with relief.

Logan sat across from her with his legs outstretched, sprawled in his favorite armchair. He had removed his jacket and tie and unbuttoned the first few buttons of his shirt.

On a tray between them were the remains of Maggie's sandwiches, the chocolate cream pie, and empty glasses that had once held milk.

Lerisa was replete and winding down from the most exciting night of her life.

"That was the most delicious piece of pie I've ever eaten." She rubbed her tummy to emphasize her pleasure.

"Agreed," Logan admitted with a lazy smile at his fiancée's happy face. "The roast beef sandwiches eaten in privacy with you tasted better to me than the catered gastronomic delights my caterers soaked me a bundle for."

Startled by the ringing of his phone, Logan reached lazily across to lift the receiver. "Probably someone lost a watch or earring," he told Lerisa. "Mom! How marvelous to hear from you, despite it being the middle of the night."

Lerisa smiled, listening to the one-sided conversation with amusement as he talked with first his mother then his father. It was obvious that Logan loved both his parents with equal affection.

Logan stood, leaned his hip on the corner of his desk, and motioned for Lerisa to come forward. When she was snuggled comfortably in his arms he said, "Here she is." He put his palm over the mouthpiece. "Mom wants to speak to you."

"Hello, Mrs. West," Lerisa greeted her, listening with a wide smile as she was welcomed effusively into the family.

"Don't let my boy walk all over you, love. He's just like his father. A bit arrogant and a lot spoiled."

"I'll keep him in line," Lerisa promised, squirming helplessly when Logan raised one hand, placed it inside her décolleté gown, and cupped her naked breast as if he'd been dying to touch its nakedness all night.

"I won't keep you, since I know you're tired after all the festivities."

"I am," Lerisa admitted, "but apparently your son isn't!" Lerisa gave Logan a warning glare before trying to slap his fingers away from their sensual stroking. She could hardly speak, it was so arousing.

"Tell him to keep his hands to himself, love," Logan's

mother told her, obviously well aware of her son's inclinations.

Lerisa pulled away from the phone. "Your mother says behave."

Logan's laughter and erotic fondling went on undisturbed as Lerisa tried desperately to pay attention to what his mother was saying.

"We'll be there wherever and whenever you marry. I can't tell you how pleased I am to have a daughter. You sound like exactly the kind of woman I wanted for my son."

"Thank you, Mrs. West."

"Call me mother, please. And tell Logan to phone as soon as you set the date. We'll jump ship and pick up a flight at the closest major airport. That's one monumental event he won't cheat us out of witnessing."

Without a break in his intimate exploration Logan took the receiver from Lerisa. "Good night, Mom. I've more important things to do with my time than talk to you now that you've welcomed Lerisa."

He listened a moment, then laughed heartily as he hung up the phone.

"What did your mother say to make you laugh?" Lerisa asked, drawing away from Logan's hold.

Sweeping her up into his arms, he carried her from the room and headed toward the stairway. "She told me to keep my hands off you until after we were married. Also that you sounded tired and it was either me or the engagement party to blame and she'd bet her entire fortune it was me!"

When Logan reached the master suite he lowered her to the carpet, gave her a lingering, utterly devastating kiss that left her feeling possessed from head to toe, then pushed her inside alone.

As her dynamic fiancé closed the door behind her, Lerisa gave a weary, satisfied sigh before slowly walking into the bathroom to prepare for bed. From start to finish it had been the most wonderful night of her life.

CHAPTER TWELVE

Early that same morning Lerisa sat in the middle of the vast bed with her back propped against mounds of pillows. She was wide awake and intently watching Logan's image emerge as her fingers drew sketch after sketch with lightning-fast speed.

Once again her fiancé had entered her room while she was sleeping to leave her a gift. Her eyes shone with appreciation for his whimsical humor. This time she had awakened to find Baby Cakes resting on the pillow next to her face. Beside the fuzzy toy puppy was a child's set of fat crayons and a thick pad of drawing paper.

As she recalled the wording of Logan's accompanying note, she knew his night's rest hadn't done one thing to curb his impatience to consummate their relationship. His bold scrawl was short and to the point.

Get to Work On My Picture Immediately.
If I Can't Have Your Body, I Want to Look At It!

Deciding to leave Logan something equally silly, Lerisa was concentrating on creating his caricature. With the ability to capture a person's perfect likeness with a few quick strokes, she had drawn Logan in a variety of poses.

233

Each depicted his handsome face with a frustrated, leering grin as she laughingly ran away, one arm's length in front.

Interrupted by the shrill ring of her bedside phone, Lerisa leaned over to lift the receiver. Carelessly propping it between her ear and shoulder, she focused her attention on completing another drawing before going in search of Logan.

Without bothering to raise her eyes from the paper in front of her, she answered in an offhanded manner.

"The despicable beast loves you," Jaclyn exclaimed before Lerisa had finished saying hello.

"Who?" Lerisa asked, wondering what on earth her best friend was talking about.

"Knickerpepper!" Jaclyn answered as if Lerisa was dense. "Check today's newspaper. Your picture . . . *the sexiest darn one I've ever seen of you* . . . fills the top of his column. The man devotes his entire article to you." She paused to take a breath. "Which is half a page of newsprint." She stopped again to let her words sink in. "To telling his readers how lucky the notorious, woman-chasing Mr. Logan West is for being engaged to the . . . sweet, gorgeous, talented, witty, outspoken, intelligent, etc. . . . Ms. Lerisa Forbes. In addition, Knickerpepper said he fully intended to haunt your social circle just for the opportunity of dancing the tango with the most graceful woman he'd ever held in his arms."

Lerisa set the crayons and paper aside, giggling in disbelief as she listened to Jaclyn read the column verbatim.

"I can't believe this, considering the names I called the cocky little penguin. I really let fly with the adjectives . . . *all bad too.*" Lerisa's mouth curved into a mischievous smile. "That is until I decided to kill the man with kindness by telling him he was kind of cute before I asked him to dance."

"You didn't!" Jaclyn gasped.

"More or less," Lerisa admitted with a teasing chuckle. "Actually he was a surprisingly marvelous dancer."

"You weren't doing too bad yourself. I thought Logan was going to have a heart attack when he found you and Knickerpepper were the cause of everyone's undivided attention."

"It really was a wonderful night, wasn't it?" Lerisa asked in a dreamy voice. "I still can't believe Logan arranged all that for my benefit."

"Obviously the man loves you. What time did you finally get to bed?" Jaclyn asked innocently.

"Not until five. We gorged on thick roast beef sandwiches and mouth-watering chocolate pie, discussed the night's events between each mouthful, talked to his parents, then hit the sack. And before you ask, I slept alone . . . *again!*"

"Poor you," Jaclyn sympathized openly.

"Good-bye, friend," Lerisa yawned, suddenly tired. "I'll call you back after I place my sketches of Logan on his bed and search him out for a good-morning kiss. After that I intend to go back to sleep for at least eight undisturbed hours."

"No you won't," Jaclyn explained with sudden seriousness. "Your father just phoned here wanting to know how to get in touch with you. I gave him Logan's office number and explained it was too bad he missed your engagement party. He seemed pretty shocked so I imagine he'll be calling you right away."

"Oh lord no," Lerisa cried in a plaintive whisper. All color left her face as the trauma of her past came flooding back in a rush.

"What's the matter?" Jaclyn asked with concern.

"Everything," Lerisa confessed quietly.

"Surely you've already notified him about your marriage?" Jaclyn questioned, hoping she hadn't made a horrendous blunder. She had always been curious about Lerisa's relationship with her father. It was something her friend refused to speak about so she never probed.

"Actually I hadn't contacted him yet." Lerisa hesitated a moment before sharing a little of what she felt toward her parent. "I've never discussed it with you, but my father and I don't get along. He also has the power to destroy my relationship with Logan."

"How?" Jaclyn asked in a stunned voice. "Logan's so in love with you, he glows with it."

"He won't be after my father spreads his vicious poison."

"I don't believe it," Jaclyn scoffed, trying to reassure her friend.

"I—I have to go," Lerisa stammered in a dazed voice. "Logan means so much to me, I couldn't bear to lose him now. I love him, Jaclyn. More than anything in the world."

She wanted desperately to be more explicit, but her feelings had been bottled up too long to share them now. Besides, her friend wasn't the one she wanted to help her sort it all out. Logan was the only person strong enough and wise enough to do that.

Lerisa hung up, scattering her sketches across the bedspread without concern as she rushed to the dressing room for her clothes.

Within seconds she had tugged on white shorts and a navy-blue, figure-hugging T-shirt and rushed barefoot from the master suite into Logan's room. She knew his bedside phone was an extension of the one in the downstairs office. If luck was with her, Logan would be eating breakfast and she could handle the call on her own.

She came to a skidding halt beside his neatly made bed

236

and lifted the receiver, only to collapse on the edge of the mattress. She was too late. Cradling the mouthpiece in both hands, she listened, undetected, as the two men spoke.

Logan's voice was clear and precise as he parried words with her father. His anger was evident as she eavesdropped with bated breath.

"If you'll be quiet for a moment, Mr. Forbes, I'll explain why you weren't notified of our marriage plans." Logan's tone cautioned her father that he'd be wise to heed his advice. "For some reason, which Lerisa hasn't confided to me yet, she's hesitant about notifying you of our engagement. Being a suspicious man, I'm inclined to believe it's because you haven't been an ideal parent."

"After you hear what I have to say, Mr. West," her father addressed the younger man confidently, "I'm certain you'll feel it's my daughter who should bear your criticism, not myself."

Lerisa listened in a daze, braced to hear her parent's familiar cultured voice spill forth the horrendous story she'd been subjected to for years. Shaking with a sudden chill despite the warmth of the room, she waited for Logan's interest to become as cold as the blood flowing in her veins.

"Start talking," Logan insisted enigmatically.

"As hard as it is for me to say, Lerisa is a depraved nymphomaniac. A common whore who delights in enticing all men with her voluptuous figure."

"You should be damned glad we're seven thousand miles apart or I'd tear you apart for that remark. I've never heard such a despicable lie in my life," Logan spat out, making no attempt to suppress his anger.

"It's true." Her father was completely unperturbed as he continued his diatribe. "Who should know better than me?

The girl's been driving men wild with her wanton ways since she was a teenager."

"Including you?" Logan's question not only shocked Lerisa's father but herself as well as she listened in disbelief.

"Of c-course not," her father stammered. "The day her mother died . . . God rest her innocent soul . . . her daughter—"

Her daughter?"

"Our daughter," Mr. Forbes corrected quickly. "As I was saying, her mother was only hours in her grave when Lerisa enticed my best friend into her bedroom."

"How old was Lerisa then?"

"It was her fifteenth birthday."

"And your best friend? How old was he?" Logan demanded in a grating voice.

"Fifty-five."

"Old enough not to be seduced if he didn't want to be, I should think," Logan pointed out in a scornful voice.

Ignoring Logan's comment, Mr. Forbes continued, "Not after Lerisa flaunted herself in his face." His breathing quickened. "She exposed her overdeveloped breasts and nubile body to where he couldn't help himself. My God, I'll never forget the sight. She always went around the house wearing skimpy shorts and tight tops that barely covered her decently. From that night on the girl's shared her body with any man who cared to ask."

"That's not true," Logan contradicted, making no attempt to conceal his fury.

"It is," her father insisted. "Why do you think she paints those vulgar nudes? Her mind's obsessed with sex and men's naked bodies."

"Lerisa's paintings are priceless works of art. The vulgarity is only in your mind. Each word you say convinces me further that you, Mr. Forbes, are a very sick man."

Logan paused, choosing his words carefully. "I'm not certain yet your reason for believing such blatant lies about your own daughter, but I have an idea. Time will tell if my suspicions are correct."

"If you won't take my word for it, ask Lerisa's friends about her dating habits. She's entranced some gullible fool every night of the week since I kicked her out of the house. Even her speech would embarrass a longshoreman."

"Are you finished?" Logan demanded between tightly clenched teeth.

"Yes," Mr. Forbes assured him. "I thought it my duty to warn you before you made the dreadful mistake of marrying the girl."

"Your words . . . *true or not* . . . haven't affected my feelings for Lerisa one iota. We'll marry the moment she sets the date, but first let me make this point very clear." Logan's arrogant tone brooked no argument. "You may end up my father-in-law, but that fact doesn't mean you're welcome to phone this number again!"

"Wh-what do you mean?" Mr. Forbes spluttered, taken aback by Logan's confidence in his daughter.

"I mean listen . . . *and listen close* . . . as I'm only going to warn you once. Leave my fiancée alone. I tend to lose my temper when a person, related or not, bothers someone I love."

"You have no reason to be mad at me. I'm only trying to keep you from committing a grave error." Her father sounded stunned that Logan wouldn't give credence to his outpouring.

"I didn't ask for your advice, nor do I want it." Logan's voice was cold as hardened steel. "In fact, I'm so damned furious right now I could break your neck with my bare hands. Since I am so mad . . . if we should accidentally cross paths in the distant future . . . keep away, as I won't be held responsible for your physical well-being!"

With that parting shot Logan slammed down the receiver. He tore out of his office, taking the stairs two at a time while praying that Lerisa was still asleep. It would kill him to think she'd ever learn a single thing about this conversation.

Instead of finding Lerisa in her own room, Logan spotted her sitting on the edge of his bed. Her face was buried in her hands as she softly cried. The sight of her slender shoulders shaking with grief told him more than the receiver dangling by its cord over the side of his nightstand that she had heard every word.

"Damn the bastard," Logan swore, sitting down and pulling her into his arms. "You overheard, didn't you?"

"Y-yes," Lerisa confessed, blinking back tears as they spilled down her cheeks. She clung to Logan's neck, trying hard to stop shaking as she absorbed strength from his comforting hold.

Logan took an impeccable white handkerchief from his pocket, tilted her chin upward, then gently wiped her face dry. "I'd give anything to have saved you that pain."

Lerisa's lips formed a tremulous smile as she met his sympathetic glance. "The only pain was hearing my father repeat the same old lies. I'm crying because I can't believe what you told him."

"It surprised you to hear I love you?" Logan questioned, rocking her back and forth. Cradling her close to his chest, he unconsciously stroked her back in slow, soothing motions until she quit trembling.

Lerisa drew back. "It astonished me that you heard him out, then still cared for me enough to declare you loved me." Her eyes were filled with tenderness as she met his glance. "You, my darling, are an extraordinarily special man."

"Do you want to tell me about it now?"

"N-not yet." Lerisa held his glance squarely. "I'm too happy over your faith in me to want to relive the misery of explaining my father's lies. Do you mind?"

"Not in the least." Logan kissed the tip of her nose, each pale cheek, then her soft, sweet mouth. "I'm in the mood to entertain you, sweetheart. Which sounds best? A cruise to Ensenada, Mexico, hunting up rare objets d'art and stuffing on tacos or a flight to San Francisco for a day exploring Fisherman's Wharf and eating heaping bowls of bouillabaisse?"

"You decide while I put my makeup on," Lerisa told Logan brightly. She clung to his neck in a tight hug, showing him more than words could express how much she adored him. As her mouth met with his all the pent-up emotion her father's words had roused were released in a devouring, seemingly endless caress. His lips as well as his arms wiped out the traumatic half-hour phone call as if in a dream.

"Come back here," Logan demanded with a frustrated moan while taking a swat at Lerisa's rounded bottom as she pulled out of his arms and fled from the room like a young happy child.

"No way," Lerisa called down the hall as she raced toward her room to finish dressing.

Logan ambled inside her bedroom, watching with amusement as she rooted through one dresser drawer after another searching for just the right outfit.

"Don't change." His eyes took in the long length of shapely leg and womanly curves. "Just grab some tennis shoes, throw in a swimsuit and some kind of cover-up for walking around town. I don't think Mexico is prepared for the sight of such a gorgeous gringo wandering around its streets in that delightful state of undress."

Ignoring his personal comment, Lerisa teased his male vanity. "Apparently you want to show off your yacht instead of your airplane." She faced him, trying without success to curb her wild tangle of hair with an incessant brushing. "Am I right?"

"You bet," Logan admitted with a boyish smile. "Besides, you wore me out last night, and a lazy Sunday cruise down the coast sounds enjoyable today. I can relax, swim, and sunbathe on the deck while you serve me my meals."

He stood with arms crossed over his chest, eyeing her with a hopeful expression. "You can cook, can't you?"

"Of course I can cook!" Lerisa raised her chin haughtily. "If your yacht's galley is stocked as well as your kitchen, I'll whip up the finest Sunday brunch you've ever eaten."

"Be sure you fix enough for six. I told Josh and Brad to stand by until we decided where we'd go today. Brandy and Jaclyn are probably as anxious as you to know what to wear."

"That sounds perfect," Lerisa agreed ecstatically. Nothing would be a better antidote after listening to her parent's terrible lies than spending a day having fun in pleasant company. "Absolutely perfect, in fact!"

And it was perfect. Every leisurely moment. Logan's yacht far exceeded her expectations, despite her knowing that he would undoubtedly have the finest in its class.

She fixed eggs Benedict, baked a cinnamon-pecan coffee cake with a buttery streusel topping, and heaped a wide bowl with fresh pineapple spears, sliced kiwi fruit, whole strawberries, and banana chunks. The brunch left them all so replete, they welcomed the opportunity to dock and explore the Baja California town of Ensenada.

After Lerisa completed her rapid-fire haggling in fluent

Spanish, each purchased Mexican huaraches and crazy sombreros to wear as they prowled the side streets for souvenirs that caught their eye.

After an invigorating swim while the yacht was anchored offshore in calm turquoise-blue waters beyond the breakers, Lerisa sprawled on a cushioned deck pad alongside Logan while the balmy breeze dried her sun-kissed body.

Logan, in his skimpy swim trunks, nearly took her breath away. His limbs were strong and straight and as deeply tanned as his wide chest. It took all her willpower not to beg him to take her to his cabin below. She ached with the need to be loved, and meeting his darkened, penetrating gaze, she knew he felt the same. She watched without comment as he rolled over onto his stomach to conceal the mammoth bulge of his arousal in case the others looked their way.

As the sun dipped over the horizon in a last burst of brilliant crimson, they lifted anchor and cruised back to the San Diego marina where his boat was berthed.

The following day Lerisa spent ages carefully applying makeup and choosing the perfect dress. Logan flew her in his private jet to San Francisco. In a rented car they made a thorough tour of the surrounding area before parking on Fisherman's Wharf.

After a leisurely walk along the wooden rail at the water's edge, they entered Nick's seafood restaurant and Logan surprised her yet again. The owner, Nick Sandini, and his wife, Carlyn, hosted them to a special lunch along with their friends De-Ann and Derek Howell.

To her delight they were joined by the couples' precious babies. Two-year-old Nicky, Jr., as dark and as handsome as his father, plus Deidree, a sparkling, vivacious little doll with the same auburn hair as her mother, De-Ann. Both babies sat and crumbled breadsticks into a terrible mess between eating bites of noodles Alfredo and drinking large glasses of milk.

Exhausted, Lerisa fell asleep on the flight back to San Diego. It was a pleasant nap since the image of bearing Logan's children was foremost in her mind.

On Tuesday Lerisa left with Logan in the wee hours of the morning to pick up Josh and Jaclyn. All four, dressed in blue jeans and plaid shirts, drank hot coffee and ate fresh-baked French crullers as they drove over the hills to Palm Springs.

Arriving at the stables an hour before daybreak, they were met by Brad and Brandy, who were waiting with their two horses, Whoa Boy and Gray Witch, plus rented horses for their guests.

Mounting easily, they trailed one after the other behind Brad as he led the way through the pungent sagebrush along a seemingly indistinguishable trail toward a high knoll overlooking the city.

Noticing the numerous passionate glances exchanged between Brad and Brandy after they had all dismounted and were easing their stiff muscles while waiting for the sun to rise, she knew this private niche had a special intimate meaning for them.

Another memory to add to her rapidly growing list, Lerisa thought as she inhaled the cool morning air and watched in silence as the sun changed from the purest rose pink to a shimmering saffron-yellow ball. She leaned back, welcoming the warmth and the strength of Logan's possessive arms while thinking of the peace and love he'd brought to her heart.

After a screaming, boisterous race back to the stables, which Brandy won by barely a nose over Brad, the horses were cooled, then they all left for a swim and barbecue lunch at the Lucas home.

As Lerisa entered the sprawling hilltop adobe home she looked around, entranced. With its heavy-beamed decor, it was unlike any style she'd ever seen. Indian rugs and baskets, a vast gun collection, and several bronzes by Josh prominently displayed in the enormous front room were invitingly appealing.

"Is your home near here?" Lerisa asked Logan after she had washed up.

"Pretty close," he explained, partially unbuttoning his shirt for coolness.

"Is it like this?"

"Very much. I'll take you for a private look-see after we've had lunch. I think you'll like it. It's much smaller than the La Jolla house and totally different in furnishings and architecture."

Their conversation was interrupted as Brandy called to them it was time to go swimming.

Within minutes they had changed to bikinis and were splashing back and forth in the cool water while waiting for Brad to join them.

She couldn't believe her eyes when he walked across the patio with the cutest twins she'd ever seen. One in each arm. Like little fishes, they wiggled out of his arms and leapt into the water, squealing with delight as they headed toward their courtesy uncles, Logan and Josh, and Aunt Jaclyn.

Gathering them together, Logan managed to bring them to Lerisa for an introduction. Both sets of eyes, one pair gray and the other the amber color of brandy, stared at her. Neither of the children said a word.

Intrigued with seeing her uncle's naked chest for the

first time, four-year-old Betty turned and reached out one teeny finger to touch the wet whorls of dark hair.

"You look like my daddy without your clothes on, Uncle Low-gan."

"How's that?" Logan questioned, hugging the little nymph close.

" 'Cause you got lotsa hair." She looked at Lerisa closely, then back to Logan, staring him square in the eye. "Aunty La . . . La . . . er . . . Aunty Risa and I don't have none at all on our chests."

"Thank God for that." Logan roared with laughter as the others overhearing the conversation joined in.

He set the twins on the tile edging when they began to wiggle too much to control, letting them cling to his neck with the utmost loving patience.

"Mommy says she luvs Daddy's chest 'cause it's s-sexy."

Not happy with all the attention paid his sister, Bobby asked in an innocent voice, "Are you pregnant, Aunty Risa?"

"What do you know about that stuff?" Logan demanded with twinkling eyes as he waited for Lerisa to come up with an answer. It was the first time he'd ever seen her at a loss for words.

"I know lots," Bobby told him proudly. "Mommy and Daddy 'splained the fax of life to me an' Betty already."

"Tell us what they said," Logan demanded with complete aplomb. "Aunty Risa needs prompting."

"What's promptin' mean?" Betty asked in her sweet high-pitched voice.

"It means your Aunty Risa don't know nothing," Logan laughed, moving his hips to easily avoid Lerisa's underwater kick.

"I'll get you for this, Logan," Lerisa promised in a soft

246

hiss for his ears alone. "For this and all the other things your offbeat sense of humor seems to find amusing."

Wanting to be the center of attention again, Bobby precociously announced, "Makin' babies is a men's job."

"That's enough," Brandy said, moving closer to her twins after giving Brad a pleading look.

Unperturbed over Brandy's admonition, Logan persisted in making matters worse. "I couldn't agree with you more, Bobby."

"Mommies need help makin' babies," Betty piped up. "My daddy said so."

"Well I'm glad to hear that." Logan's eyes twinkled with mischief. "I guess I'll have to ask Aunty Risa real nice and maybe she'll let me make a baby with her." He turned to Lerisa and asked with feigned seriousness, "Will you make a baby with me? *Please.*"

"*Definitely not!*" Lerisa stormed between clenched teeth. Logan was acting like a brat, egging the babies on while she stood helplessly by, and he knew it.

With both pairs of eyes staring at her in surprise, she stood speechless as Logan calmly explained:

"Aunty Risa means not now, kids. Baby-making is private stuff, which we'll talk about later."

Josh gave Jaclyn a questioning look, and when she nodded yes he announced proudly, "Aunt Jazzy and I have already made a baby, Bobby and Betty."

Everyone was overwhelmed by the news, and the next few minutes were taken up with congratulations.

"Why didn't you tell me the good news Saturday?" Lerisa scolded Jaclyn softly when they were off to themselves.

"Josh and I decided not to. That was your day to shine. Our happiness was assured and could wait."

"Have Jazzy 'splain how to make babies, Risa," Logan suggested boldly after sneaking up behind her and running his hand intimately up her inner thighs while she was treading water.

"Damned lecherous beast!" Lerisa sassed, thankful the babies were playing out of hearing in the shallow end of the pool. She dived away from the laughing group, hoping to get rid of her irritation at Logan's constant teasing by vigorously swimming back and forth the full length of the pool.

After a delicious barbecue shared with Brandy's godfather, the Colonel, and his valet, James, who both had ramrod straight spines despite their advanced years, she and Logan left to explore his desert home.

Arriving in La Jolla well after midnight, after dropping Josh and Jaclyn off, Lerisa could barely keep awake. It had been another long and wonderfully exciting day.

Sunday, Monday, and Tuesday all passed blissfully, without a single angry outburst to break Logan's courting of her.

Unfortunately, by midafternoon Wednesday Lerisa expected and was well prepared for all hell to break loose.

Her repeated requests for Logan to pose had been met with adamant denials. Determined that her fiancé would model unclothed, she was ready with a plan formed the first morning in his house. A scheme simultaneously put into motion the moment she decided to paint a nude of Logan before the one he had commissioned.

The details were finalized, Maggie informed what to expect, and the gardener instructed to have the gates opened.

As luck would have it Logan played right into her hands by going to his office immediately after they had shared breakfast. He would return at two o'clock sharp to take her to lunch.

On the dot of one Maggie escorted the first man into

her studio. Lerisa ignored the housekeeper's disapproving snort to give her visitor a welcome smile.

"Frank Smith!" she exclaimed happily, giving her long-time friend a hug. "It's been ages since we had dinner together in France."

"One year to the month," he told her, looking with appreciation around the spacious, luxurious studio. "But it's not Frank now. I'm known on the circuit as Françoise Smythe, the remarkable Frenchman."

"You fool," Lerisa laughed. "You were born in California and don't have a single drop of French blood in your veins."

"I know it, but the ladies who adore my sexy body think I'm the perfect epitome of a French lover."

"Where are the others?" Lerisa asked, changing the subject to check her watch. "If they don't arrive in the next few minutes, my scheme won't be nearly as effective."

Hearing a commotion on the stairs outside her studio, Lerisa smiled. The rest of the troupe had arrived en masse. She greeted each one with enthusiasm, pointed to the corner where they could disrobe, and settled her hips on a tall stool before a large easel supporting a blank piece of canvas.

As the men paraded out before her in the briefest G-strings she had seen outside the beaches of France, she smiled. Each was perfect and exuded tremendous sex appeal. They were startlingly fresh-faced, well-tanned, and handsome-featured. It was also obvious that each worked out to keep fit since their muscles were well defined and none had an extra ounce of fat. But best of all, not a one looked like any of the others.

Totally unselfconscious, they surveyed the room while waiting for Lerisa to pose them as she wished.

"What about some music, Lerisa?" Frank asked. "When

we perform for the ladies at Chippendale's it's to a hot, sexy beat."

"A great idea," Lerisa agreed with a mischievous twinkle. She slipped off the stool, rushed to the corner, and slipped a cassette into the slot after turning up the machine to an ear-splitting decibel level.

"Now this is what I want," she explained carefully. With a lot of laughter and good-natured, ribald comradery, they were soon lined up and waiting for a high-sign to begin their show.

They had gorgeous sexy bodies and were all young enough to enjoy trying to outdo the other by displaying their muscles to the best advantage. The fifty-dollar bill each had received ahead of time hadn't hurt either.

At five minutes after two Logan appeared at her studio door, stunned to hear "The Stripper" being played full blast and an even dozen men parading one at a time back and forth in front of his fiancée.

Pretending not to notice Logan, Lerisa stared straight ahead, making notes as each struck a series of poses directly in front of her. As she watched their near-naked torsos through narrowed eyes, she wondered if she might have overdone it a bit this time.

Out of the corner of her eye she watched Logan take a deep breath and start to move forward. She braced for the imminent confrontation with a casual lifting of her face and a wide, innocent smile.

"Hi, Logan," she greeted him matter-of-factly. "Is it two o'clock already?"

Logan ignored the men, the music, and her question to ask through clenched teeth, *"Having fun, darling?"*

"Actually"—Lerisa gave Logan a quick, impersonal glance and looked back at the men, who continued their act as planned—"I'm working."

"Not any longer you're not," Logan warned in a steely voice.

In three quick strides he had reached the cassette player and switched off the blaring, sensual recording. Next he turned to the dozen men suddenly wondering if they hadn't been hasty in deciding to help out a friend and explained in such an even voice that only Lerisa knew how mad he really was:

"I'll give the lot of you five minutes to dress, depart my studio, my house, and my property."

"Yes, sir," Frank answered politely. He looked at Lerisa, shrugged his shoulders as if to say you're on your own now, and motioned to his friends to get moving.

In four minutes' time Lerisa heard the last of their vehicles screech out of the driveway. As the squeal of tires leaving rubber was absorbed in the heavy silence that followed, she turned to face Logan with a brave, impudent tilt to her chin.

Logan ran his eyes up and down her body with a thoroughness she found disturbing and he knew it.

"You look like the winner of a wet-T-shirt contest in that skimpy top and shorts that expose the entire length of your legs and most of your sexy bottom as well."

"I didn't want to make my models feel ill at ease by being overdressed," she answered brightly.

"Models?" Logan scoffed. "Those . . . *boys* . . . looked like superstuds trying out for gigolo of the month."

"They're highly trained dancers."

"What the hell kind of dancers run around practically naked, have tanned skin smooth as a girl's, muscles from head to toe, flat midriffs, and shoulders out to there?"

"Popular ones," Lerisa shot back, hoping she wouldn't start laughing before Logan had finished his tirade.

He shook his head in disbelief, commenting jealously,

"There wasn't a damned one of them over twenty-one years of age."

"Twenty-five actually," Lerisa pointed out with an impish twinkle in her eyes. "Françoise is . . ."

"Françoise?" Logan interrupted angrily.

"Frank Smith. We met in Paris when he modeled. I told him he was so sexy that he should return home and try out for the Chippendale dancers."

"You did?" Logan exclaimed in disbelief, though he should have surmised as much. "I might have known. It was probably you who also suggested he use Françoise instead of Frank since women think Frenchmen are the ultimate lovers."

"I don't," Lerisa answered, standing before him with legs braced and hands on her hips. She gave Logan as thorough a scrutiny as she had received when the men left the room. "I have an idea that in about five minutes you'll suit me just fine."

"Five minutes?" Logan scoffed as he moved one step forward. "I'm a man, not a rabbit, and you my little horror are going to spend the next twenty-four hours repenting for your many sins."

"Now you sound like a preacher." Lerisa moved a step closer to Logan. "And if so, what are *you* going to repent for?"

With lightning speed Logan moved forward and took Lerisa into his arms. Holding her squirming body close, he answered her question. "I'm going to repent for sending for you! Ever since I commissioned you to paint a picture my life has been alternating between heaven and hell." He kissed her hard on the lips. "With definitely more of the latter each time I sleep alone."

"That's your fault," Lerisa told him boldly. "Since you

locked me out of your room that second night, I've never been asked to share your bed."

"What about that damned celibacy clause you kept throwing up each time I tried to get friendly?"

"That was a spur-of-the-moment inspiration to keep you intrigued. If the truth be known, I'm getting pretty damned tired of the thing myself."

"God help me," Logan groaned. He hugged her close, wondering if he'd ever best her in a verbal exchange.

"What about Maggie?" Lerisa asked, drawing back as she suddenly remembered Logan's housekeeper.

"You mean my dignified old employee who I found brandishing a dust mop like a lethal weapon outside the studio in case your virtue needed protecting?"

Lerisa smiled, thinking how sweet it was to have someone concerned enough to stand by. She hadn't explained that the men were friends and not the least interested in her . . . virtue . . . as Maggie suspected.

"Where's Maggie now?"

"I sent her home and told her to stay away until I'd had time enough to make love to you in every room of the house."

"Oh lordy," Lerisa moaned. "What did she say to that?"

"Stay out of her kitchen," Logan answered flatly.

"Where's Frank?"

"I found my gardener standing guard outside the opened front door holding on to a hoe big enough to kill a water buffalo so I slipped him a hundred bucks and told him to take Maggie to dinner."

"You were already suspicious when you looked in the studio then, weren't you?" Lerisa asked, suddenly feeling depressed that her scheme hadn't had the startling impact on Logan that she'd intended.

"Seeing as how my driveway was filled with customized

vans and expensive sports cars it didn't take too much intelligence for me to figure out you were up to no good."

"I can't believe you."

"Believe it," Logan warned. "Everyone's gone, the security gate's locked, and now we're as safe inside my home as if we were sealed off in a fortress."

"It sounds like I've been outwitted again." Lerisa cast him a dejected glance.

"Not on your life," Logan assured her as their eyes meshed, held, and darkened with mutual excitement. "I've been the one constantly outsmarted in this relationship."

"How do you figure?"

"Because I handled you all wrong from the start."

Logan swept her into his arms, planted a kiss on her cushiony mouth, and headed toward the door. He carried her out of the studio and headed directly to the floor below. As he walked he chastised himself bitterly and continuously beneath his breath.

"This is what I should have done the first night we met, you little troublemaker. It would have saved me days of difficulty, hours of mental anguish anticipating your next escapade, and long nights of the most agonizing sexual frustration of my life."

"Been that bad, has it?" Lerisa asked, letting her sensitized lips curve into a satisfied smile. Her arms clung to the strong column of Logan's neck as each long stride took them closer toward the master suite.

"Worse," Logan grumbled, casting her a piercing glare before bluntly explaining, "I've got a permanent ache in my ba—"

"*Back?*" Lerisa cut him off, only to be interrupted as he continued both his tirade and his hurried steps.

"Back, hell! My pain's a lot lower and way around in the

front. Fortunately for all concerned, I'll be far more comfortable in about one hour's time."

"For all concerned?" Lerisa quizzed as he stopped long enough to open the master-suite door, step inside the room, and kick it shut with his heel.

"Yes, for all concerned," Logan explained, setting her down without releasing his hold. "My employees unjustly felt the wrath of my temper this morning and all because of you."

"Me?" Lerisa asked in a voice so innocent, he looked for her to sprout wings and a golden halo.

"You and only you," Logan reiterated, figuring he had talked long enough.

With all the pent-up passion and anger of a man unused to holding back, Logan kissed Lerisa. Long, deep, and intensely passionate. Before he was finished his tongue had penetrated deep between her trembling lips with the same motion he intended using to possess her body.

Whimpering with pleasure, Lerisa returned his ardent hunger until she was forced to pull away or collapse at his feet. Without doubt her legs wouldn't hold her up one more second.

Swept high into his arms again, Logan met her bemused glance with such tenderness that she could feel tears start to brim in her eyes.

"Now, my scheming little witch of a fiancée," Logan promised against her lips, "prepare yourself for the most exciting loving of your life."

"I can live with that," Lerisa told him readily. "But you still haven't said yet whether you'll pose."

With a deep groan Logan dumped her in the middle of the mattress. He stood braced with legs apart and hands resting on his hips, staring at her enticing face, and was forced to admit that this time she had won.

"Yes, I'll pose for you. I'll do anything to keep those dozen G-string-clad threats to my sanity from returning to your studio."

His eyes narrowed and his voice thickened as he warned her she couldn't have everything her own way.

"But my modeling career, Miss Lerisa Forbes, will damn well start *after* I've made you mine every way I know how."

"What's stopping you then, Mr. Logan West?" Lerisa asked sweetly as she reached her arms out, beseeching him to join her on the bed.

CHAPTER THIRTEEN

Lerisa studied Logan in silence while he undressed. She stared without embarrassment, letting him know through the yearning expressed in her eyes that she not only longed to caress every inch of his fine body but to have the taste of him on her tongue as well.

Intrigued by her first sight of his naked manhood in a state of taut arousal, she pulled herself into a sitting position. Giving in to temptation, she slid with fluid grace off the edge of the bed to go to the man she loved.

As a deep groan of pleasure left her fiancé's lips, she took his hot, throbbing flesh into both hands and gently stroked the velvety textured skin before lowering her face to caress it with her mouth.

She loved him desperately. All of him. And in doing so no part of him was less appealing than the other.

"Enough," Logan moaned deep in his throat. "I'm here to make love to you, not to explode in your sweet mouth."

"I know," she whispered in an awestruck voice. "I just wanted to show you how much I care."

"Well that's one hell of a shocking start," he groaned as a long shudder shook his entire body. Gripping Lerisa's shoulders, he was adamant in his demand. "Now I'll return the favor tenfold."

He drew her slowly up the length of his body. Sliding

his fingers around her neck beneath the weight of her lustrous hair, he lingered en route to gently caress the sensitive hollow behind her ear.

As she trembled with the pleasure of his touch, it seemed fitting somehow that he wanted to make love to her for the first time in the shadowed light filtering through nylon sheers drawn to keep the afternoon rays of sun off the furnishings. The soft golden glow appealed to her sense of beauty by enabling her to see every portion of his magnificent torso.

And afterward, she planned ahead, when they lay happy and sated in each other's arms, her artist's eyes would be forever imprinted with her lover's features and able at any time to guide her fingers in portraying his exact image whether depicted in quick line drawings, more detailed charcoal sketches, or a finished oil.

"I didn't think," Logan interrupted her somber musings, "I'd ever say it with you wearing these clothes, but you have far too much on."

"Shall I remove them or do you want to?" Lerisa offered. Her eyes were large pools of deepest emerald, shimmering with anticipation of the delights ahead.

"I'll do it," Logan assured her, lowering his hands to pull the T-shirt off in one sharp tug.

He paused in breathless wonder, watching the voluptuous perfection of her breasts. With knowledgeable hands he cupped their fullness in his large palms and rolled each nipple between his thumbs and fingers until they were taut peaks of desire.

The impact of his touch was enough to melt her insides but she stayed still, breathlessly waiting to see what he would do next.

His head bent, meeting her upthrust breasts with opened mouth. Taking his time, he took each swollen nipple fully between his lips and suckled with such sweetness that she felt the sensation flow straight to the core of her femininity.

Regretfully ending the exciting ministrations, he whispered against her sensitive skin, "I think we can dispense with the rest of your outfit also."

With accustomed ease Logan slid her panties and shorts off Lerisa's hips. He let them drop down the length of her legs in a crumpled heap of lace and cotton on the floor. In one swoop he threw back the spread and top sheet and tenderly laid her on the patterned gray satin like she was the most precious creature in the world.

Slipping down beside her, Logan cradled her face with strong but gentle fingers before possessing her lips in a kiss that left her feeling as ravished as if they had already made love. His beautiful mouth controlled her own from the first, shaping it with infinite sensitivity as he probed with a tongue intent on driving her crazy with a need for his loving.

Moments after he began to explore her body with the same sensual expertise, every nerve ending cried out for him to never cease. Waves of pleasure spread along her legs until his fingers spread and lingered intimately against the inside of her thighs.

Despite her sudden tension, she could feel each fingertip like a separate entity. When he reached to probe beneath the short black feminine curls in order to bring her a maximum of pleasure, she whimpered in dismay, knowing she must withdraw.

Pulling herself into a sitting position, Lerisa huddled against the headboard while Logan looked on with keen, questioning eyes.

"What's the matter? Did I hurt you?" he asked with

concern. "You tensed up so suddenly that if I didn't know better, I'd think you were shy."

When for the first time since they'd met Lerisa wouldn't meet his eyes, Logan pulled himself up beside her and calmly urged, "Look at me, sweetheart. Tell me what's bothering you."

"Y-you won't believe it."

"Is it my past? The women I've known?" Logan inquired gently. "If so, you have no need to be jealous." He cradled her against his chest and tried to explain. "I've never been unfaithful to you, Lerisa, because when I was with them we hadn't met yet."

"It's not that."

All the while stroking her lustrous hair, he kissed the top of her head. "Since Jaclyn first mentioned you I've never thought of anyone else. It's been so long now since I've touched another woman, I can't remember who it was."

Lerisa gave Logan a tremulous smile. "I'm glad," she replied honestly.

Returning her smile with one equally tender, Logan lowered his head to whisper against her ear, "Your bewitching presence immediately erased the image of every female I'd ever known from my mind."

"That's not why I pulled away."

Lerisa looked at her fingers, nervously splayed across the top sheet, which was drawn across her lap. Her eyes were caught and held by Logan's shimmering engagement ring, which was as binding to her as his wedding band would be, and she knew it was time to explain about the false impression he had regarding her past.

"What is it then?" Logan prompted, brushing a soft, fleeting kiss across her brow.

"I—I'm having an anxiety attack."

"You're frightened of making love?" Logan asked in disbelief. "The same little minx who's bragged all about her experience with men from the age of fifteen on? The woman who Jazzy said gave her a veritable library of erotic books? The one female in the world brave enough to take on me and Knickerpepper too?"

"Yes."

"You actually expect me to believe you're scared of making love with the man who worships you?"

"Yes."

"Why?"

"Reading about making love and doing it are a world apart."

Logan gave a short, knowing laugh. "I found that out by myself before I was fourteen years old."

"But that's why I'm so nervous," Lerisa shot back, turning her head to meet him square in the eye. "I didn't! My bold talk is all a bluff. Once started, I couldn't seem to quit."

"What's the problem then?" Logan nonchalantly asked.

"The problem is . . . hard as it may be for you to believe . . . but I've never been with a man," Lerisa disclosed, waiting for the shock of her words to sink in.

"Me either," Logan chuckled, lessening the trauma of her confession with his gentle teasing.

"Fool!" she scolded, tugging the hair on his rock-hard wrist. "I really mean it."

"Oh baby." Logan cuddled her close, crooning tenderly, "My poor sweet love. Don't you think I knew that from the first day we met?"

"I don't believe you. Even Jaclyn would swear my nightly dates in France all ended in orgies rather than the casual friendships and rap sessions they really were. How could you be so certain I was a virgin?"

"It was easy," Logan assured her with complete composure. "I had the experience you only claimed to have."

"So what happens now?"

"You have to ask?" Logan laughed, raising one arrogant eyebrow in surprise. "I'm going to give you so much loving from this moment on that you'll be able to brag about your vast experience whenever you want and every word will be true."

"Your lack of reverence is astounding." Lerisa tried to scowl but failed miserably when she saw the humor of the situation.

"It wasn't meant to be." Logan met her wary eyes with total seriousness. "I've never felt so damned reverent in my life."

"I'm glad I saved myself for you. I just couldn't indulge in casual sex, despite the constant pressure to do so."

"You're a very fastidious lady. I never doubted for a moment you were as innocent as your talk was bold."

"Why didn't you say something then?" Lerisa scolded softly.

"What?" Logan gave her a wide, teasing smile. "And spoil all my fun by listening to you brag about your *sex*-ploits."

"Do you mind?" Lerisa gave him a pleading look. "You did say you didn't like inexperienced women."

"I wouldn't touch them with a ten-foot pole until you laid siege to my heart." His darkened glance met hers. "Loving you, and being your first lover as well, will be the ultimate sensual experience of my life." He lifted her chin in order to place a caress on the parted softness of her willing lips. "My former life-style made me the last man in the world to deserve a virtuous fiancée."

"The only thing I regret about your past is that I wasn't

there to share it," Lerisa told him with sudden wisdom and faith in their future.

"Oh, darling," Logan spoke with feeling, "if you only knew how many times each day I've felt the same way." He held her glance and huskily vowed, "When I take you, remember this one thing. My possession will be with all the fire in my heart. And that fire burns for you as free of the taint of another woman's touch as your body is of a man's. Never once has a woman invaded my soul, and you captured that the moment I sat beside you on the plane. When you boldly met my eyes with such openly expressed desire, it damned near blew my mind."

"That bad was it?" Lerisa quizzed softly. His declaration of love left her filled with awe, and she knew whenever they were forced to be apart it would be like losing a part of herself. The most important part.

"Worse!" he whispered against her mouth. "I think we've talked long enough. I'm a hungry, *hungry* man and knowing you're mine to cherish . . . *first, last, and always* . . . hasn't helped one little bit."

There was barely leashed passion in Logan's eyes as he settled Lerisa comfortably and began the slow seductive tutoring that left her writhing in ecstasy below him and totally convinced that it was her destiny in life to be his wife.

Not an inch of her body escaped Logan's loving touch, neither her overly sensitized breasts, her quivering abdomen, the core of her femininity, or the rounded flesh of her soft derriere, by the time he finally hovered above her and prepared to break the final barrier between her innocence and womanhood.

"Tell me what you want, Lerisa? Let me hear your sweet lips plead for my love."

Clinging to the bunched muscles of his broad shoulders,

she raised her lashes, briefly staring with wide languorous eyes at the perfection of his intelligent face. At the sight of his broad, heaving chest covered with dark hair veeing down to an arousal unbelievable in its size, she readily spoke her need:

"I want you inside me, Logan. Deep and tight until I'm as filled with the love *of* your body as I'm filled with the love *for* it."

Before the words had barely left Lerisa's throat he cupped her hips close and urged, "Put your legs around me. Let me feel their silken skin around my back while I take us both to that heaven on earth reserved for lovers."

With infinite patience Logan took her innocence. He molded his mouth to hers in a passionate kiss that went on until her short cry of pain changed to a soft, pleading whimper for release.

Intent on pleasing the woman who surrounded his thrusting manhood with a moist warmth devastatingly sensual, he observed her peak reaction, moved accordingly, and moved again. Proud of his past control, sweat beaded his brow as he trembled uncontrollably at the shock of feeling a first tentative clenching around his erection.

"God help me! I can't believe what you're doing to me," he cried out. He was ready . . . *far too soon* . . . to climax as her shocking eroticism continued unabated.

Lerisa felt like her heart stopped when Logan's absorbing invasion paused for an endless moment before plunging to the very depth of her being. Wild with the spiraling urgency he had created, she instinctively arched upward, crying out his name as she experienced the first convulsive tremors of satisfaction.

"I love you, Logan. Forever and ever." Barely able to speak as wave after wave of intense pleasure continued to flow through her veins, she clung to his neck while the world tilted on its axis, straightened, and slowly started to spin again.

After Logan's shuddering spasms eased he rested on his elbows above her, still entwined as he devoured her features with all the love in his heart.

Mere seconds later Lerisa's lashes fluttered open, observing Logan's passion-filled face with disbelief.

"Oh yes, my wild little love," Logan assured her in a voice thickened with rising desire. "It's entirely possible for a man to regain his virility this fast when he's as entranced with his woman as I am."

As his great body hardened and stirred, Lerisa's passionate nature was revitalized also and she was soon lost in the exciting magic of the new and startling intimacy with total abandon.

"I'm glad you're such a sensual man," Lerisa confessed. "Because I don't think I'll ever get enough of your loving." She placed her arms around his neck and met his eyes, darkened to deep indigo blue. "You really do deserve your reputation as a devastating lover, don't you?"

"Time will tell," he promised. "Though I do have every intention of trying to surpass my past records with you tonight."

After reaching the heights once again she lay cradled close to his side attempting to regain her breath. Every touch of his fingertips, every exploration by his warm seeking lips, and every movement of his great body seemed to drive her wild, making her cry out over and over her exquisite surrender to his expertise.

"That was marvelous," she praised him after they had lain in each other's arms for a half hour in the aftermath of a loving so perfect that she knew it would be etched in her memory for life.

"As this will be also," Logan told her with confidence.

Cradled in his arms with a gentleness startling in such a big man, Lerisa found herself carried into the bathroom. The oval tub had been filled to the brim with scented water foaming with fine oils.

With great reverence she was lowered into the bubbles and joined by the man whose mere glance made her tremble from head to toe.

"Now, my darling," Logan told her as he settled himself in the roomy bathtub, "lay your head back, close your eyes, and let your body relax while I bathe you."

"There's no need for you to bother," Lerisa whispered, reaching to take the soft cloth from his hand. "Despite the expertise of your lovemaking, I've regained my equilibrium enough now to wash myself."

"I know you have, but I want to do it." Logan met Lerisa's questioning glance with a look so loving that she reached up to touch his face. He kissed each fingertip as thoroughly as he had kissed each inch of her body. "You gave me the gift of your innocence, and now it's my honor to cleanse and care for you."

Taking a bar of soap from a shell-shaped tray, Logan rubbed it into the washcloth until it was filled with suds.

"Lie back, Lerisa."

Doing as he asked, she was amazed by his tender ministrations as he gently spread her limbs and washed away the obvious signs of her virginity and their first coming together.

The succeeding intimacy was as touching and erotic in its symbolism as the first moment Logan had penetrated deep into her femininity. And as he continued to gently soap the rest of her body, she knew it was also his totally personal, masculine way of declaring that she was his and no other's from that time on.

When Logan finished he rinsed Lerisa free of suds, lay

on his back with his head resting on the marble edging, and raised her until she kneeled directly over his face.

As pliable in his hands as a piece of sculptor's clay, she waited breathlessly for her next introduction into the sensual side of his life. A gasp of pleasure was torn from her throat when he eased her down and buried his face in the damp triangle of black curls between her thighs.

Taking the drops of bathwater into his mouth, Logan replaced them with the moistness from his tongue as he lazily searched and found the exact areas to give her maximum enjoyment.

Her eyes darkened to a deep, impossible blackish-green and she gripped his shoulders to keep from collapsing. Tremors shook her body from head to toe, starting deep in her abdomen and traveling along her thighs. Involuntarily arching backward, she cried out her satisfaction in repeated moans for mercy.

Logan met her disbelieving, innocent gaze with a smile of satisfaction. It would always be his intent to pleasure her first before letting his own climax bring release in the most natural way.

Sliding her sleek body down his, he stopped when her breasts reached his mouth to place a lingering, reverent kiss on each tautened nipple. In a passionate plea he confessed his innermost feelings:

"I can hardly wait for you to have our child, Lerisa. I will cherish you as your body changes, and when your lovely breasts are full of life-giving nourishment, I want to suckle them once. Tasting your mother's milk will be the ultimate erotic experience for me."

Moved by his deeply spoken declaration, tears brimmed her eyes as she leaned down to place a soft caress on his dear mouth before they each got out of the tub.

Carrying Lerisa's hastily dried body back to bed, Logan

laid her down. Her hair spread across his pillow like a cloud. A dark, turbulent storm cloud . . . not white and useless . . . but filled with fire and flashes of thunder, like her tumultuous personality.

Hovering over her, he knew his desire would never cease. "I love you, my passionate little witch. You're the most beautiful woman in the world. Most wonderful of all, though, is that you're mine."

Lerisa reached a finger up to touch his beloved mouth. He had given her such pleasure, she still tingled with the thrill of it. "I'm pretty entranced with you, too, Mr. West. But aren't there still a couple of tricks I need to learn to keep you happy?"

"You don't need to learn a thing." He praised her. "Not after the woman magic you perform each time I'm snug inside you. I've never felt anything so damned exciting in my life as your grip of love."

"Are you game to experience it again?" she asked, knowing she was as insatiable for him as he was for her.

Taking her in his arms, his actions were answer enough.

In the wee hours of the morning, after endless hours spent in her lover's strong arms, Lerisa begged for a respite. "Did you say your bar is kept well stocked with goodies?"

"You're all the nourishment I need," Logan drawled deep in his throat as she slipped from the bed on legs suddenly stiff.

"Well, I need something more than the taste of your tanned flesh to keep me going," Lerisa shot back before turning to glance over her kimono-clad shoulder and smile. "Not that I think a nip or two wouldn't make a good dessert. As I recall I definitely owe you a sharp bite on your sexy bottom."

Logan eased off the warm sheets, slipped his jeans over

his naked body, and carefully zipped them closed. "I'd better help." He watched her pull out a jar of Beluga caviar, pimento-stuffed olives, and teeny cocktail onions. "I'm not eating that crap tonight. It takes meat and potatoes to keep a man fit enough to satisfy your hot little body."

"Sounds good to me," Lerisa said agreeably, picking up the jars she'd removed from his refrigerator to take with them to the kitchen.

Within twenty minutes, and the help of his microwave oven plus the grill-topped range, they were forking tender bites of a prime, two-inch-thick New York steak into their eager mouths between equally tasty bites of baked potato heaped with butter, sour cream, and chives, plus crumbled bacon bits. Washing it all down with glass after glass of cold champagne, Lerisa doubted if she'd ever be happier in her life.

Too lazy to clean up the kitchen, they walked side by side back to the bedroom to fall asleep just before dawn.

With the morning sun high in the sky, Logan, awake and freshly shaved, reluctantly honored his agreement to Lerisa by posing in her studio as promised.

Grumbling beneath his breath, he stripped the jeans from his body, dropped them on the back of a chair, and walked toward his fiancée with his brows drawn together in a deep scowl.

"Stand right there," Lerisa told him, pointing to an area where she thought the light was best. It was hard to keep from laughing out loud as she observed the stormy expression in Logan's eyes while he awkwardly did as she asked.

"Relax, stand still, and think of something pleasant or you'll ruin my painting. I need an accurate depiction of your image. If you're wiggling all around, I can't draw you in proportion."

269

"Well, hurry up then," Logan complained irritably. "I didn't agree to stand around naked as a jay bird forever."

"Don't be so impatient," Lerisa scolded. She bit back the urge to smile at Logan's ill humor, knowing any sign of amusement on her part would bring an immediate end to his modeling career. "You've been here only ten minutes, while Michelangelo spent four years painting the ceiling of the Sistine Chapel of the Vatican."

"Bully for him," Logan complained irreverently. "I'll bet he damned well had all his clothes on while he did it."

"I certainly hope so," Lerisa shot back brightly. "Considering the chapel's vast height and lack of forced-air heat. In winter it'd freeze the bottom off a polar bear."

"Cut the smart talk and get busy. You haven't drawn one thing yet." Logan glared broodingly. "My time here is becoming more limited each time you open your mouth."

Lerisa gathered some sharpened art pencils, a sketch pad, and settled her hips comfortably on a high stool ten feet away from her scowling lover.

With as dignified a glance as possible, considering the circumstances, Lerisa began a thorough, intimate scrutiny of her fuming fiancé.

There was no doubt Logan's body was a gift to her artistic nature with its subtle shading of deeply tanned skin that highlighted every masculine curve. He was hard and fit with each muscle well defined, like she had always preferred in a man. After years of life classes it was obvious that his was the most perfect male form she'd ever seen.

Knowing him intimately, she admitted with a rush of desire, definitely enhanced her appreciation of his physical attributes.

Logan continued to pose self-consciously, glaring

through narrowed eyes as Lerisa studiously ignored his silent threat to end the session.

"Hurry up, damn you!" Logan blasted in a demanding voice. He was miserable, ready to leave, and she knew it.

Again biting back the urge to chuckle out loud at Logan's obvious discomfort, Lerisa returned his glance with a dazzling, sensually interested smile. Flirting outrageously, she scrutinized his naked form with the thoroughness of a sculptor eager to get both hands on his finest work.

"Cut the eye magic, witch," he hissed between tightly clenched teeth.

As Lerisa's bold eyes trailed down, Logan's manhood went up . . . *and up farther* . . . until he was fully erect and quite unable to do a thing about it. As long as Lerisa stayed on her stool staring at him instead of easing his frustration, he'd damn well let her know by his body's reaction and his facial expression what he wanted.

"You're finally beginning to get the drift of posing now," Lerisa said with mock seriousness as she continued to observe his arousal.

"Well I feel like a stupid idiot standing here in my birthday suit."

"You'll just have to grin and . . . *bare it,*" Lerisa told him, unable to hold back a soft chuckle at her pun.

"That's not the least funny," Logan stormed back. "And why the hell aren't you drawing? I didn't agree to this just to be a one-man peep show."

Deciding it was wise to do as Logan asked, Lerisa made a series of marks on the blank sheet of paper before she realized she didn't need his presence to depict his image in perfect duplicate. She had enough memories from the first time they made love to keep her happily sketching for the rest of her life.

She lifted her head from the sketch pad and stared straight at his manhood for an endless length of time.

"You do make a good peep show now that I look at . . . *it.*" Lerisa let her eyes rest on his erection again before raising them to his face to innocently ask, "Can't you keep that . . . *mammoth, heat-seeking missile* . . . of yours under control?"

"Not with you looking at it all the time," Logan complained, giving her a censorious frown. "Or with you in that state of undress. Don't you ever wear a bra when you paint or dress in anything but skimpy shorts and tight T-shirts that boggle my mind?"

"Nope," Lerisa acknowledged without concern. "I need to be comfortable to do my best work."

"Well all I need to do my best work is to be aroused and I'm that now." He took a menacing step toward her and complained bitterly, "Only a damned fool would agree to do anything this stupid."

"Shall I call the guys back for a . . . *rousing* . . . encore performance?" Lerisa taunted clearly.

"Not if you value your life." Logan moved another step closer, then stopped to pin her eyes with his heated gaze. "I've decided since you don't like my body aroused you should . . . *unarouse* . . . it."

Lerisa nonchalantly met his stiff, arrogant look and with a knowing smile replied, "There isn't any such word as *un*arouse."

"There will be after you've been loved until I'm exhausted and can't get it up anymore."

"From past experience, Mr. West, that probably won't happen for at least three or four more decades. You've been running around with . . . *it* . . . hanging out since you got out of bed."

"It's your fault," Logan complained.

"Why?" Lerisa shot back as if he was crazy.

"Because I only hang . . . *out* . . . when you're around. The rest of the time I hang . . . *down!*"

"Forget I asked," Lerisa moaned. She raised her hands in dismay. "I brought you up here to sketch your body, not make out with it."

"Tough!"

Lerisa cast him a look of consternation. "Darn it, Logan. It's impossible to work with you in such a distracting physical state."

"Don't tell me I'm the first male to sit for you that this happened to."

"Actually you're not," Lerisa admitted, giving him a noncommittal smile as her fingers rapidly shaded in the drawing on the sketch pad resting on her lap.

"What'd you do about him?" Logan asked in a decidedly gruff voice. He felt like a damned fool standing before his woman with a hard-on taut enough to pole-vault on.

"I'm a professional, Logan. Art is my life's work," Lerisa told him in a haughty voice.

"So?" Logan questioned irritably.

"So I naturally acted in an appropriate manner."

"How?"

"I giggled."

Logan stared at Lerisa in disbelief, wondering if she was putting him on. "That's all you did?"

"No," she admitted mischievously. "I also told the oversexed young fool to get the damned thing under control or I'd have to hire someone else."

"What happened then?"

"I got someone else," Lerisa said with a casual shrug of one slender shoulder. She raised her face to add, "He didn't have much to paint anyway."

Logan slapped his forehead and moaned, "Will I ever be prepared for your blunt little tongue?"

"Probably not," Lerisa assured him with a devilish look. "But you're bound to get used to it."

"That does it," Logan told her, suddenly reverting to the powerful executive who had single-handedly developed and now headed a multimillion-dollar business.

In two strides he had reached her, grabbed the sketch book from her fingers, and thrown it to the floor. As the pad dropped several pages scattered, causing him to stare in disbelief.

Instead of his own image, as expected, Logan saw pictures of Baby Cakes, but in place of the single tear by one eye, the toy puppy now had a wide silly grin on its face.

"My God," Logan swore in a thundering voice. "You damned, conniving little devil. I can't believe your unmitigated gall."

Not the least perturbed, Lerisa calmly watched Logan's anger rise. She listened in silence as he berated her in a voice that would have had his employees seeking shelter on the run.

"You weren't even drawing my picture! While I stood there posing like an ignorant ass, you were undoubtedly laughing your scheming little head off. Behind your look of innocence hides the brain of a world-class unholy terror."

"You really were amusing," Lerisa admitted, chuckling. "And you deserved every second of discomfort you got for all the stupid things you have done to me, starting with your introduction as *Mark!*"

"I think I know one argument I can win, and by damn I'm ready to debate it right now!"

The message in Logan's eyes was unmistakable. He wanted her, intended to have her, and nothing, not even her objection, would stand in his way.

Without bothering to dress Logan swept Lerisa into his arms and headed toward the door. "Prepare yourself for easing my frustration, you troublemaking brat, as we're going to spend the rest of the day in bed."

"Why bother wasting all that time traveling downstairs?" Lerisa suggested as she eyed the empty lounge.

With the agility of a star athlete Logan spun around and carried her to the narrow couch. Before she had time to do it herself he had pulled the T-shirt over her head, slid the shorts and panties from her hips, and was straddling her body.

Hunger for his loving had brought Lerisa to a fever pitch of excitement with amazing speed and she clung to his shoulders begging, "Take me, Logan. Take me quick. *Pleeease!*"

"Want it, do you?" he asked with marvelous control as he poised with his hardened manhood pressing urgently against her moist, sensitized femininity but not penetrating it.

"After the last twenty-four hours you shouldn't have to ask that," she cried plaintively. Her head twisted back and forth on the pillow-backed lounge in an abandoned gesture of ecstasy.

To Lerisa's dismay, Logan continued to hold back, tantalizing her by giving her only a haunting, teasing touch of the pleasure soon to come.

Too impatient to wait, Lerisa instinctively arched upward and let her legs cling to his hips as she slid her warmth around his pulsating flesh. The moment he was deep inside she began clenching her muscles with the same expertise that had driven him wild during each previous possession. Digging her fingers into his straining biceps, she knew the muscle control learned as a whim would soon drive her lover to the brink of an earth-shattering climax.

"Heaven help me again," Logan groaned, cradling Lerisa close as he thrust forward to reach the very depth of her being. "I can't believe what you do to me." He ground his hips against hers in a surging hunger that he never wanted to end. "I wish I could do this all night, but you're too tight and know too damned many . . . *tricks of the trade* . . . for a novice!"

When Lerisa lay writhing and replete Logan cried out his satisfaction and collapsed, sweat-covered and sated, with her body carefully cradled but still entwined with his.

Long minutes later the breathless aftermath was ended by Maggie calling on the house intercom to tell Logan he had an important call on his office phone.

"I knew I shouldn't have let my housekeeper come back today," Logan complained bitterly.

With a groan of protest he stiffly withdrew from her body and slipped on his jeans to head barefoot down the stairs.

While Logan was busy Lerisa dragged her own listless body to the master suite and was enjoying a warm invigorating shower when she looked around to see Logan opening the glass door.

Welcoming him ecstatically, she wrapped her arms around his neck and rubbed her wet body up and down his until they were soon breathing rapidly and eager to sate their need without leaving the tiled enclosure.

Lifting her easily into his arms, Logan cupped Lerisa's bottom as her slender arms clung to his neck and her long silken legs wrapped around his hips. As the water continued to pour he braced his legs and entered her waiting warmth with exquisite pleasure.

Easily controlling her motions in this position, Logan

moved Lerisa back and forth until she writhed helplessly, unconsciously sinking her teeth into the taut shoulder muscle alongside his neck when he brought her to a peak of ecstasy.

After Lerisa had begged for mercy from the continued erotic plundering, Logan let his own frustration ease in a long shuddering sigh that nearly collapsed his legs. Barely able to stand, he leaned against the tile wall and slowly let Lerisa slide down his body.

With her feet on the wet, sloshing floor, her face resting on his heaving chest, and the water streaming down her back, Lerisa locked her arms tight around Logan's waist. She was filled with a deep sense of gratitude for her fiancé's virility. His lovemaking, whichever way he took her, was an unbelievable pleasure.

"Prepare to cool down, honey," Logan warned her as he adjusted the temperature. "I need something more bracing than warm water after being drained of my life's fluids in your hot little body once again."

With a shriek Lerisa huddled in the corner, trying to avoid the chilling spray as she soaped her body in record time before stepping out to luxuriate in the warmth of a fluffy bath sheet.

Logan finished shortly, joining her to dry his brawny body unselfconsciously while Lerisa walked into the bedroom to pull on her kimono.

Tying the sash around her waist, she watched him gather up his clothes, which Maggie had miraculously moved into the room during their sojourn to the studio.

Instinctively sensing his mind was elsewhere, Lerisa asked, "Was the call bad news?"

"Not at all." Logan met her smile as he snapped the waistband of his gray slacks over a white dress shirt, then casually zipped the front as if they had been married for years. Walking to the dresser mirror, he knotted his tie, smoothed his hair with a quick touch of the comb, threw his suit jacket over one arm, then turned to gather her into his arms.

"Will you be gone long?" Lerisa asked curiously. She sensed the office wasn't his destination this trip.

"Two days." He lifted her chin to plant a hard possessive kiss on her lips. "Buy your wedding dress while I'm gone." He handed her a key. "This fits your new Mercedes sports car, which will be delivered this afternoon. I've placed money in your purse along with a list of shops where credit's been established in your name."

"Why so generous?" Lerisa asked with a flood of love for his constant consideration.

"The minute I return we're jetting to Vegas to be married and I damned well don't want you standing beside me wearing shorts and a T-shirt."

"I promise to do you proud," Lerisa assured him. Tears brimmed in her eyes as she reached up to kiss his beloved mouth. "Have a safe journey. I'll miss you, darling."

"I should hope so," Logan told her, taking her hand as they walked side by side from the room to the front door. After another devastating kiss he walked to his waiting car, eased behind the wheel, waved good-bye, and was soon lost from sight as the big Cadillac zoomed out of the gates.

Feeling exceedingly lost after Logan's departure, Lerisa walked into his office and placed a call to Jaclyn. After her friend had brought her up to date on hers and Josh's life since their trip to Palm Springs, Lerisa paused, waiting for Jaclyn to ask:

"What have you and Logan been doing?"

"Well," Lerisa confessed. "The second most important thing is that I finally got him to pose in the nude."

"I won't ask about the first most important happening

since you sound like a very satisfied young woman. As to the second I can't believe Logan gave in to your demands," Jaclyn remarked in a stunned voice. "Did you learn anything you didn't already know?"

"I sure did. First in the bedroom, then reaffirmed in the studio."

"I hate to ask what." Jaclyn spoke with hesitation.

Lerisa deliberately paused so that her next words would have the impact deserved. "I learned that the sight of Logan in his naked glory certainly *dis*proves the old theory that . . . *all men are created equal!*"

"Lerisa!" Jaclyn scolded before laughing at her friend's rhetoric.

"Another thing I discovered was that compared to Logan all my former boyfriends were sexually in . . . *neutral.*"

"Don't even tell me what you mean by that remark," Jaclyn moaned.

"I mean that, compared to Logan, they had . . . *no drive!*" Lerisa teased, ignoring Jaclyn's request before changing the subject to ask if she'd accompany her on a marathon shopping spree the following day.

The two days passed with lightning quickness. Each afternoon was taken up with traipsing in and out of every dress shop from Newport Beach to San Diego. Nights and mornings were spent in her studio drawing sketch after sketch until Lerisa had finished thirty-five perfect drawings.

Pleased with her work, she phoned Josh and wasted no time making her request.

"Do you know of a discreet bookbinder that can handle erotic drawings not for anyone's eyes but mine and Logan's?"

"I think so," Josh answered. "Why?"

"I've just completed a set of intimate drawings of us making love. I'd like to have them bound in leather to give to Logan as a wedding present."

Josh whistled through his teeth. "That's quite a present and one any man would cherish. When do you have to have it finished?"

"Sunday morning. I'll pay anything they ask."

"No problem," Josh assured her. "There's a man right here in Laguna Beach who does fine work. As a favor to me he'll have your portfolio of love ready in time to give the groom before you start on the honeymoon."

"No wonder Jaclyn loves you so much," Lerisa told Josh happily. "You're a genius in more ways than one."

"Thanks." Josh paused, thought a moment, then asked, "Would you mind if I looked at your work? As an artist and gallery owner I'd be very interested in seeing your erotic works."

Flattered by Josh's interest, Lerisa agreed. "One peek each for you and Jaclyn. I owe her one anyway for letting me gaze at you in *Stolen Idyll*."

She smiled after the call was completed and the final arrangements for pickup had been made. She would have *Bedroom Magic* imprinted in gold Gothic letters on the cover to match the brass plate bearing the title of her painting of Logan, which she intended to complete the moment the honeymoon ended.

As she thumbed through the sketches she thought them the best she had ever done. She knew instinctively that Logan, being a man of surprising sensitivity, would treasure his gift as a true and permanent expression of her love.

Saturday afternoon Logan arrived home just in time to glance up in amazement and see Lerisa sliding, bottom-first, down his curved banister.

Wearing skin-tight jeans and a bare-midriff tank top that hugged her full breasts, she teetered precariously and screamed at the top of her lungs:

"Lo-gaaan!"

Braced to catch her weight, Logan knew the unexpected had happened again.

Lerisa barely managed a thankful, welcoming smile after she tumbled into Logan's arms before he crushed her in a hug that threatened to break every rib in her body while he kissed her breathless.

"Why did you do that?"

"All my life I've had a compelling urge to try it. Your banister's perfect so I hopped on. Unfortunately the trip down was far faster than I anticipated."

"What would have happened if I hadn't been here to catch you?" Logan scolded, carrying her right back up the stairs to their bedroom.

"Your wife would have had a very bruised and a very ugly behind on her honeymoon." She cast him an impudent look. "That is if you haven't changed your mind about making what you've already done to me legal?"

"Oh I intend to make it legal, you crazy impetuous female." Logan nuzzled her hair aside and followed the dainty curve of her ear with his tongue before giving the lobe a sharp nip.

"Ouch!" Lerisa complained, then gave a happy sigh when he quit to blow his warm breath into her ear instead. "I'm glad you decided to make an honest woman out of me since I spent a fortune of your money on a wedding dress. I'd hate to waste my gorgeous gown on a less devastating admirer in the future."

"Like Knickerpepper?" Logan suggested, kicking the door shut behind them when he got to the bedroom.

"Right." Lerisa gave him a twinkling-eyed mischievous

look. "That little man may do a great tango, but in the sack I imagine you've got him beat all to hell."

"You really do have a terrible mouth for a girl," Logan groaned, sitting her on the bed while he methodically began to remove his clothes.

Staring wide-eyed, Lerisa asked, "When do I hear about your trip?"

"After you've been had. If I'm as devastating as you say, you won't want to miss the experience."

"Braggart," Lerisa scolded, unzipping her jeans and removing her clothes with as much enthusiasm and speed as he was his.

Naked and entwined in each other's arms on the cool satin sheets, Lerisa whimpered with the pleasure of being back in Logan's arms once again. She had missed him so much, she couldn't eat or sleep. It had been a dreadful two days that she hoped never to repeat.

"Miss me, did you?" Logan asked when she cried out her love over and over as he brought her quickly to the edge of satisfaction. Each deep thrust sent tremors of excitement racing through his veins also and they were soon *much too soon for both* . . . temporarily replete.

"Where are you taking me on my honeymoon?" Lerisa asked blissfully when she could finally speak. She lay along Logan's side, held close in his loving clasp while they caught their breath.

"We'll detour to Tahiti on our way to Paris to close out your apartment. As expensive as your tastes are, I'll need all the money you can earn selling Josh your designer scarves and nudes."

"Why Tahiti?" Lerisa inquired with casual curiosity.

Logan pulled himself into a sitting position, propped against the headboard. Drawing Lerisa up with him, he took her hand in his and placed a kiss in the palm before speaking.

"I have some news about your father. Are you ready to share the problem of your relationship yet?"

"Yes," Lerisa met his compassionate glance with complete confidence he would understand. "Knowing you love me, I feel able to talk about it for the first time."

"Good." Logan gave her a satisfied smile. "First, will you tell me if your father ever abused you in any way?"

"If you mean sexually or physically, the answer is no." She met his glance squarely. "Quite the opposite, in fact. My father was cold as ice. I never received one sign of affection or a single hug all the time I was growing up."

"What was your mother like? Didn't she help?"

Lerisa shook her head no. "Mother was an introverted, very genteel quiet lady who was totally dominated by my father. Quite the opposite from me."

"When did your father change?"

"The night my mother died." Lerisa shuddered as the terrible memories of that traumatic day surged back into her mind. "Before then he totally ignored me."

"What happened when you returned from the funeral?" Logan prompted softly.

"His best friend dragged me to my bedroom, beat, and nearly raped me. Hearing me scream, my father investigated and let loose with such an outpouring of horrendous lies and verbal abuse, all directed at me, that I've never been able to stand the thought of seeing him again. That night I ran away from home, hurt and grieving, and I've been on my own ever since."

"Oh my poor darling," Logan sympathized with pain in his voice. He couldn't believe the misery she had borne alone. "You were only a baby."

"Believe me, I grew up in a hurry. I had finished school

two years ahead of my class, was sole benefactor to an ample trust account from my grandparents, so I left the United States. For the past ten years I've traveled around the world, Europe mostly, learned to speak six languages and to parry men's advances, and all the while I studied art incessantly."

"No wonder you're such an outspoken, independent woman. Have you seen your father since you left home?"

Lerisa shook her head no. "But no matter where I moved he always found my address. Then the harassment and filthy accusations would begin all over again until I became filled with hatred just hearing his voice on the phone. That's why I dated every night. I hated being alone."

"I could kill the man for the pain he's caused you," Logan spat out vehemently as his fingers clenched spasmodically around her slender waist. He was filled with a deep anger and knew one blow with the side of his hand would end her father's miserable existence. Worst of all, he knew he could deliver it without a single regret.

Lerisa shuddered, thinking of the only gift he'd ever given her in her life. "He once sent me a collection of crude, sexually explicit books. I gave them to Jaclyn, but I always wished I'd burned them instead."

"Then you won't be unhappy to learn, he is *not* your blood father."

"A-are you serious?" Lerisa whispered as her cheeks paled at the news.

"Totally." Logan drew her into his arms, explaining in complete detail what had transpired since she had eavesdropped on the angry interchange.

"While talking with your mother's husband I immediately became suspicious. The man was either a pervert or wasn't related at all. My investigators did a good job."

"What did they find?"

"That you, my love, have a wonderful father anxiously waiting to meet you. He's a distinguished, gray-templed, black-haired, green-eyed man who has spent the last twenty-six years living in a sprawling home beneath some coconut palms about twenty minutes from Papeete, Ta-hiti."

"Why didn't he and my mother marry when she got pregnant with me? Didn't they love each other?" Lerisa inquired, stunned by the news Logan was relating.

"They were very much in love, but your father never knew your mother was going to have his baby. Your grandparents pulled off a terrible deception by telling each teenager the other was dead. When your mother knew she was pregnant with her dead lover's baby, she gave up all hope and consented to marry her parent's choice."

"But why was my stepfather so cold to me when I was young, then so hostile after I matured?"

"Jealousy, I imagine. It's hard for some men to accept another man's child. As for his change of attitude on your fifteenth birthday, I sensed that reason immediately."

"What?" Lerisa clung to Logan, resting her head on his naked chest while he continued to stun her with his knowledge.

"I believe your stepfather was tormented when his jealousy turned to sexual attraction, which began when you started to mature. The mounting frustration ate at his mind until his only outlet was to mentally and verbally abuse you with accusations of actions he felt too guilt ridden to physically attempt. He knew you would reject him and couldn't handle that in addition to his frustration so he became more and more determined in his efforts to prevent any other man from having you."

"That explains so much," Lerisa said. Tears filled her

eyes at the thought of the many lives ruined by her grand-parents' deception. Her mother's. Her real father's. Even her stepfather's. And nearly her own.

"Are you ready for some really startling good news?" Logan asked with a loving smile as he wiped Lerisa's damp cheeks.

"Definitely."

"Ever heard of the artist LaBreque?"

"Who hasn't?" Lerisa exclaimed, giving Logan a brief résumé. "The man is world-famous for his vivid use of color, painting South Pacific Island scenery. Why do you ask? Is he a friend of my father's?"

"He is your father." Logan cradled Lerisa close. He stroked her back sympathetically as she softly cried out the past bitterness and replaced it with a flood of happiness over the news of her true heritage.

When her sobs had subsided Lerisa looked at Logan with all the love in the world in her eyes. In silence she beseeched him to take her once more. At the moment making love was the only possible way to show him how much she cared and appreciated what he had done.

Afterward, lazy and replete, Lerisa lay entwined in her lover's arms square in the center of the romantic bed. Her thoughts ran ahead to the future as she questioned:

"What are you going to do with your bedroom now that Maggie's moved you bag and baggage into the master suite?"

It was just idle curiosity, as there were so many bed-rooms in the house, it wasn't needed as a guest room.

"I thought I'd knock a hole in the wall, install a connect-ing door, and use it for a nursery."

Logan turned on his side and drew Lerisa's warm, yield-ing body the full length of his. His voice was thick with feeling as he pleaded against her lips:

"Will you make a baby with me, Aunty Risa? Please?"

"Starting when?" Lerisa asked wistfully.

Her eyes expressed her willingness before her arms had time to reach up and cling to Logan's neck. The depth of her love stunned her. He engendered a need, a wanting so physically necessary to her well-being that it was terrifying in its intensity.

"Since Bobby's already 'splained the fax-of-life stuff to me . . . *how about now?*"

"Fine with me, Uncle Low-gan. *Fine with me!*"